MARSHALLVILLE

JOHN WEST

Acknowledgements

I had a great deal of help on this book from Alicia Dean. She corrected my grammar, formatted the text, and gave me valuable suggestions throughout the manuscript. She helped me paint verbal pictures by pointing out when to use my characters point of view. Many times she reminded me to show action, not tell action. If you need an editor for your work, I suggest you contact Alicia at Alicia@aliciadean.com

My cover design was created by Mary Eileen Russell. She takes wonderful pictures and was able to put together my vision for the covers.

I also want to thank my friends in Cowboy Fast Draw. Some inspired the characters used in my story.

Praise for Marshallville

What did I like? I could not believe that this was the first for this author in this genre. His research was spot on and it showed on every page. I loved the writing style and the layout of t he book. After completing it I tried to imagine it written any other way and I don't think it would have worked. I was impressed by how he incorporated new inventions as the story flowed. The details and descriptions keep you anchored in the story line with so much humor you'll be in tears, I was! Additionally, it has every emotion that you would expect from a western. The action and mystery with a little love thrown in occasionally emerged in every chapter as the new character became a resident on Marshallville. His characters are a work of art, loved the lawmen all retiring there yet banding together to protect their new homes and support the local law enforcement. The story brought the West alive again in a very special way, while making new friends, neighbors and families.

Dee Gott, Beta reader and book reviewer.
https://donadees.com/

Foreword From Robert Hanlon

When it comes to the West it takes a writer with historical understanding to do the job. "Marshallville" is the kind of Western you sit down and enjoy from start to finish. The story is laid out beautifully, the action is impeccable and the historical aspect is handled beautifully. I would recommend this novel to all who enjoy a great western yarn from a writer who can truly give readers what they demand. Thank you, John.

Robert Hanlon – Bestselling author of the "Timber: United States Marshal" western series.

Table of Contents

Prologue

The Wagon Train, 1868

The scream was filled with pain. A sound any woman who had gone through childbirth knew well. The effort to stifle the cry was useless; pain overwhelmed her. The ladies in the wagon train knew Jane Marshall's baby struggled to be born.

Jane's pregnancy had not been expected, but it marked the tipping point that forced the move west. Diseases such as cholera were killing a fourth of the population in the eastern cities. Having no sewage system added to the illness and disease problems. Buckets of human waste were merely tossed onto the street. The great, civil war had ended, bringing back thousands of people, making the crowding and waste worse.

A year earlier, John Marshall had talked to his wife, Jane, about moving. His sister had died of Cholera; an ugly disease of dehydration, diarrhea, and organ failure. Cholera, caused by bacteria in contaminated water supply, ran rampant. John did not want to see his wife or children suffer and die as his sister had. He wanted to get a group of friends to go out west with him.

"John, have any of our friends agreed to join a wagon train out of here?"

"A couple, but most of them sound like our next door neighbor, Carl. 'I ain't gonna sell everything to jump into a wagon going who knows where. I don't like it all that much here, but I know what I have, and that's better than not knowing what might happen.'"

It took John a year to put together a group of five other families willing to move, willing to take a chance. The question was timing.

When Jane Marshall became pregnant, that signaled time to go. It was November and the wagon train would leave in May. The families had six months to get ready. The twelve adults and thirteen kids were excited to get out of New York.

*****

The wagon train left St. Louis, May 1, 1868, crossed Missouri and Kansas, and now, two months later, sat in the eastern Colorado territory. Tornados, storms, buffalo stampedes,

2

drownings and accidental gunfire had ended the journey for twenty-seven people of the fifty wagons that had started the trip, but until now, the Marshall group had survived intact. After all the tragedies they had endured for two months, they could go no farther. Jane needed to stop and prepare for the birth of her baby.

The pain forced Jane to stay in the wagon. John moved bags of beans and flour to one side of the crowded wagon to clear an area for Jane to lie down. He laid out a blanket, giving her a soft cover on the wooden bottom. Her head rested on a sack of flour.

"I'm sorry this trip has been so hard, Jane. Bouncing across an uneven plain hasn't been easy for you. I wince every time I hear you cry. Maybe, we should have waited until the baby was born."

"No, John, we had to get out of New York," she whispered. "It was our chance to give the boys, and our new baby, a chance at a good life. I'll be okay."

The sun cast a yellow glow through the wagon canvas. The area had a peaceful look, which belied the struggle. Cindy Davis approached the wagon to assist Jane, and John left to meet with the other men.

"Cindy, I'm glad you're traveling with us," said Jane. "It's reassuring to know we have a mid-wife with us."

"I'm happy I'm here too. I'll take good care of you. You just focus on bringing that precious child into the world."

Cindy had been through many births and immediately had Jane strip down to her bloomers and camisole. With a bowl of cold water close by, Cindy wet Jane's forehead and had her take slow, deep breaths. This was going to take a while.

Being as brave as she could, Jane smiled and assured the other ladies looking in, that she felt fine. The four other wives, Tillie Burns, Barbara Franks, Jenny West, and Angela Miles, were doing what they could to help. Tilly and Barb fetched up a pot of water and set it over the fire on a tripod.

John Marshall and the other men met with the wagon master. "Mr. Winston, Jane isn't going to be able to travel soon. I think we may have to stay here a few days. If we do, we'll have to leave the train."

"Well, John," said Winston, "you do have a couple of choices. We're goin' ta head north to catch up the trail to Oregon; you could try to catch up with us later. Or, not far from here is the Santa Fe Trail goin' south to New Mexico territory and then to California, or you have the choice to stay here. This spot is on a trade route from Santa Fe to Denver. You're near a river and Box Elder creek, with plenty of water, good pasture and rich soil. You're a two-day ride to Denver. There's a saw mill one day from here in the foothills of the Rockies if you're lookin' to build. There's a cavalry fort 'bout a day's ride from here. There'd been serious Indian trouble past few years, but that's over for the most part. We can stay one more day, but this train's got ta keep movin' to beat the winter weather in the mountains.

"Thanks. We'll talk it over and I'll let you know in the morning."

As John approached the wagons, Cindy met him outside. Her face showed lines of strain and she wrung her hands together. "John, something is terribly wrong. The baby has not turned. This is going to be a fight. We can't move for several days."

John felt the blood drain from his face. He told himself that with some rest, Jane would be fine, the baby would be fine. He could not imagine life without her. He shuddered at the thought.

John Marshall called a meeting of the other families.

"Cindy says Jane won't be able to travel for several days. I don't know when we can travel again or where."

Jenny West spoke up. "I think we need to wait to see how Jane and the baby work out before we make a decision."

"We can camp here for a while," said Ken, Jenny's husband.

"All right," John nodded, "let's make camp, and make Jane comfortable."

*****

Winston pulled the wagon train out the next morning and waved good-bye to the Marshall group. Remaining behind, the group formed a large circle with the wagons, strung rope between them as a temporary corral for their livestock, and set up camp. The families had started with twenty-four oxen, twelve mules, two horses, four dairy cows, one bull, two beef cows, six pigs, four dozen chickens, and four roosters. Two pigs and two beef cows were gone. Three dozen chickens and two roosters had not made it either. The rest were fine.

They had milk from one of the four dairy cows. Twelve chickens out of four dozen were still alive and laying eggs.

Two roosters had survived and made people aware of their presence each morning at 05:00. Low on flour, coffee, beans, and grain for the livestock, they needed more supplies whether they stayed or found the Santa Fe Trail.

"It is a four day round-trip to Denver. We need to get there and buy supplies," said John. "We can empty a wagon and Mike, you and Phil can go."

As they were heading out, Cindy told them to pick up a couple of baby bottles.

The warm summer days went by slowly, and Jane continued to struggle. The remaining men, Darryl Burns, Ken West, Bill Williams, Mark Jones, and John gathered wood and topped off the water barrels. They set up several cook fires with tripod hangers circled by large rocks.

The livestock were walked out of the wagon circle for grazing. The kids were in charge of keeping the stock fed and returned. Two older kids carried short whips. Sometimes, the oxen were reluctant to stay in the area, but a sharp swat with the whip fixed that problem. With eleven other kids waving and hollering, the stock learned to come and go when told.

As daylight slowly became evening, the men were able

to sit, stretch their legs, and have a smoke. Watching some of the kids play tag took John's mind off Jane for a little while.

The kids ran barefoot, but with livestock close by, they had to watch where they stepped. Some of the boys made a game of stacking prairie coal then throwing rocks to knock over the piles. *Kids can always find a way to play,* thought John.

During the day, John rolled back the canvas on the wagon, so Jane could get some sunlight. She held her face to the sun and let the warmth flood over her. She was able to sit up and, with great effort, get out of the wagon and stand. Jane had always been resilient. John nearly cried when he saw her so weak, and in such pain. He knew he had to stand strong for her sake, he spoke to her with hope and cheer.

Leaning on the wagon together, late one afternoon, John stroked Jane's hair. "Remember when we met? You offered me a glass of tea while I worked. Being close to you, I could hardly keep my knees from shaking."

"You stood there, looking so official with your surveying equipment; my heart was all aflutter." Jane smiled reliving that time in her memory.

"We've had a wonderful ten years, Jane. It's only a start. We have a great future out here where it is clean and fresh." Seeing Jane's ashen look, he said, "You lie down now and rest."

Jane still had to use the bucket for relief. Three days after the wagon train pulled out, Jane's water broke. Cindy had been working to turn the baby's head during that time. They didn't know it at the time, but the struggle had caused internal bleeding.

Jane, laid out in the back of her wagon, knees up, bloomers off, pushed as hard as she could. Barb and Tillie had hot water and were washing her legs. Angela was wiping Jane's forehead with cold water. Cindy was pushing the baby's butt down the birth canal. The baby's head crowned, but another twelve hours passed before a baby girl finally made her way into the world. The chord tied and cut, another painful contraction, and the after birth came gushing out. Cindy took the baby while Tillie washed Jane's legs.

Too much blood covered the wagon, and Jane's eyes were half-closed, her face pale, her breathing labored. Cindy cleaned the baby and held her out to Jane. Jane smiled, but did not have the strength to hold her. Cindy handed her to Barb, who wrapped the tiny babe and held her close. Cindy turned back to Jane and worked vigorously to stop the bleeding. It had been a difficult pregnancy and a difficult birth.

Barb showed John the baby. He smiled, but crawled into the wagon, moved some bags of flour, lay next to Jane, and held her close. Jane slowly faded away. Less than an hour after the birth, Jane Marshall died.

John didn't know she had died until he noticed her breathing had stopped. He hung his head and quietly sobbed. He cradled her in his arms and chest, and rocked back and forth, trying to will her back to life.

After what seemed like hours, Cindy told John to take his baby and sit by the fire. She and Tillie would clean and tidy up.

The men had made a small cradle out of some branches and lined it with blankets. John set his baby in the cradle and lay down next to her. He lay there in deep sorrow until the next morning.

Early in the morning, Tillie had breakfast going. The bright sun signaled a new day. Barb milked the cow, strained the milk, and soaked a cloth in the milk. She let the baby suck on the cloth, dipping it in the milk often, until the baby seemed full. She changed the baby's diapers with the ones Jane had brought from home, and wrapped her up

Mike and Phil came rolling into camp with supplies. When they were told about Jane, they caught their breath, and looked worriedly toward John.

Even with the bright sunlight, the morning took on a somber feel. Quietly, the adults and kids ate breakfast. John had some coffee, nothing else. Unsteady, he walked to the wagon to see Jane. He held her hand. It was cold, but he remembered the warmth of her grasp. He stroked her face as tears rolled down his cheeks. Heart aching he had to get a hold of himself. He had to take charge, even while grieving for Jane.

Stoop shoulder, he called the families together. Taking in deep breathes, he said, "As you all know, Jane has died. But, we also have a new life, a baby girl. Her name will be Jane." There was a light sound of approval, some yeses, and good choice.

"We will finish breakfast, bury--" His voice cracked, and he swallowed hard before continuing, "--Jane, then, we have some decisions to make. Mark and Bill, will you get a couple of shovels and help me find a spot?"

"John, Mark and I will take care of it. There is a nice shady spot overlooking the river. You get something to eat, and hold your baby," said Bill.

They had the funeral at noon. Bill and Mark found a spot on level ground overlooking the river; they knew Jane would love it there. Wearing her favorite dress, she was lowered into the ground. A simple wooden cross marked the grave. They would erect a headstone later. One by one, each told a story about their time with Jane, a fond remembrance they would never forget. Tears rolling down his cheeks, John told how they met. Breathing heavily, he looked one more time at the grave and walked back to the camp, followed by the rest of the group. It was decision time.

*****

"This must be a group decision," said John, "you know the options, what do you think?"

Ken West spoke first, "I, for one, am tired of spending day after day walking and riding this prairie. The creaking and groaning of the wagons are wearing on my ears and my nerves."

"This seems like an ideal place to lay down some

roots," said Phil. "Look at the hills and mountains to the west, everything is green and clean. The forests reach for the skies. No more filthy streets and crowded neighborhoods. You can actually breathe in the air and feel good. We can smell pine, not dirty waterways. Our kids can grow up roaming through forests instead of garbage filled alleyways."

Barb added, "We have clean water, farm land, a large flat area near timber," waving her hand around said, "Look at this place, it's wonderful."

John looked at the group and softly said, "You know folks, I think this might just be a place to start a new town. We have the skills and tools to do it. I am a land surveyor. Phil, you're an accountant and businessman, and Barbara is a seamstress. Mike, you've built roads and bridges, and Angela is a gardener and a canner. Ken, you and Jenny are metal workers and gunsmiths. Darryl, you are a meat packer, and Tillie, you can put anything edible in a jar. Bill, you are a wheelwright and carpenter. With timber, grazing, water and a great location for trade, we can make a fine living. We can start our town fresh and clean and keep it that way."

The men nodded their approval. The women looked around, smiled, and added their approval as well.

"This is a mighty fine place all right," said Ken.

"I think Jane would have loved this place," said Cindy.

"It seems prophetic, a birth of a child, and a birth of a town," Marshall said softly, holding his baby.

A chorus of yahoos went up, and the men shook hands and hugged the women. The group put their heads together for a moment, turned, and George said, "John, we all agree, we want to call the town, Marshallville."

"One more thing," said Cindy Davis, "today is the fourth of July, a perfect time to start a new town."

*****

July 4, 1868: The Township Act of 1862 granted 320 acres of land to be used to build a town. Lots would be roughly 25 feet by 125 feet. After five years, the town folk simply had to record the town plat at the county seat, and the land would become property of the town.

John Marshall and Mike Miles started laying out the town site. "Mike, I think we need to take the trade route right down Main Street." Pointing out the direction of the route, "It will be a perfect setting for the growth of the town and the best place for shops and businesses."

"That's true, and we need to make the streets wide enough for a wagon with a team of animals to turn around. Supply wagons can stop next to shops and still have plenty of room for other wagons to pass. A small wagon train could even trail down Main Street, stop, and have access to the stores and shops."

That night, John sighted in the North Star, and determined true north. The next morning, he set his markers and took measurements with his ropes and Gunter Chains. One hundred links on a chain equaled sixty-six feet. Eighty chains equaled one mile. Ten square chains equaled one acre. Three hundred twenty acres is two quarter sections. The town would measure a mile long and half a mile wide.

The outline of the town would resemble a checkerboard. Main Street would follow the trade route going north and south, with cafes, hotels, stores and retail shops. The streets west of Main Street would be the industrial zone. That would include the livery, blacksmith, corrals, feedlots, wagon repair, carpenters, metal shop and wood lots, tanneries or any large scale or smelly business. The streets east of Main Street

15

would be zoned for homes, churches, schools, parks, and a doctor's office. The south end of town, at least four blocks from the start of Main Street, would be the entertainment zone with saloons, gambling, upstairs women, pool halls, and a theater.

Streets on the east side of Main, the housing district, would be numbered. Roadways on the west side of Main, the industrial area, would be named avenues, and describe the business like, Corral Ave., Livery Ave., etc. Those streets would be four wagons wide. The blocks would be 250 feet long (ten shops wide).

Mike Miles hooked up a team of oxen, and dragged the streets until they were nearly flat and level. Standing on boards, bumping over rocks and dirt, leveling took leg strength and balance. He started with Main Street, taking it out about 2000 feet. The streets on either side of Main Street, he leveled about four blocks or 1000 feet. That would be plenty to start. Several days later, when a few cross streets cut Main, the outline of the town looked clear.

*****

At one of the family meetings, Phil Franks spoke up. "John,

money will be a big concern. We can sell lots for businesses and lots for homes, but that will take a while. The quick money will come from trade. The major trade route runs right down Main Street, so the first shops should be on Main."

"Wagon trains will be able to stop for supplies and repairs before going north or south. Trail drives to Denver and Kansas will bring men looking for entertainment, and chuck wagon supplies. Miners are still going to Pike's Peak for gold and they will need mining equipment."

Marshall was quick to agree. "You're right Phil, what do we need to start?"

"Having a café, saloon, and a hardware store with dry goods, right away, will bring in needed money," Phil replied.

"Phil, you're a businessman. Set out a budget and a list of supplies that will sell quickly, with the best profit," said Marshall.

"We'll need several tents to start," said Bill Williams. "And as time and money allows, wooden buildings will replace the tents. Of course, those tents will eventually be sold to newcomers."

"Okay, Phil, you and Bill, take a wagon to Denver for trading supplies. Let's get this town going."

For the next four days, the women and children started clearing and raking the first six lots on Third Street as home sites.

"Do we have to work every day?" moaned the kids.

"If you want a place to sleep and eat you better keep going," re-moaned the mothers.

"The livestock needed a permanent corral. Dan, you and Thomas come with me to the wood mill for some posts and rails," said Darryl. "With a working corral for the animals, we can move our wagons to our home sites."

"Hey Ken, I heard you can find water with a forked stick. Just walk around and it will point at water," said Mike.

"Well, we can't keep haulin' water from the stream in buckets every day if we want to grow a town. Find a forked stick and try it out."

Pacing back and forth near the first home site, Mike pointed his stick left and right; then it happened.

"Dang if that don't beat all. This stick is bending like crazy. We ought to start diggin' right here."

With no special tools, Mike and Ken set to hand digging. Throwing a pick and kicking a shovel broke out the sweat on those boys. The hole had to be wide enough for a man to work a pick or shovel while inside the hole. The well would have to be about five feet wide. Being close to a river and a creek, they hoped the water table would be high.

The first day, they managed to dig about six feet. Fortunately, the soil was loose with small river rock so the shovel kicked through without having to use a pick to bust it up. Eight more feet were added the second day. The third day, at about six more feet, water started to seep into the hole. They got three more feet and they were knee deep in water and quite digging. The town would have the water it needed.

Four days later, Phil and Bill returned with tent material, trading goods, and the first businesses were set up.

By the end of August, Marshallville came alive. With the corral built and the stock secure, the families were able to set their wagons on their home lots. Bill Williams had a wheelwright tent set up. Ken and Jenny West had a gun shop and metal works tent ready for business. Barbara Franks had a millinery tent open. Angela Miles ran the café, while Phil Franks ran the saloon. Darryl ran the dry goods and hardware tent. Cindy Davis became the town doctor.

John Marshall set up a land sales office, complete with the town plat map and prices. The café and saloon were big hits for freight haulers, lumbermen, a few prospectors, and trail hands. Miners following Pike's Peak gold and silver finds in the area, kept the tool business busy. A couple of wagon trains stopped in August; Bill Williams' wheelwright shop had plenty of customers. The dry goods store had a regular business, and the ladies' millinery tent hummed with orders from the train women.

Phil and Ken travelled to Denver once a week for food, grain, fabric, tools, nails, medicine, liquor—lots of liquor—and mining supplies. They left on a Friday, and were back by Monday evening. Lots were being rented and bought quicker than expected. The big Cherry Creek flood of 1864 in Denver had wiped out half of the town. Rebuilding slowed in fear of another flood. With shops sitting right on the trade route, several merchants from Denver saw a chance to get business from wagon trains, trail drives, miners, and frontiersmen, and moved to Marshallville.

With a new town close by, some of the farmers in passing wagon trains dropped out and, using the Homestead Act, laid claim to 320 acres near Marshallville. Several farms sprang up. Plowing and sowing were going on every day. Fall crops were planted, and the first harvest came before the winter set in.

*****

1869: A year had passed since Marshallville had been founded. Mark Jones, Jane's brother, became the first sheriff to be appointed by the city council.

An interesting situation occurred that helped the building of the town. A wagon train drop-out camp began to form outside of town. Men knew they had to get their families out of the disease and unemployment of the eastern cities. The problem was, often, these men did not have enough money for the entire trip to the west coast. They would join a wagon train, but drop out near a town, and walk in looking for work. If they were lucky, they were able to earn enough money to continue their journey. These families were called 'migration workers'.

Marshallville lay near water, pasture, and had a forest close by for game hunting. It happened to be the perfect place

21

for a wagon train drop-out camp.

The city and families were making money on trade and repairs, but sometimes they just needed more manpower to get some jobs done. The wagon train dropouts provided that help. With their help, the temporary tent stores came down, and a hotel, and café went up.

A new dry goods and hardware store sat next to the café. The migrant workers even helped build a few other stores for rent. The buildings all had a large, flat, false front, typical of most western towns. Drinking and gambling was big business, so two saloons went up in the south end of town.

A couple of loggers brought in some timber and produced a sizable wood lot. They lived on the lot in a tent while stacking the wood. Every new family or merchant needed some wood to start, so the 'Logger' boys did a good business. A town hall, school, and fire house also sprang up that year.

John Marshall travelled to Denver and had several flyers printed extolling the advantages of moving to Marshallville. He sent them out to several newspaper offices in the states back east. With the town plat and existing businesses included, Marshallville looked like a real town, ready and available for investment.

Two key factors made the town stand out. George Franks had brought plans for a windmill, and it would soon pump water from the town well, to fill a covered tank with a spigot. A second ordinance required all buildings to have a least one privy out back, and all human waste had to be dumped in the privies. This added a desired feeling of cleanliness. The privies had to be dug and built first before anyone could live on a lot in town. The new parts of town had a funny look to them. Often times, a row of privies graced the lots before any tents, or building went up. They would not repeat the mistakes of the eastern cities. The town ordinance for a privy became a huge selling point for incoming settlers.

The rules were clear. The dirt dug out for the privy was piled to one side. Once a month, dirt was to be shoveled back over the waste. When the privy was full, a new one had to be dug and the routine repeated. Plants were placed over the old holes. The privies behind a hotel or boarding house had to have several holes including small ones for kids. The privies had to be at least fifty feet back from the building with the door facing away from the house or hotel, so the door could be left open for air. A crescent shaped cut-out on the door meant women, a star shaped cut-out meant men.

Several new boarding houses were built. Five dollars a week or one dollar per night got you a small room, a cot, and one meal.

Churches back east were anxious to expand out west. Preachers were sent to new towns to start a congregation. The fliers that Marshall had sent out attracted attention, and two new churches were built, a Methodist and a Baptist. Sunday sermons went on all day.

The Denver-Rio-Grande train planned to run a branch line terminus to Marshallville by 1873; having a train spur increased interest and land values. Commercial lots were now $2000.00 and home lots, $1000.00. The town also collected property taxes, license taxes and a sales tax on whiskey.

Chapter 1

Short Keg

Marshal Ken Knight poured a cup of coffee and sniffed the aroma with eyes closed. He loved that first sip of coffee, followed by a bite of bread. Grabbing a piece of bread, he raised the mug to his mouth, when Tom Murphy rushed into his office. "Marshal, we tracked our cattle to a box canyon below the rim bout six miles north."

Knight had just slathered his bread with butter and had a jar of honey ready for dipping. Reluctantly, he tossed the bread back onto the plate, but kept his grip on the coffee. "What about the rustlers?"

"They're there too. They've been runnin' a few head off each week, but that's added up to a nice herd. They look to be ready to drive'em over the rim, north inta the Utah territory."

Knight stood and sighed heavily. He had packed on a

few pounds lately and standing usually involved a sigh or a grunt. Just under six feet, he might be described as stocky. Just north of forty, he still moved well, once he got started.

Early mornings, in northern Arizona, can chill a man to his bones. Seemed like nothing ever happened when it was warm outside, he thought, there had to be a better way to earn a living. Knight took a gulp of coffee, banged his mug on the desk, looked at the bread, grabbed a quick bite, flung the bread back on the plate, and licked the butter off his lip. Throwing on a coat and a pair of gloves, he said, "Let's go." Knight led Tom out of the office, cold wind hitting him square in the face. "We should get there just before noon."

He and his deputy, George Sundown, mounted up and joined the ranchers; a good group of seasoned ranch hands, well-armed, and ready for action. The horses blew mist from their nostrils as the posse, girt for battle, headed out of town.

The rustlers were former confederate soldiers out to raise havoc in the north and make some money at the same time. The cattle grazed in a box canyon with two lookouts nested above the canyon on either side of the mouth. Each lookout had signal flags to use in case they were discovered. Two of the men at camp had spy glasses and were watching for

26

a signal. The lookouts had two different flags, one for a lone wanderer, and one for a large group of riders.

Just passed noon, the sun sitting high and bright overhead, the canyon came into view.   Cut over the years by storms, ice and running water; a creek flowed through it yielding rich grass, plenty of water for wildlife and now a perfect place to hide some cattle.

"This is it Marshal. The herd and rustlers are in this here canyon."

"Okay, Tom, leave two men here, and the rest of us will split up, injun along the sides of the canyon, til we get to their camp. That way we'll catch'em in a cross fire. Leave the horses here so we don't spook the cattle, or give up any sounds."

The Reb lookouts saw them coming and signaled to the camp that a large group were coming their way. The signal was picked up, and the Reb captain called the men together.

"Looks like a posse's makin' their way up the canyon," warned the Reb captain. "Our best chance is ta stampede them cattle out the mouth of the canyon. That'll knock them boys good, and drive off their horses. We can head the cattle north and watch our back trail for any sign of the posse. We need the money from this herd. We cain't let nothing stop us. Y'all roll up your gear and mount up quickly."

The marshal's posse started up the sides of the canyon, stepping as quietly as they could. Marshal Knight led four men up one side. Tom, the ranch owner, with the deputy Sundown, led three men up the other side. The canyon walls were steep, the cut narrow. The men were near halfway up the canyon when several shots rang out, followed by a loud rumble. The Reb lookouts fired down on the two men staked out at the mouth of the canyon, wounded them both, and ran off their horses.

The stampeding cattle appeared like a tidal wave of horns and hooves ready to trample anything in front of it. When facing harm, the brain has a switch that will alter time and motion. The scene in Knight's eyes slowed and sounds growled. Feeling like slow motion, Knight turned to face his men and yelled, "Flatten yourselves...." before he could finish, a solid hit threw him against the canyon wall. Pain shot across his hip then blackness as he bounced back toward the cattle. He lay in a heap next to a mound of scree. The cattle veered away from the rocks or Ken Knight would have been trampled to death.

Cattle and rustlers cleared the canyon and were out on the range in only a few minutes. The posse fired no shots hugging the walls for dear life. The men staggered away from the walls silently giving thanks for being alive. Standing slack-jawed, they took stock of their situation. Most of the posse escaped with minor cuts and bruises. George Sundown had a broken arm and leg and lay unconscious near Tom. Tom called to his men and they went about setting the deputy's bones.

On the other side of the canyon, they found the Marshal, unconscious and bruised, with one leg bent the wrong way. The foreman of the ranch shook his head in despair, he had seen this before and it was never pleasant. He yelled to one of his men to hold the marshal by his shoulders while he pulled the leg straight. Even unconscious, the marshal winced during the pull.

"Find a limb or piece of wood, and we can set the leg," yelled the foreman.

The men strapped a small branch to the leg with the marshal's gun belt and the foreman's bandana. It wasn't perfect, but it held the leg. A few hours later they had retrieved their horses, patched up the cuts, and headed back to town. George and Ken were still woozy. They rode double, behind two men, legs straight out, and bandanas wrapped around their heads, holding tight.

A week later, using a cane for support, Knight hobbled to the marshal's office and turned in his badge. Lying in the doctor's office then in his bunk at home, he had plenty of time to think about his nineteen years as a peace officer. Over the years he had squeezed out of some tight spots unhurt. Now, feeling pain and seeing the bend in his leg, he pulled the curtain on his career. He didn't know what might come next, but he knew going from town to town, job to job, ground up his insides.

The next morning Ken sat in the café, all balled up about his future, nursing his third mug of coffee, staring blankly out of the window. The café door creaked open, the Postmaster came in and scanned the tables. Spotting Knight, he shuffled over and plopped down in a chair opposite him. The chair strained under the bulk of the Postmaster. A short, stocky, bald man with a perpetual smile, he said, "Howdy Marshal, it's good to see up and around."

"Thanks, but that is ex-marshal. And as far as up and around, I'm a bit up, but I'm not much getting around."

Still smiling he said, "Got a letter for a Ken Knight. Just came in on the stage. Looks like it is from a Sheriff Mark Jones postmarked Marshallville, Colorado Territory."

"Interesting," Ken put down his coffee mug. He examined the letter like it might be evidence of a crime, then opened it. He hadn't gotten many letters in his life, and the ones he had gotten were usually bad news.

Dear Ken Knight:

I am sorry to inform you that your uncle Clyde Knight has died from an unfortunate accident. Further, he was the owner of a saloon here in Marshallville, named the Short Keg. Papers in his desk show the saloon now belongs to you. Please advise your intentions regarding the saloon.

Signed, Sheriff, Mark Jones,
Marshallville, Colorado Territory

"Well, damn, if that don't beat all." He looked at the postmark and shook his head. "If I'da got this two weeks ago, I'd still be in one piece."

31

"How's that?" asked the postmaster.

"Looks like I just became the owner of a saloon in Marshallville, north east of here, in the Colorado territory."

George Sundown, with an arm in a sling and a leg strapped to a cane, walked lamely into the café as Ken stuffed the letter in his pocket.

"Hey, George, come over and sit yourself, you look like you're about to fall down. We sure are a wild pair to draw to, limps and canes and all. The postmaster here just gave me a peak into the future, maybe opened up a new career. Still not sure, but I'm thinking, when we heal up a bit more, we can scout out a new trail if you're a mind to."

George confused a lot of people. With an oriental mother and a fur trapper father, George spoke two languages and had a split personality. He could be kind and polite on one hand, but ready to skin you alive on the other hand. A little beefy like a trapper, taller than an average oriental man, he had a smooth face and slightly tilted eyes. He looked gentle but could skin out anything with fur and four legs in a minute. He looked at Knight with a puzzled look on his face.

"Just so happens, I turned in my badge today, and I'm

lookin' for a new trade. Don't want to trap, mine or do laundry, don't want to be a lawman. So, whatcha got for me?" asked George.

"I own a saloon called the Short Keg. It's in Marshallville, in the Colorado territory. We can partner up if you are agreeable. My Uncle Clyde left it to me. He was a miner. When he had an extra poke of dust, he'd stop in and see me and my mom. He told me, he and my mom were the only kids, their parents were dead and the family name was Knight. He seemed like he wanted to do more for me and my mom, but wasn't able."

George, not quite sure he heard right, simply stared straight ahead. When the words finally sunk in, he broke into a smile. "Dang!" he said. "We go from busting up fights in saloons to owning one. I like it, Kenny, I'd be proud to partner up."

Knight had never heard of Marshallville. This turn of events may be the right trail, or it may be a bust. It could be a one horse town and a dead end for a future. He had passed up forty a few years ago, and with a gimp leg, his options for a career going into his twilight years, were limited. He didn't want to get his hopes up too high, but this deal from his uncle might pan out.

Ken sent the sheriff in Marshallville a letter saying he would be there in a month or so. When they healed as much as they were going to heal, Ken and George Sundowner set out for Marshallville. Still feeling a mite sore, they hitched up a small wagon loaded with camping supplies, and with a short string of horses trailing behind, they headed north.

*****

Pulling into Marshallville, they looked around to find a well laid out town. Sitting a little Taller in the saddle, Knight felt a sense of relief.

"When I got that letter, I wasn't sure what this town held in store, but it seems to be a right fine set up," said Ken.

"It appears peaceful enough, might be what we're looking for," said George. They both had talked about being done with trouble and long days in the saddle. Being on edge every day for years had sapped them both from any feelings of adventure.

"There's a fresh sawn wood smell along with clean clear air that sets a smile on a fellow's face", said Ken.

"I've seen so many run down towns over the years that I forgot what a new town looked like", said George. "I like it."

Ken swept his head left and right, nodding approval of what he saw. Looking up over the two-story, false fronted building, he saw green; green trees, green mountains and green pastures. With Pike's Peak in view, he thought green was a lot better than brown sand and brown thorn bush in the Arizona territory.

"George, you ever seen so much green? I've seen thousands of Saguaros, twenty and thirty feet tall, but here are thousands of trees, hundreds of feet tall. Might make a man feel grand and small at the same time," said Ken.

They dropped their rig at the livery, met up with Nevada Slim, shook a few hands, got directions from Slim, and headed for the City Hall.

They met Mayor John Marshall and Sheriff Mark Jones. Handshakes and smiles filled the hall. Ken had George's name put on the deed to the Short Keg and the ownership was transferred.

"Welcome to Marshallville," said John Marshall. "Best of luck with your saloon. It's only one year old, but it's seen some rough days recently. Your Uncle Clyde was a decent fellow, but he apparently fell from a ladder while putting in some new oil lamps. Busted his head bad. The man running the place now, was the manager for your uncle. He is a bit on the gruff and ornery side. He is the one reported the accident."

Ken and George listened without saying a word, but both had an idea what really happened. A lot of accidents aren't really accidents, especially when money or property is involved. This wouldn't be the first time, or the last time, someone tried to steal another man's poke.

"Thanks Mayor, Sheriff, good to meet you, we'll take it from here," said Ken.

"Oh, by the way," said the mayor, "John and Van Gentry run a ranch outside of town. They used to sheriff down Arizona way. Maybe you know them?"

"Well, it's certainly a small world," said Ken. Looking at George, "We do know them, crossed paths in Arizona a few times. Darn good boys, we'll ride out and say hello real soon."

On the way to the Short Keg, Ken and George devised a plan. They weren't law men anymore, but they still had survival instincts, honed over several years, by being one step ahead of the big jump.

"OK, George, you go in first, check out the place, and cover my back. I'll go in and have a face to face with the ornery one. I'll take him, you look for any back shooters." They checked their loads and headed downtown.

When Ken entered the Short Keg, he noticed George having a beer at the end of the bar. The early afternoon found the place half full. The Short Keg looked like most bars in the west. A long and narrow room, with a bar along one side stretching halfway down the building, with a ten foot high ceiling, and a floor of solid fir. The walls were of sawn wood, nailed firmly, with slats covering the butt edges of the wood boards.

Several tables and chairs lined the wall opposite of the bar, along with the Faro table, dice tables, and one roulette wheel in the corner. There were a couple of prostitutes upstairs leaning over the railing, and a couple downstairs standing around the tables. The place was smoky and dirty with stains on the tables and floors. Ken noticed one of the girls had bruises on her arms, another with a dark shadow below her eye. A slow boil started to simmer. Ken approached the bar and asked for the manager. A tall, scruffy looking man wearing a black frock coat walked over and growled, "What'd you want, mister?"

Ken looked him over and knew him to be scum. He had seen his type many times, and many times had thrown guys like him in jail. He immediately went into his marshal mode, alert for the coming violence.

"I'm Ken Knight, Clyde was my uncle, and I now own the place." He waved his hand around. "We need to clean this place up, and I don't want any prostitutes in the saloon."

"What? I don't know who you really are, but Clyde told me the place was gonna be mine. Don't try to buffalo me, I'm gonna run the place the way I want. If you don't like it, get out," he said and pulled his coat aside showing his gun and holster.

The bartender became alert, stopped polishing the glass in his hand and reached under the bar. A couple of toughs leaning on the bar straightened up, watching the two men.

Ken knew there was no point in talking. This man probably caused his uncle's death. With his experience as a lawman, striking first would be the best plan.

Ken raised his left hand to get the guy to look left and yelled out, "You got this, George?"

George hammered back both guns to full cock, making two loud clicking sounds. A bit confused, the ornery one hesitated and looked back for just a second. That was all the time Ken needed. In a long practiced and smooth move, his right hand drew his gun and slammed the butt across the head of the ornery one, who dropped like a rock. A quick shot from George took out the scatter gun pulled by the bartender. Ken now leveled his gun at the two toughs, neither man moved.

Looking at the rest of the men in the bar, Ken said, "I'm the new owner here and things are gonna change. We'll be closed for the next week or so to clean up this place. So you'all, head for the door and come back later. You girls, go upstairs until I call you. Bartender, and you two men stay. Unbuckle your gun belts, and the three of you sit over here." Ken pointed at a table next to him.

"Hey, we ain't done nothing, you cain't take my gun," said one of the men. He was more of a slouch than anything else. Yellow stains ran down his lip from the chaw that poked his cheek out.

Ken wanted to put a round in the floor next to the man's

foot but realized the floor belonged to him, and he didn't want a hole in it. He walked over to the guy, knocked off his hat with the barrel of his gun, then stuck it in the man's eye. Grumbling, the men unbuckled their guns and sat down at the table.

The place cleared out, and the ornery one lay still on the floor, moaning.

George picked up the men's holster rigs and set them on the bar.

"George, keep an eye on these three, I'll search this guy."

With two guns fully cocked and pointing chest high, the men sat, trying not to move, strain and beads of sweat showed on their faces.

Ken pulled the pistol from the moaning man's holster, set it on the bar, and searched through his coat pockets.

He found an ivory handled derringer with the initials 'C' 'K'—Clyde Knight. Ken had seen that derringer as a kid, once, when Clyde had visited his mother. He had always admired the ivory handles. He knew it belonged to his uncle.

Ken turned and looked at the men. "Listen carefully, boys. You have one chance to get out of here alive. Did this guy kill Clyde Knight?"

Worried that he might be blamed, the bartender said, "No, it was an accident, he fell from a ladder."

"Where is the ladder, and where did he fall?" asked Ken

"Uh, uh, I'm not sure," said the bartender.

"Before you speak again, let me tell you about my friend here. His name is George Sundown, and he has a split personality. Sometimes he just does strange things, painful things. We all got pieces of crazy in us, George got bigger pieces than most others. So, did this man have anything to do with my uncle's death?"

Still worried they might get blamed, or that the man on the floor might kill them if they talked, all three just shook their heads no.

Ken nodded to George, who stepped up and cropped off the better part of one of the bartender's ears. He screamed, "Son of a bitch", nearly fainted, and held his bar towel to the side of his head where most of his ear used to be.

Ken turned to the two men and asked the same question, "Did this man kill Clyde Knight?"

Pale and visibly shaken, throats bobbing and eyes wide open, they both nodded yes.

"Were either of you part of the killing?"

Both quickly shook their heads no.

The bartender, still holding the side of his head with his towel screamed, "He did it. There was no ladder. He clubbed him hard then brought in a ladder to show the sheriff. We had nothing to do with it, and he threatened to kill us if we talked. Please, keep your crazy friend away from me."

"George," said Ken, "how about that, he called you crazy. Take your crazy self and round up the sheriff please. We will need you three to testify at the trial, then I suggest you boys find another town to stink up. I'll tell you only once, do not leave town before the trial. 'Crazy Sundowner' here, is a very good tracker."

A few minutes later, George pushed through the

batwing doors with Sheriff Jones following behind. Looking at the man on the floor, and the three men sitting at the table, Jones said, "What do you have for me, Ken?"

"This guy clubbed my uncle to death, and brought in a ladder to make it look like an accident. These three here will testify this guy killed my uncle."

"I thought it looked suspicious, but I am stretched pretty thin, and I don't have much sheriffing experience. I'll get this guy to jail and hold him for trial. The circuit judge is due in a couple of days."

"I may be able to help you, Sheriff. I know an experienced lawman out in California. He is getting worn out with all the trouble in those mining towns. His name is Cal, and he is in Sacramento right now. I could send him a letter and see if he is interested," Ken said.

"That is a great idea, we could use an experienced lawman in Marshallville," said Jones. "Being a lawman is a lot harder than I thought, and I'd just as soon pass it on to someone else."

Both Ken and George nodded knowingly.

With the sheriff and the other men heading for the jail, Ken said, "Well George, this might work out, we can live upstairs while we clean up this place. You know, I never had a place to call home. As a kid, I lived in the back room of the reverend Smith's place while my mother worked. I learned to read because Mrs. Smith wanted me to read the bible. I guess she thought I might be a preacher someday. About twelve or so I ran away. Years later, I worked in many towns over the years, but never one to call home. Having a place of my own, at my age, is a beautiful thing."

"You're right," said George, as he slapped Ken on the back. "My feet are done itch'n for the trail, more like itch'n to be put up on a chair with no place to go."

"I have a funny story about why I ran away from the Smith's place," Ken said. "It was scary at the time, but now, looking back, I shake my head in disbelief. I've never told anyone before, so it's just between you and me."

"In the midst of the pain and loneliness of those years, something kinda funny happened. When I was eleven or twelve, the minister's wife came into my room one night and told me to stand up and take off my pants. I didn't rightly know what to do. I ask why and she told me at my age is when the devil tries to enter a soul. I was really puzzled because I couldn't figure just how he was coming in, under my pants. Then she grabs my man part and says 'this is where'. She tugs on it a little and says the devil isn't in yet. I didn't much like the tugs, but happy the devil wasn't in yet."

"She came in about once a week, I dropped my pants, and she tugged a little longer each time it seemed. I think you can figure where this is going. One night, that tug started my dick to harden; scared the shit outa me. She let me know the devil was coming in. The next time it hardened she said she had to get him out, so she tugged and tugged and it finally came out, squirted all over the place. Boy, did my eyes get big, there was the devil coming out of my dick."

"That climax feeling, I figured was the devil trying to hang on and not come out, but little by little he was coming out. When she asked me to squeeze her breast while she was letting the devil out, I got spooked."

"After that, I ran away to a ranch outside of town. They knew about the minister and his wife and let me work there til I turned sixteen."

"When I told some of the ranch hands about letting out the devil, I didn't think they would ever stop laughing. Every time they tried to talk to me, they broke up laughing. Finally, they explained the ins and outs of sex, along with uses and descriptions of all the women and men parts. It sounded like a made up story to me and I told them so, and they just laughed and laughed."

"There were several sisters living on a neighboring ranch who would sneak over now and then. One of the ranch hands convinced one of the girls to show me how it all worked. Lesson learned and she did a fine job. For years, I found myself saying, 'here comes the devil', 'here comes the devil' during sex."

"I can see why you never told that story before, that is crazy, and believe me, I'll never repeat it. When I was a kid," said George, "we lived in a cabin for several years. My dad was a trapper and gone a lot, but we weren't too far from a town. Depending on the season, sometimes we had a roaming camp, but it still seemed like home because of my mother. When I left home I spent time in mining camps, and that is where I got my first sheriff's job. I did some sherifin' up in Idaho city for a while, big time mining up there."

"I didn't much like my first law job," said Ken. "Bad pay, and they expected me to keep the peace, find lost dogs, chase down livestock that got loose, and I had to sleep in the jailhouse. The next town seemed a little better, but when the mayor's wife dropped in a few times, I knew that meant trouble, and time to leave."

"I hear ya, some women can sure mess up a guy's life."

"It always seems to be one thing or another. A different town, different people, but the same story, no real home. I surely hope this place pans out. It is a nice town, we have a place of our own, and I'd like to plant some roots, we ain't getting any younger."

George nodded and headed upstairs to check out his room.

Unsure about the saloon business, he hoped this move would bear out. He laughed to himself when he realized he went from a law dog to a bar dog.

Chapter 2

Molly and Mary, Ginger and Kathy

"You ladies, come down stairs, please," Ken said. "Sit over at the table."

Four young women looked puzzled and worried as they sat down. They knew things could go wrong in a hurry. They could see things were changing.

"I am the new owner, and you all are free to go. I won't have women working for sex here."

It took a few seconds for his words to sink in before the girls responded.

"What're we 'posed to do," asked one of the girls. "We're brought here from Kansas. I don't know no one here. How'd I get back to Kansas?"

"The town is growing, maybe you can find some work

here," said Ken.

"Can you cook, or clean, or work on a farm? I'll let you stay here til you get settled. If you want to go home, I'll give you stage fare."

"Who's gonna hire us?" asked another girl, "we're prostitutes."

"I can use a cook and waitress," said Ken. "The hotel can probably use someone. Can anyone do some ranch work? I can ask my friends at the Gentry ranch, they may need a cook and someone to do some chores."

"I grew up on a ranch," said one of the girls. "It wern't much of a ranch, and we lost it ta the bank, but it would beat sackin' out with a bunch of sweaty old men. And I'm not goin' out there for sex neither," she snapped.

"I haven't seen John or Van for a while, but I'm sure they'd appreciate a woman's touch, and if you can cook, you'd have a job for life. They are ex-law and honorable men. What's your name and how old are you?"

"Ginger, I'm twenty-two, so what?"

Ginger was tall and thin with brown hair that hung down to her shoulders. She had a pretty face but she looked older than twenty-two, maybe a bit weary. There was a spark in her voice, but also a worn tone. She carried a chip on her shoulder and stood with a determined grip in her body.

"Ginger, it will take spunk to do ranch work, and I think you'll do just fine. I'll take you out there tomorrow. If you don't like it, we'll come back and try something else."

"I can cook. I had nine brothers and sisters and I had ta help my mom take care of the house," said one of the girls. "Can I cook and clean here and keep ma room?"

"It'll be noisy upstairs. Why do you want to stay here?" Ken asked. "You could go home."

"I have nowheres ta go. Like I said, I have nine brothers and sisters, there aint no room, no food, nothin' back home, that's why I'm here. I had ta earn money for the family, don't like it much, but I had to do sumpin. This might sound strange but I feel safe here with you and 'Crazy Sundowner'."

Ken let out a muffled laugh. "Here it is, then, what's your name and how old are you?"

"Molly and I'm twenty."

Molly was short and thin, but had some curves in the right places. She was young, only being in the business for a couple of years, she still had a sweet look to her. She seemed shy, but able at the same time.

"I want ta stay here, too," said another girl. "I can cook, clean and waitress. Ma name's Mary, I'm twenty-one and I feel safe here, like Molly." Mary and Molly could have been sisters in their look and posture.

"Wow, do you hear that, George? Well, Molly and Mary, we have plenty of cleaning to do to get the place passable. You can both stay as long as you want. We have one person left, what's your name and what do you want to do?"

"My name's Kathy and I don't really want to work. I don't mind men, I'm used to 'em. I didn't like that jerk you pistol whipped, but I'll just head over to the 'Lucky Lady' saloon. I plan on findin' a rich miner, or businessman, and have 'em take me home. This is a growin' town with a lot of opportunities. Maybe I'll run my own house. Thanks for your help, I'll be out in a few days." Kathy was a fiery redhead who had a look of confidence and some grace in her stance.

"OK, that's settled. Molly and Mary, let's see what we have for food and drink, we may have to hunt down something to eat. You're all welcome to stay for supper tonight. We'll see if Molly and Mary really can cook. Ginger, we'll head out to the ranch tomorrow."

George took Molly and Mary to the mercantile. They loaded up with food supplies and headed back to the Short Keg.

"You ladies go upstairs and clean up, there'll be no men tonight," said Ken.

The four ladies pitched in, cooking and setting the table for supper, happy they were having a good supper, and not wrestling around with smelly, drunk men. It was a pleasant supper, not much talking, more thinking about tomorrow than anything else. The next morning, Ken took Ginger out to the Gentry's ranch.

Ken had not seen the brothers in a while, and they greeted each other warmly. Handshakes and back slaps made the rounds. The ranch was at the foothills of the Rockies. Timber lined the hills due west. Pasture stretched out for acres, and cattle dotted the land. A ranch house, barn, and corral completed the scene. It was a comfortable picture, a place a man could call home.

"Come into the Short Keg for a beer and we'll catch up," said Ken. "Meanwhile I want to introduce you to Ginger. She wants out of the 'man' business, and into the ranch business. I figure you boys would welcome a cook, and a woman's touch around this place. Ginger grew up on a ranch and tells me she can do the work, what do ya say?"

"I don't know, Ken. It's all guys here, and ranchin' is a tough business."

Hands on her hips, Ginger retorted, "You boys got nothing ta be fraid of, I won't bite. I'm a good cook and I'll keep your place clean."

"Ha, ha, I reckon she'll work out Okay" said John and Van in unison, "she does have spunk."

"That's not all either boys, I want ma own room and ma own privy. You boys do what you want, but, stay outta my privy. And, I don't want it a hundirt miles out in the forest! I want it close by the house, maybe even a covered walkway to it."

This time the boys slapped their legs, laughed out loud and shook hands with Ginger. "We think you'll work out right nice," said John and Van, almost in harmony.

When they got back to the Short Keg, Ken, George, Molly, and Mary, took stock of the place. They made a plan and got started. Molly and Mary took to cleaning while Ken and George did repairs. In a few days, the place was shaping up well. A few of the floorboards had to be replaced along with a couple of chairs, and one new table. They all worked hard, complementing each other well. The girls started to relax in the new environment, often laughed, and sometimes sang a happy melody. Ken and George enjoyed the company of the girls, but did have to correct their language from time to time. The Short Keg was taking on a friendly, bright look, turning off the mean, ugly feel from just a week ago.

There were five rooms upstairs. Kathy was still in one, but would be out soon. Molly and Mary took the rooms farthest from the downstairs noise and closest to the kitchen. Ken and George took the rooms at the other end. When Kathy left, there would be an empty room between them. The wood building felt solid. With some window coverings and a rug or two, it would be comfortable. A new privy or two out back, would finish the basic repairs.

54

Pondering one day, Ken asked his friend, "George, what do ya think about Molly, Mary, and our saloon?"

"Ha, a month ago we were lame and out of work. If ya had told me we'd have our own saloon, with our own rooms, with two young ladies cookin' and cleanin' for us, I'd have said you were crazy. I'm gonna like this place, Ken. Them girls won't stay forever, so let's enjoy it while we can."

"You're absolutely right you Crazy Sundowner."

*****

It had been a few months since Ken and George had reopened the Short Keg saloon. It was a clean place, the spittoons were even emptied each week. Having no girls upstairs eliminated a lot of trouble. Having two ex-lawmen running the place also eliminated a lot of trouble. Mary and Molly kept the kitchen going and the place dusted and swept. It was a saloon, a friendly place with good food and a comfortable feel.

"Ken, apparently you've a new alias. A lot of our customers have taken to callin' you 'Short Keg'. It might be cause you're a bit short and round?"

"Not funny, George. Haven't you noticed how people

love to have fun with names? The carpenter's called 'Thumb Buster', the lady dress maker's name is Tilly, but she's called 'Frilly', some call the doc, 'Stitches', and the wheel wright is called 'Wheels'. And you know what? I like it, makes me feel at home, and I intend to make this place my home."

Chapter 3

Nevada Slim

A man named Nevada Slim had set up a livery near the town corral with the help of the dropouts. He doubled as the blacksmith and stayed busy from day one. The livery and blacksmith shop were on the edge of town coming in from the east. It had been laid out in two connecting buildings, horse stables and corral at one end, a forge, anvil and tools at the other end. The livery had a good selection of horses. Slim hired the Williams boy, Jacob, to help with the feeding and bedding. Jacob proved to be a strong boy and good worker. Slim kept the metal work going constantly. The ring and ting of hammer and metal continually echoed down the street.

John and Van came into town for supplies every month or so and always stopped at the blacksmith shop to say 'Hi' to Slim. Nevada Slim—an ex-lawman—was not from Nevada, nor was he slim. At 6'7" and 300 pounds, with half an ear, he presented quite a sight. He had a shock of hair pouring over his large head with a beard to match. He always had a smile and finished every sentence with a laugh.

Van entered the blacksmith shop where Slim was pounding iron.

"Hey Slim," Van called out, "I brought in one of my ponies, threw a shoe last week, how bout fixing him up?"

"Sure thang."

"Slim, how long you been in the smithy business?"

"Well Van, I growed up in Omaha. I was big for my age; practically ate my folks outa house and home. I had to get a job just ta feed myself. I hustled at the stable in town at twelve. Throwin' manure, straw and hay after school put some beef on my bones. At fifteen, I started working in a smelting foundry. At twenty, I stood six foot seven and weighed in bout two hundred and seventy. I had to git on one of them scales they used to weigh beef. Working the foundry, I learned smithing skills, and put on these here muscles you wish you had."

"Ha, ha, big as you are, you need those muscles just to hold yourself up. Got any new stories bout how you lost half that fleshy thing on your head?"

"Don't know. What'd I tell you last time? The bear, the cougar, the ex-wife," Slim laughed. "Hey, got some news. We have us a couple a new guys runnin' the Short Keg. Names are Ken Knight and George Sundown, both ex-lawmen. Clyde was Ken's uncle and Ken busted Clyde's killer. Turns out that wern't no accident. Clyde's manager clubbed him and set it ta look like an accident. He's oer to jail house awaiting trial. Ken told them working girls from upstairs, they were free to go. Also seems, many of the men in town are takin' to callin' Ken, Short Keg, just like the name of the saloon. That saloon is becoming the most popular place in town, and Ken is a right friendly guy."

"I know a little bout it. Ken brought one of the girls out to the ranch lookin' for work. Dang if she doesn't do a great job. She's loaded with spunk and fun to be around. We knowd Ken and George from our lawdog days in Arizona. It's good to have some friends in town, specially ones that owns a saloon."

"Well, they cleaned the place good, and two of them 'upstairs' ladies are working there cooking and cleaning. We also have a new sheriff moving in. A feller named Cal, friend of Ken's, coming from Cali-fornia. Mark is real happy to turn his badge over to Cal. He was figurin' to do some ranchin' and a little prospecting, not sheriffing. So you know Ken and

George?"

"Yep, them are boys you could ride the river with. I'm going over to the Short Keg now to catch up. Also good news bout cleanin' up the place. Clyde kept it nice, then that manager really took it to the dumps. Come over when you have a break, we'll bend an elbow and meet the boys."

Van met up with John outside the livery and they headed for the Short Keg.

"I reckon we should head there first off and get supplies later. Catch up with those two, and tell them a bit about town and the folks that live here," said John

The boys got to the saloon, stomped in, and gruffly asked, "Where's this Short Keg fella?"

Ken looked up like there was trouble a brewin', saw the brothers and with a wide grin, just as gruffly said, "Who's askin'?"

The other men in the bar looked up, braced for some trouble, and sat still. Talk like that usually meant trouble.

"Just the toughest hombres you'll ever want to meet."

Van laughed.

Ken and George stepped from behind the bar and slapped both the boys on the arms, shook hands and continued grinning from ear-to-ear.

"Well if this isn't a wild pair to draw to, how you boys getting by?" asked George.

"First, we've got to tell you, Ginger is dynamite, thanks for bringin' her out. We've been eatin' good and the place is clean. We got her a room and a privy. She's definitely the boss around the house."

"I saw a bit of the ranch the other day, looks good. What got you into the ranching business?" asked Ken.

"Chasin' bandits, gettin' shot at, eatin' dust, sleepin' on ground full of rocks, and comin' up on forty years old, got us into ranchin'. We decided to get some land of our own, and run a few cows of our own. We knowd too many lawmen whose only land was six feet under. So, while we could still take our vittles sitten' up, we looked for a place that weren't crawlin' with rowdies; a place with some peace and quiet. We found Marshallville and we aim to put down roots."

Sundowner nodded his head. "You got that right, Van. How's it going?"

"The place is mighty fine. We bought 200 hundred head from Charles Goodknight. Went to New Mexico and picked up four bulls. We've been there 'bout two years now and the herd numbers bout 300; don't it, John?" John nodded and Van went on. "We built a house and a barn, dug a well, and gettin' ready to build one of them windmills. One of the city founders, Mike Miles, has the plans and will help us out. First off we had a little Indian trouble. The Kiowa and Arapaho were gettin' a little testy bout the white man pushin' them around. Colorado territory had some cavalry units close by, so that added some protection. A few years after the great war, the men mustered out. Three of them boys stopped by the ranch looking for work. Well, we could use some help, and we could use the protection, so we hired them on. It's worked out real well. Funny thing though, I think one of them boys has gotten all smitten with Ginger. Sorry to hear about 'ol Clyde, but good to hear you busted the killer; that guy was mean and ornery." Van scowled, then his expression cleared. "So, how'd you like the town?"

"Don't know, only been here a couple of months. Spent most of it with George, cleaning and repairing the place. Organizing a business and going to Denver for supplies takes

62

time. I did talk to John Marshall a bit about the town and zoning restrictions, and the other founding families, seems like a good place to live." Ken took his place back behind the bar. "I'm beginning to feel a part of this town. Beats the hell out of moving, chasing and wearing out saddle leather."

Leaning an elbow on the bar, John grinned, "Have you met Nevada Slim?"

"Not yet." Ken shook his head. "I did meet Phil Franks and Bill Williams. They have a carpenter shop and the tools I needed to clean this place up, good people."

Chuckling, John said, "Nevada Slim's another ex-lawman. You'll notice he only has half an ear. I think whatever happened that took off half his ear is what made up his mind bout givin' up peacekeepin'. One day he might give us the lowdown. Right now he just makes up crazy stories every time he's asked 'bout it. He has a good sense of humor and loves to throw out funny words."

Pouring a couple of beers for the Gentry boys, Ken said, "I know I need to learn more about the town. George and I just want to enjoy the saloon business and not the peace keeping business. We've had our fill of gun play and cattle stampedes; but that's a story for later. Sounds like this here town is the safe place to be, what with having a bunch of ex-lawmen around."

"We do get some old law dog friends of ours stop by the ranch now and then, mostly wantin' to retire. One thing all us keepers of the peace have in common is we're always lookin' for a place to live in peace," offered John.

Taking a long pull of the beer, Van said, "We need to get on with pickin' up supplies. Come out to the ranch soon and we'll catch up on some more stories. I'll tell you about our shoot out and how we got to Marshallville. Hey, I like your new alias, Short Keg, fits you."

Chapter 4

Buzzard Cooper

John and Van headed over to the dry goods and grocery store. Van called out, "Hey, Coop, how's the shoulder?"

Gary Cooper owned the store. Coop was a large fellow, stout with broad shoulders. He was graying some, but quick with a smile and handshake. He had added a few pounds around the middle since sheriffing, but was surprisingly quick on his feet.

The store, a solid, two story, wood building, took up two lots on Main street. Cooper had the store built to replace the original dry goods and grocery tent. He lived upstairs, and had windows and curtains like a real home. Just about anything a feller might need was stacked up somewhere in the store. A bench and a few chairs sat next to the stove he kept lit up during winter. Friends took to calling him 'Coop'. Then again, sometimes they called him Buzzard. He wasn't sure why, it just happened.

"Hey, howdy Van, John. Oh the shoulder is OK, the bullet just took a little meat off the top, it's the stiff knee that catches now and then, especially when it gets to be frosty and snowy. Not like today, it's so hot even the snakes are lookin' for shade. You and John in for supplies?"

"Ya, we're picking up our monthly load. We stopped in to the Short Keg and caught up a bit with Ken and George. You been there yet?"

"I heard the ruckus the day they took over, and headed that way curious like. Them boys settled that mess, and I was glad to meet 'em. They did some grocery shopping that night with a couple of the girls. I figure on spending a bit of time there after work. It's right friendly, and a good place to have a drink and catch up on some old 'back in the day' stories."

"You know Coop, we never did hear the story bout how you got shot. I just heard that the story makes a person scratch his head. I see you rubbin' on the shoulder now and then and gettin' a little gimpy during the winter."

"It's a funny story, have a seat over by the stove and I'll get to tellin' it if you have time. I know you boys got work to do.

66

"Now that we have Ginger keepin' the place tidy and all, and the cavalry boys around, we have more time to hang out and enjoy some time in town. We been meanin' to get your measure so give it to us good."

"It's the damnedest thing," said Coop, "sometimes I don't rightly figure how it happened myself. I was sheriffing over in southern Oregon, in a little mining town called Jacksonville. On a Sunday morning, I sat in church, like most of the people in town, that's what you did on Sunday morning, listen to the preacher. He was doing a fine job of pointin' out sin and how folk ought to follow the Godly path. Finally, he ran out breath and closed up with 'now go forth and sin no more.' I thought we were done, and I started to get up and head back to the jailhouse. I had some new mail and wanted posters I needed to look at."

"Tis funny bout them preachers, Coop, they sure can go on bout sinnin'," John agreed.

"Well, unbeknownst to me, a lovers' triangle had been goin' on in town. We all knew Don Brown's wife liked to be a little flirty, but as it turned out, she was a lot more than flirty. Before we could get up and go, Don stood up, drew his pistol and yelled at Al Gator, a man sitting next to me and said, 'Now

Al, you go forth and sin no more with my wife.' At which point he took a few shots at Al. With Don shaking in anger, that added up to me getting nicked in the shoulder and knee cap."

"You're right, Coop, that's the damndest thing. Makes ya worry bout who ya sit next to," said Van.

"I jumped up and screamed at Don. He realized he'd shot me, not Al, so he tried to run out the church. He tripped over his wife's dress tryin' to get out of the row, fell and shot himself in the leg. I cain't say for sure that he tripped on his own, or his wife tripped him, but there he lay on the floor, screamin', with his leg bleedin' all over the floor. There I stood with blood dripping out of my shoulder and leg. Fortunately, Doc Smith was in church also, and it turns out, he never goes nowhere without his bag. 'Never know what might happen,' he always said, and he was right. He stopped my bleedin', then stopped ol' Don's bleedin'. We both went to his office for stitches and bandages. There I am, sitting next to the guy that just shot me, and I have to arrest him for attempted murder and shootin' a sheriff. His wife did come to see him in jail, but he told her to go back to her mother. He accounted for her to be at fault that he sat there in jail with a wounded leg lookin' like the hindquarters of bad luck."

"Wow," said Van, "that's one of the craziest stories I've ever heard, I'm glad I was sittin' down."

"In fifteen years, I'd never been shot, shot at, yes, but never hit. I figured getting shot in church was a hell-fire message it might be time to hang up my badge, and look fer somewhere quieter and safer. I headed back to my home town in Illinois and stopped in Denver. I saw a poster bout Marshallville, and decided to take a look. Now I'm here and plan to stay."

"I like it here, too, Coop. But how do you go from bein' a sheriff to wranglin' hardware and ownin' a grocery store?"

"I grew up in Illinois. My dad had a grocery and dry goods store for years. At ten, dad put me to work in the store. Dad expected me to take over the business when he retired. I put in a lot a years, and learned a lot bout the business. But, I read a lot of those dime novels bout the old west. Horses, cattle drives, and shoot outs sounded a lot more excitin' than polishin' apples, stackin' bolts of material, or countin' tins. I saw a lot of wagons moving west. A lot of excitement, so when I turned 18, I bought two horses, packed my kit and caboodle, and tagged along with a wagon train headed for Oregon. Riding out west gave me a thrill in my bones. A few months later I entered Oregon. I wandered a bit. Looked for gold for a bit. A couple of years later, by accident, I got into the peace keeping business."

"This is some good story tellin' ain't it John. We got more time for listenin', or do we got to get back?"

"We got time, Van. Had me one them pickles you got in that jar Coop and tell us how you go in the law business."

"Funny you ask for a pickle cause you jest never know which way a pickle will squirt. When havin' supper in a café in a town called Medford, a fight broke out bout an insult, or a girl, or money, I never found out, you know how it is, men start fightin' and fussin' at the drop of a hat. A sheriff, also in there havin' supper, stepped in to break up the fight. Unfortunately, he stepped in to a roundhouse punch and went down. The two guys seeing the sheriff go down, washed off the war paint and skedaddled. I helped the sheriff to his feet. His legs were shaky so I helped him back ta the sheriff's office. He sat down, put his head in his hands and moaned a bit. He figured he might need help for the next few days til he cleared his head, so he offered me a job as a deputy. I couldn't believe it, me a deputy! I'd read bout lawmen, always as heroes and then suddenly, I was gonna be a deputy. Fifteen years, many towns and many experiences later, I get shot in a church. The excitement of the old west wore off pretty quickly when I saw my own blood. The dime novels were jest make-believe stories. Suddenly, polishin' apples and countin' tins sounded very appealin'. I knew the business, had a few dollars and here I am, safe and sound."

"Sounds a lot like John and mine's story, but we had a sure'n'nuf, shoot out with a gang carrin' them new Henry's. I were lucky I walked away with only a nick in my shoulder and a hole in my hat. John ate some dirt, got skinned up some but stayed alive. We made it this far, so no more dangerous rides; time to enjoy life."

"What's on your list for this trip, boys?"

"Supplies and a beer or two. We'll get the usual, bacon, beans, flour, some .44s, and a few of those new 'airtights'. How's business these days?"

"I've got a new section in the store, fresh farm goods. One of those wagon train folk headin' for Oregon had some wagon trouble and decided to stop here. With the land grant option, this Danish family staked out a farm and went to work. Hans and Janet Anderson are hard workers, come all the way from Denmark. Were farmers there, now farmers here. They have 4 or 5 kids and know the farming business. They're also raising pigs, so I'll be havin' fresh bacon and chops from time to time. I'm also busy with lots a new folk in town."

"We need to head back to the ranch, come out for supper and drinks one night, it's light til nine. Look forward to seeing ya. We all got stories to swap. Ginger makes a great supper, and a pile of bear sign fer desert.

Chapter 5

Gentleman George

"Senor, you are on zee wrong side of zee river. Why are you here?"

George had been looking for sign and never saw the men approach. Sometimes a person gets so intent on one thing, he completely shuts out everything else. George had made that mistake. Now he found himself in a bad place and he didn't like it one bit.

"Just chasin' some bad men. Ah didn't want them to be troublin' for y'all in your country," said Texas Ranger, George Kay.

"Amigo, that is kind of you but you see, those men are friends of mine so I theenk you are not my friend."

George knew he had found trouble. He had been with a small group of rangers from southwest Texas chasing a large

73

band of Mexican bandits that had been raiding towns and ranches for months. The rangers had split up casting for sign. Now here he sat on the wrong side of the Rio Grande, by himself, looking at a bunch of tough hombres. *Well I found the gang,* he said to himself, *now what?* He knew they were not going to just let him trot back across the river without a fuss. He had been in tight spots before, but this had a very bad feel about it.

Sitting a large roan with a Walker colt on his saddle holster plus a cap and ball open top in his belt holster, he came well-armed, but looking at twenty or more bandits, also well-armed, gave pause to wonder what was next. George was never one to be gripped by fear but this looked to be a mighty tight squeeze.

Out of the corner of his eye he saw part of his ranger group dismounting on the US side of the river. He would get some cover fire, but not before he gained a few pounds of lead from his new found buddies.

The bandits were all smiling. Shaggy mops of hair stuck out from under their large sombreros. Bandoliers crossed their chests. With sweat clinging to their foreheads, they sat silently ready to ignite if lit. Only the buzzing of insects and the occasional croak was heard.

He knew, they knew, trying to ride back across the river would make him open for some target practice. He had to do the unexpected to have any chance for survival. A plan quickly formed in his head, now if you could just pull it off.

"Well boys, if you'all don't mind, Ah'l jest head back home."

"Sure, Senor," laughed the bandit leader,

Instead of turning to cross the river, and opening his back to a couple dozen shooters, heart beating a mile a minute, he charged the bandit gang. Facing more than twenty fierce looking bandits, he pulled his Walker Colt. With the punch to stop a full grown horse, he dropped the hammer as fast as he could.

The bandidos initially sat shocked, then dropped their smiles and drew their guns. George emptied two saddles as he charged. *At least I got a couple of them before they got me,* was a thought that ran through his brain.

The rangers across the river opened up with a volley that wounded two more. Within a few seconds George rode into the men. Their horses reared, throwing off their aim. Many of the bandits held fire so as not to hit their own men. That didn't stop George from firing, and he took out another bandit. With his eyes looking left and right and his senses lighting up his brain, he sent his horse jumping and kicking dirt in all directions. A couple of the bandit horses reared, throwing off their riders. George pistol whipped one more then broke through and immediately turned right, emptied his Walker toward the gang then headed as fast as he could to the river. He hit the water at full speed and, for a second, thought he might make it.

The valiant effort took him only halfway across the river. His body jerked right and left and lurched forward. He knew he was hit, but hell bent on getting free, he ignored the searing stabs, and hung on to the saddle horn to keep from falling. His horse reared, and went down, throwing George into the water. The rangers were throwing a lot of lead at the bandits. Seeing George go down, the bandits halted firing, grabbed up their wounded and rode south, yipping and cheering.

A couple of rangers rode into the river, grabbed George and carried him back to land. Blood flowed out of a lot of bullet holes. The river water had washed some of blood away from his body and left a red pool floating where George had gone down. It slowly drifted away with the current. George winced as he was lifted out of the water. Pain shot through his back but he didn't have time to worry about dying; he passed out.

The rangers had been through this before and set to stopping the blood flow. Not spitting blood, meant no lungs were hit. None of the holes were squirting blood, so no arteries were hit. Either one of those would have meant death in a few minutes. While two of the men were seeing to the wounds, two others set up camp and built a fire. They knew a lot of hot water would be needed. Once they got the bleeding stopped, they looked to the bullet holes.

He was lucky—if being shot up could be lucky. He had some flesh wounds and a grazed head. However, three pieces of lead were buried in his back. One piece cracked a rib near his back bone, but again, a lucky hit for George, otherwise it might have gone deeper and hit a lung. The unlucky part, it sat too close to the back bone to try to dig it out. That piece of lead would be a permanent part of George.

Each shoulder blade took a hit, and again, a lucky hit or they too may have gone deeper and hit the heart or a lung.

Again the unlucky part, each piece stuck almost through the bone, and any attempt to dig them out might also cause more damage. Three pieces of lead would live in George from now on.

An hour later, the bullet holes were thoroughly cleaned out with hot water and plugged with bandage. George shook uncontrollably from the loss of blood and shock to his body. The rangers wrapped him tightly in blankets to keep him warm. He became delirious and groaned a lot, but finally went to sleep a few hours later.

The rangers figured the bandits might come back to finish the job. They had lost a number of men, were frothing, riled good, and may have figured with only a small group of rangers, they might return to wipe them out. In the dark, the rangers moved their blankets about fifty feet away, but kept the fire going into the night. They stacked brush into piles to look like men sleeping around the fire, and they rotated guard duty throughout the night.

At dawn the next morning, the fake fire, almost out, sent faint wisps of smoke rising from the ground. A little mist draped on the water. The rising sun cast a sliver of light shimmering across the river. A quiet stillness pervaded the area.

Suddenly, several shots rang out, kicking up dirt and ashes in the fake campsite. The bandits hooped and hollered sending dozens of rounds into the stacked branches as they raced hell bent across the river. The rangers quietly slipped out of their blankets, braced their rifles against their shoulders, and waited for the bandits to cross the river. When they came within fifty feet, the rangers opened fire. Their first round dumped four of the enemy. Almost in unison they levered in another round and three more men jerked up and dropped as pieces of lead found their mark. Shot, surprised, and panicked, the gang turned tail and headed south back across the river, as three more saddles were emptied. The whole gun fight took less than a minute, but, the bandit gang was decimated and George slept through the whole thing.

The rangers grabbed the fallen bandits and their horses. Two were still alive, but badly wounded. Many bodies lined the river bank. The rangers waved a white flag and shouted out to the remaining gang that could come get their dead and the wounded. The bandit leader showed himself also waving a white flag. "Senors, do not shoot."

The ranger leader shouted back, "Leave your guns and

come get your men. No tricks, we've got you covered."

"No senor, no treeks, we jest want our amigos so we can take them home."

Four unarmed men slowly walked their horses across the river with one hand clearly in the air. The four men loaded up the dead, and the wounded men carefully on the captured horses without looking the rangers in the face.

"You best never come back," warned the ranger captain. "Or next time you'll die where you lay." They watched as the bandits slowly made their way back to Mexico.

The rangers figured the fight was over, but they still made up a fake camp that night. Packing up their gear the next day, they took George into El Paso to see a doctor.

"That's a lot of holes to plug up," said the doctor. "You boys did a good job tying him up, and good thing you got him in when you did."

The doc stitched up the holes and rewrapped the bandages. Each day, the bandages were changed, and each day George gained some strength. Several of the townsfolk ladies were willing to help with George's care. The graze alongside his head would form a permanent line just above his ear. It also birthed an aching headache for the first week.

After the first week, George sat up, but found himself unsteady on his feet. Stiff and sore he ached from head to toe. *I feel like crap,* he thought. *This shit's gonna take a while.* He hadn't shaved or had a haircut for nearly two weeks, so he decided to keep the beard, trim it neatly, and keep the hair long enough to cover the bullet scar on the side of his head.

"You take it easy, George, don't bust up those bandages and start bleeding again, it's only been a week."

"I know, Doc, but I gotta get out of this bed for a stretch."

When George had woken up a few days ago, and realized he was going to live, he figured he wanted to stay that way. When he began to move around town, he turned in his badge and became a normal citizen. He lived through a narrow escape, and narrow escapes are not what he had a hankering for. A reward for busting up the dangerous gang put a sizable bulge in his poke.

He had become somewhat of a celebrity in town, after all, he did charge right into the bandit gang. He, and the other

81

rangers, had busted up a dangerous gang that had been raiding towns and ranches along the border for months. When he finally walked out of the doc's office on his own, several people applauded him as he went by. Much to his pleasant surprise, several of the ladies also took the time to smile and batt their eye lashes. He felt the sun on his back and saw a clear road ahead. One day you're shot to pieces, the next day you have some money in your pocket, and the ladies are smiling at you. Life is good.

His clothes were shot up and bloodied, so, when he started to get around without passing out, he went clothes shopping. He liked the attention he was getting from the ladies, and picked out clothes a gentleman would wear. Keeping a mental tally of the compliments he received from the ladies, he designed his wardrobe accordingly. It wasn't long before many of the townsfolk referred to him as 'Gentleman George.' With three bullets stuck in his back, he walked more upright, adding to his gentlemanly look.

After fifteen years of marshaling and rangering; chasing outlaws and bandits no longer fit his plans. He lost all interest in making a living in a saddle, and sleeping under the stars and, just as often, sleeping under the rain. He wanted to find an indoor job. He took a real shine to his new gentleman look, and threw out his saddle bum clothes. He found a job in a men's clothing store, and quickly learned the trade. He learned some tailoring skills and decided he needed to open his own store. First though, he bought a half partnership in an El Paso clothing store to learn the business part. *I can get used to this indoor work,* he grinned to himself. Eating in a fine café and sleeping on a bed, put a smile on George's face. Once a week, he slid into a barber's chair and walked out trimmed and smelling good.

*****

"I like the variety of clothes here, you have an eye for style," said Charles Goodnight. "I've my trail ridin' duds on now, but I need something a bit more 'gentlemanly' on occasion."

"Y'all came to the right place, sir. I just got in an order from back east, and I've several styles of coats, ties, braces, pants, vests, boots and hats. I can spruce you up, wherever you need to go."

"You sound like a Texan," said Goodnight, "you from around here?"

"I used to be a Texas ranger, got shot up pretty good at the border, now I'm done bustin' my hump and eatin' dust. I'm out of the law business, and into the fashion business. It's a lot safer and cleaner. I want to have my own store someday, and enjoy my peaceful, getting older years, in a smaller, safer town."

"I hear ya, pardner, a few more trail drives and I'm done eatin' dirt myself. Say, I passed a small, but growing town on a drive up Denver way. It could probably use a guy like you. It's called Marshallville, bout eighty miles south a Denver, snuggled up near the Rockies. It's on a trading route, and the Union Pacific is runnin' a line near there in a couple of years, and the Denver and Rio Grande railroad's running a spur by '73. There'll be plenty of business, and it's a right friendly town. It even has its own windmill. I sold some cows to a couple of brothers that had been lawmen, and now run a ranch outside a town. There are two ex-marshals that run the saloon. The town is growing, and it'll probably need a men's store."

Looking around El Paso and figuring his options, the next week George sold his part ownership in the store, loaded up a wagon with merchandise, and headed for Marshallville. The sun at his back, a clear road ahead, gave him a grin from ear to ear.

*****

Going from El Paso to Colorado is a dusty and tiresome trip, but when George pulled into Marshallville, he knew he had made the right decision. The streets were wide and clean. He parked his wagon in front of the land sales office and walked in. He met John Marshall, shook hands, and asked about shop space. George learned a lot about the town and its layout from Marshall. A fast growing town like Marshallville would welcome a men's store.

Marshall showed George the city plat. George picked a building near the hotel and one of the dress shops. They walked to the building and went in.

"It smells like new wood with a fresh, clean feel," said George, "This is perfect for a clothing store, ah'll take it."

Shaking hands, Marshall said, "Deal."

"You're going to like it here, George. We are on a busy trade route, and a wagon train stop over. Many of those travelers saw the place and decided to pull out of the train and started farming right here. New shops open every month. There is also some gold mining close by. Charles Goodnight brings his cattle drives close by, and the cowboys love to stop in for a drink or two. "

"Well sur, Goodnight is the one who told me about this place."

"So, you met Goodnight?"

"He came into ma store in El Paso, right friendly man."

"The other big news is the Union Pacific is running a spur toward Santa Fe near here, and the Denver and Rio Grande is building a station here by '73. The price of lots is going up, you have made a good investment. You might want to invest in a home lot over on 4th street."

"You sure are quite a salesman, but for now, ah'll get my store loaded, see how things shake out, and maybe take a look see later."

"That's not all, Mr. Kay, I think you'll find several friends here also."

"Ah only pulled in today, not likely to know anyone here abouts."

Marshall handed George a city map again with the locations of stores and homes in town. On second look, George was surprised by the organization of Marshallville and the city council.

"This here map shows the city plat and all the businesses in town so far. We need this map for taxes and permits." Marshall pointed at a spot on the map. "This is your store right here. Notice we have a carpenter shop, a leather and harness shop, a couple of millinery shops, a bank, three saloons, two cafes, a hotel, a gun shop, and more. But, right across the street from your place is a grocery and hardware store."

"Okay, so?"

"So, the owner is a former sheriff out of Oregon and California named Gary Cooper. Here is a bathhouse run by a former deputy named Miss Kitty. In the saloon section of town is the Short Keg, run by two former marshals. I suggest a trip to the Short Keg when you get settled. There are two other saloons in town, but the Short Keg is where I feel comfortable and I think you would, too. The livery and blacksmith shop is run by an ex-lawman from Omaha named Nevada Slim. A couple of brothers, the Gentry boys, own a ranch outside of town, also former peace keepers."

A big smile broke out on George's face. He was as pleased as a puppy with two tails. He took off his hat and ran his fingers through his hair, put his hat back on and ran a hand through his beard.

"Well, Mr. Marshall, don't that beat all. Ah'm sure glad Goodnight steered me to this town. It does seem like ah have some built in friends, looking forward to meetin' up with them. Glad tuh hear about the Short Keg, kind of waterin' hole I could get used to."

With a bath house in town, he knew where to go after getting his wagon unloaded and his team stabled. Marshall offered his sons as helpers to unload the wagon and set up the store. George quickly said, "Yes sur," and paid the boys a dollar each.

The boys fetched up the wagon load, but it would be a few days til the store opened for business. The building had two stories with a living space upstairs. The boys helped carry up a living space load, and George took his wagon to the livery. Getting down off his wagon, he bumped into Nevada Slim.

Never for a loss for words, he said, "Whoa, you're a big one. Mister Marshall told me an ex-sheriff named Nevada Slim ran the livery; Ah had a different mental picture of a man named Slim. Mah name is George, just arrived in town. Ah'm setting up a men's clothing store, and ah need to store my wagon and stable ma team. Ah tell ya, I got nothing your size, but if y'all need something, tell me a few weeks ahead of time, and ah can get it."

"You're a funny man, name's Nevada Slim, welcome to town. I'll take care of your rig and team. I don't really need no spiffy duds, but I could use some of that Denim by that Levi feller, makes for a good set of working clothes."

"Ah can get some of that, gonna take a lot, but ah can fit you up. It'll take a week or two."

"What brings you this way?" asked Slim.

"I'm looking for a peaceful, but prosperous town to hang my hat. Ah was a ranger down Texas way, got shot up good at the border, now ah just want to be free of annoying, dangerous people. How about you?"

"Nearly the same story, but I hail from Omaha. We'll swap stories, and cut the deck deeper at the Short Keg some afternoon, got work to do now."

Shaking hands, George said, "Thanks Slim, ah think

ah'll head for the bath house. It has been a long and dusty ride from El Paso, and a long soak will wash the body and lift the spirits."

Chapter 6

Miss Kitty

Pointing down the street, Slim said, "Have you met Miss Kitty? She runs the bath house."

"Not yet, but ah aim to."

"She's one tough lady. She's an ex-lawman too, or should I say ex-lawwoman. Her husband, Todd, sheriffed in a small town in Kansas and she signed on as his deputy. They were a good team. She's mighty handy with a gun, and could stare down a bear. They were making their rounds one night. Some saddle bum dragged into town and was drinking pretty heavy at the saloon. He tried his hand at the Faro table and it emptied his poke, a month's wages worth. He had a few more drinks, but wouldn't pay for 'em, told the bartender he should get'em free seeing as they had all his money. They threw him out as Miss Kitty and Todd walked by. That low life was screaming and yelling obscenities. Todd told him to calm down and cool off. As they were walking away, the bum pulled his gun and shot Todd in the back. Miss Kitty turned and put two slugs in the guy's chest; blew up his heart. Todd lived long enough to tell Miss Kitty he loved her. She lit out right after the funeral. Too many memories caused too many tears. She'd heard of Marshallville from a friend passing through from Denver. She came here for the same reason I came here…looking for a nice peaceful town. She runs a good, clean bath house."

Miss Kitty had two retired 'upstairs ladies' working with her and one large bouncer. The bath house sat in a large tent with a half dozen tubs lined up around the walls. There were two private rooms, curtained off at one end. Short clothes lines stood next to each tub with a sheet hanging over the top line giving a tiny place for privacy and blocking the view from the outside, and from the working ladies. Miss Kitty would tell the men to stay behind the towels cause no one wanted to see their raw, skinny hides. Two large signs hung on one wall.

No Profanity or Rudeness Allowed

First offense, a smack in the head with the broom.

The second offense you get thrown out and no refund.

No peeing in the tubs.

Seeing a gun holstered high on Miss Kitty's hip along with the bouncer gave pause for concern and usually a willingness to follow the rules.

The second sign listed the prices:

Hot water, 1st in, soap, towel, lavender water, private $1

Hot water, 2nd in, soap, towel, lavender water .75

Hot water, 3rd in, soap, towel .50

Cold water, 1st in, soap, towel, .50

Cold water, 2nd in, soap, towel, .25

Cold water, 3rd in, soap, towel, .10

Out back of the tent, Miss Kitty had a large stove going with metal water tubs sitting on top. A well and two privies stood out back also. With a small wagon, the ladies were able to haul the water from the well to the stove, then to the tubs. Strictly speaking, the 'hot' tubs weren't all that hot but a couple of buckets of water right off the stove took the chill off the well water.

There were drain pipes running out the bottom of the tubs that ran downhill to an old dried up streambed. After the third wash, the tubs were drained, wiped out and refilled. Miss Kitty ran a clean operation, and the men and ladies loved it. From 3:00 to 5:00 every afternoon, it was ladies only. The tent covers were tightly closed, and the bouncer stood outside keeping all men away. The working girls from the saloons came in on a regular basis, along with many of the women shopkeepers.

A third sign hung by the door out back. It had an arrow pointing over to the Fu King laundry. A man named Wang owned the Chinese laundry. He would pick up clothes, wash them, while a customer bathed, and hang them up outside, near a stove. During rain or winter, he'd hang them inside.

His prices were listed:

shirt, drawers, pants, socks, bandana all .50

If you wanted them ironed .50

Hats, coats brushed and dusted .25

*****

"Welcome, I'm Miss Kitty, and if you're looking for a good place to scrub off some trail dirt, this is it."

"Very pleased to meet you, Miss Kitty. Ah'm George Kay, just in from Texas, and just opening a men's clothing store. Ah understand you're a former peace officer. Ah'm also a former, and I emphasize the word 'former', peace officer. We'll have to swap stories sometime."

"Good to know that, George, you will fit right in here. We have regular yarn spinning sessions at the Short Keg. Come in for a spell and bring your yarn."

"I have a man just left and the water is still warm if you want that one," Miss Kitty said.

"No thanks," said George," Ah'll have my own water and the first in special fer a dollar."

After a scrub and a good soak, George felt clean and refreshed. He walked out of the bathhouse and headed for the Short Keg. He had a store and a place to stay. He had a bath, and a delightful meeting with Miss Kitty. As he walked into the Short Keg, he saw a clean saloon, a long bar, some tables and chairs, and a few gaming tables. He saw John Marshall at the bar talking with a tough, but friendly looking bartender.

"Hey, George," Marshall called. "Come meet Ken Knight, some folks call him Short Keg. Your first beer is on me."

"It don't get much better than this," George grinned. "Ma first day in town and the mayor's buyin' me a drink."

"George, this is Ken. Ken, this is George. George used to be a Texas Ranger."

The two men shook hands. "Good to meet you, George. Understand you have a men's clothing store. We could use some style around here. Right John? And it's always good to meet a fellow peace officer."

"Former peace officer," said George. "Ah think you probably have a good story bout how you went from a marshal to a saloon keeper."

Laughing Ken said, "I'm sure you have a good story, too, bout how you went from a Texas Ranger to a men's clothing store owner."

"Well fellas, I hate to miss the story-telling, but I need to see some of the council members about the agenda for our next meeting. We need to approve another deputy for Cal, the town is growing and we aim to keep it peaceful." Marshall tipped his hat and left.

"George, meet my partner, George." Ken introduced the two.

George Sundown had just walked around the corner, coming from the kitchen, with a sandwich in his hand. Setting his sandwich on the bar and wiping his hand on his pants, he extended his hand. "Hi George, good to meet ya."

"Havin' two Georges around may be confusing, not that you look alike." Ken looked from one man with an oriental face and the other with a thick, nicely trimmed beard and bushy hair. "But, since you like nicknames, George, I'll call you 'Sundowner'. I've already heard people call you that. Actually, I heard that bartender that you cut off half an ear refer to you as 'crazy' so maybe Crazy Sundowner."

"Crazy Sundowner has kind of a nice ring to it. Might keep people from annoying me. Thanks, Short Keg, I can go with that."

"Ah can see this is the place to put a boot on the rail, bend an elbow, and enjoy the company," said George.

"We're here most every day, talk is what we do. Reckon you can spin a tale or two yourself. We have regular story-telling with a few other ex-law dogs most every day. Look forward to seeing you."

"If y'all feel like some new duds, stop by the store next week and ah'l fix you up."

"Oh, George, step round to the kitchen, I want you to meet a couple of people. This is Molly and Mary, they work here. They do the cooking and cleaning. They make a darn good meal, especially chili, so if you're hungry, stop by for supper."

"Pleased to meet you, ladies, it does smell good in here. If you can do up a thick T-bone and the fixins, y'all will see me often enough."

Chapter 7

Shady Mike

Six years old in 1842, Mike Hoz lived in a small, clean, one bedroom house a few blocks from the docks in New Orleans with his mom and dad. His dad worked the docks and his mom worked in a Creole café near the docks. Surviving the docks meant hanging with the right guys, scamming a little, gambling a little, and of course fighting a little. Working in a cafe in 1842 in New Orleans meant putting up with being grabbed, and needing thick skin. Mike learned early the pecking order of the dock. Over the years his dad showed him the ropes and taught him how to survive.

"Son, fightin' on the docks comes with bruises and loss of skin. Ah'll be gone a week at a time takin' cargo ups and downs the river so ya need ta learn ta fight a bit. First rule is don't never start nothin', you cain't know what a guy mite do. Never meet a bully head on, wait til he's distracted then hit him from behind. If he goes down, kick him hard. Ya want guys to know if they mess with ya, they'll get hurt. If you get grabbed and can't free yourself then get in close, they cain't get a good swing in close. In close is when ya pull your knife and stick it hard. Don't let folk know you carrin' a knife, they'll come at you with a club. When ah'm here, we'll work sum on fightin'."

At twelve, Mike, ran errands on the docks. At fifteen, he worked full time. His dad kept giving advice through the years. He had the bruises to prove he was learning through practice.

"Son, let me tell ya how life be. No one gives you nothin' for free. Ya got to con and scam ever you can. Best I can do fo ya is show how. Ya got ta keep your eyes and ears open, and yo mouth shut. Ya see sumpin' and no one's lookin, take it. Ya also need to play sum cards and learn a few tricks."

Mike followed his dad at night; that's when the action started. He watched men playing cards. His dad would point out some tricks cardsharps would do. He watched the winners and the losers, and learned from what he saw. Mike learned many important lessons in life from his dad.

*****

"It's yo bet boy, watcha do?"

Mike figured winning at cards was an easier way to earn a dollar than actually doing hard labor. Mike had been winning, and he thought he had the game figured out. Most any time of day, a game could be found on the docks somewhere. Usually the game would be in a warehouse, on an old rickety table with barrels or hay bales, and men in coveralls. This evening Mike felt lucky.

"A'h bet it all," Mike said, putting everything he had won plus all his pay from that week.

"Ya got beeg cawds, mon ami, let's look," said the big creole boat worker as he called the bet.

Mike threw down three kings. The big creole threw down three aces.

"Ha, ha, ma cawds et beeger than votre, mon ami."

Mike could not believe it. He felt sure his hand would win. Now he had lost all his money. He slowly got up and walked out of the warehouse. He sat on a crate with his head in his hands. His dad had told him to never go all in without the 'nuts'. He figured the big ol creole to be just a dumb guy that didn't know much about cards. Turned out that big guy knew a lot more about cards than Mike did. He felt like a fool, he thought he knew the game, but apparently he got scammed.

The sounds of yelling, swearing, and fighting caught Mike's attention. He hurried to the other side of the warehouse. Three men were attacking another man. They were throwing punches from all sides. Mike's instinct was to help, but his dad had told him to stay out of other people's business. He started to turn away, but recognized the man being attacked. It was the creole who beat him at cards. The creole, a big man, a curly wolf, but an older man showed tough. The three men were younger, not as big, but were getting the better of him. One of the men had a knife, and it would not be long before the old creole got pig stuck. On an impulse, Mike jumped in. He picked up a 2X4 that was laying on the dock and wacked one man hard dislocating the man's shoulder. Dropping the 2X4 he round-house punched a second man sending him over some crates, knocking him cold. The big creole sent an uppercut to the third man's jaw, breaking it, and the fight ended with three men down.

"Merci, mon ami," the big creole said. He staggered over to Mike, breathing hard, blood oozing from the lumps on his head.

Mike hooked an arm under his shoulder and steadied

him.

"Allez," he said, "we leave now."

They slowly shuffled to one of the all night cafes by the dock. The air choked with smoke, smelled of body odor and burnt food. Soot from candles covered the ceiling. Food stains covered the floor, at least it looked like food stains, could have been anything.

"They no good losers," the creole said.

"Is there ah good loser, especially if thah thenk they been tricked," Mike said. "A'h lost the money I had to buy food for my mother. My dad, he showed me about playing cards. A'h was winnin'. A'h thought ah could get a big hand."

"Oh, mon ami, yo know too leetlle. I let yo ween some, den take it all. You not cardsharper, I cardsharper. You save my life, maybe I show ya tum tings bout cawds. I give monee back, yo buy votre mere food." The creole wrote an address on a paper, "meet me dis place, ya know it?"

"Ya, a'h meet you." Making a fist around the money, Mike nodded and left.

Once a week, after work for months, when his dad was not home, Mike met with the creole. He learned bottom dealing, trick shuffles, palming cards, fake cuts, stacking decks and more. It took a lot of practice, one slip could mean a gun shot in the gut. On one rare day off, the creole took Mike to a docked steamboat and showed him the gaming tables. He pointed out the tricks the 'sharpers' were using. He taught Mike how to spot them. He taught him how to read the other players, the 'tells' he said, and when to bet and when to fold. They watched poker, Faro and Three-card monte. Three-card Monte needed helpers called 'cappers'. The 'sure thing' was a tricky con used to sucker people into three-card Monte. Tens of thousands of dollars could be made every year. There were also painted ladies near by the gaming tables.

"Monsieur Mike, do not go wif the painted ladees, they are veree dangerous."

Mike's dad had taught him about fighting, the creole showed him about 'hide out' guns and knives.

"A time will come when a bad loser or another con man will attack," said the big Creole. "Ah lost my hide-out when ya saved moi."

Mike made a 'hide out' pocket in his coat and his boot for both a derringer and a knife. He also had a shoulder holster for a six shot .22.

A year later, Mike, at twenty, sat at the steamboat gaming tables slow playing and low playing for a few hours each day. Still learning, but making some money, he liked being a gambler. On return trips to New Orleans, he showed his dad some new tricks, and his dad did better in those warehouse games.

"Mike," said the old creole, "you have thee good hands, even better than moi, ya know all I know. There is steel much to learn. Like da pere teel you, eyes opeen and ears opeen. Never go all in with a stranger. People will see you as a young kid, and theek you be a fool, that ees good fo you. Bon chance, mon amie." The old creole grabbed both shoulders and squeezed.

*****

Mike said good-bye to his mom and dad, and at twenty-two, he rode the river boats up and down as a gambler. He loved the excitement. After a few years he had seen and heard most scams and cons a hundred times, he learned well.

Mike ran a few cons and cheated his share of naive easterners. He had a conscience and never completely cleaned out the foolish men willing to gamble with strangers. After many years on the boats, he knew many of the other gamblers, and watched them scam and con gullible travelers. He could not complain; he did the same thing.

He paid the captains of the boats a share of his winnings and they looked the other way when complaints were made. His brain began to numb-over by the constant gambling, often cheating, but, he liked the cash building up in his pocket. He had nice clothes, ate well, practiced excellent manners, and had a pleasant demeanor. Many ladies travelling found him attractive and showed their appreciation.

Mike invested in coffee, sugar, cotton, and wine as a broker, and watched his cargo load and unload as he travelled up and down the river. He helped his parents out so his dad could quit working the docks, and manage the movement and selling of Mike's cargo.

*****

Earlier in the evening, Mike had been seated at supper near an elderly gentleman, his wife, and their lovely daughter.

Attracted to the daughter, Mike struck up a conversation with the old man. The old man wanted to leave the south, the war and the slave issue, so he had sold his estate in New Orleans, and with his family, decided to head to Pennsylvania where his brother lived. He would buy a place there and go into business with his brother. He carried a lot of money.

Later that night things changed, and Mike found himself leaving the river life and heading in land. He had had a good night at the tables, and standing along the railing, he enjoyed a cigar. The warm, clear night gave him a moment of pleasure. It never ceased to amaze him how easily men would throw away money on crummy cards and poor hands.

Mike heard a woman scream, a man moan, and a loud thud in one of the cabins close to where he stood. He had heard struggles many times over the years and planned to stay out of this one. The door opened in the cabin and the old man's daughter tried to run out. She was grabbed by the arm and dragged back in the room while she struggled to break free. He immediately knew the play.

Mike charged into the room to see three men attacking the family and trying to steal the old man's money. As one of the men turned and raised his fist, Mike's dock fighting instincts kicked in. He stepped in close and stabbed, and stabbed again. The other two men turned to attack Mike, but in close quarters they could not get a good swing. Mike used the third man as a shield, drew his derringer and sticking his arm under the arm of the man he just stabbed, fired point blank into the men. With his four shot, Pepper Box, he put two shots in each man. He shrugged off the stabbed man and grabbed the other two men, and threw them in a pile. The shots attracted the crew members, and they charged into the room. The three men were still alive, bleeding badly, lay heaped on the floor.

When Mike explained what happened, the crew took the three men to the brig. The old man had cuts and bruises but would be okay. Crying and shaking badly, the mother and daughter held each other tightly. Realizing they had been saved, the family called Mike a hero.

The next day, the captain came to the cabin to make sure the family was OK. He congratulated Mike for his help and reassured the family that those men would be kept in jail and punished.

The captain pulled Mike aside, "Those men were disguised confederate soldiers and they wanted the money for the confederate army."

It was 1864 and Mike was well known on the river. Having his name associated with wounding three confederate soldiers, he knew he would not be safe when the boat landed back south.

Over the next few days, the daughter expressed her gratitude personally, in Mike's room, and suggested he come to Pennsylvania with the family. He got off in St. Louis, the next stop, and looked for a poker table.

*****

St. Louis had saloons and gaming tables everywhere. A lot of money came in and out of that town. The town also had a lot of poor losers and sloppy card sharpers. Men were losing their entire savings at the tables, and on phony land schemes. Every night several shoot outs at the gaming tables took place. Mike did not want to be an innocent bystander and tried to keep a bit of sanity at the tables where he played. After a couple of years of playing and surviving the tables, he moved on to Jefferson City. The lawlessness was just as bad, the shootouts just as frequent. As long as he sat at a table, a bullet could find him any time. He hit upon a plan to scam the cardsharps and stay out of the line of fire.

Mike hired on to be a deputy sheriff. Frontier towns were always looking for lawmen. The pay was cheap but they did get a percentage of the fines and bounties.

Mike watched the poker tables, or the three card monte games, and pick out the cheats. Being well versed in cheating, he knew what to watch for. After watching one particular guy clean out some naïve easterners and a couple of young cowboys, he waited outside the saloon. When the man came out, Mike confronted him.

"Excuse me friend," Deputy Mike said. "Ah noticed you were a beeg winna tonight."

"Yea, so what. I got the cards, they didn't."

"Ah'm a deputy here and we have a law agaen'st cheatin'. I know you have extra cards in your pocket, mostly aces, and ah know you can deal off thee bottom and use fake shuffles. Actually, you were a little sloppee a couple of times and lucky you were playin' people that didn't know anye better. Some towns I've been in you woulda got gut shot tonight. So, here's the deal, ah'm goin' to 'fine' you half your winnings."

"The hell you are, I don't know what you are talking

110

about."

"We can go back een and ah can show some of those cowboys what's up your sleeve or you can pay your fine. Oh, one other thing, we can do this every night, or you can leave town."

A lot of money could be had by a good sharp and some of the cheats stayed in town and cut Mike a small 'fine'. He had a great thing going. He didn't have to risk the ups and downs of gambling or getting shot, he simply collected a small percentage of other's winnings. Being a deputy, however, did put him in harm's way a few times keeping the peace, but his training at the docks kept him alive. Unfortunately, the sheriff put a crimp in Mike's plan.

"Mike," said Sheriff Al, "you've been doing a good job here this year. But, I heard a few grumblings from some of the card players in town. Seems you have been settin' fines and collectin' money. Problems is, you've kept all the money. Now that don't seem right now does it, might even sound shady."

Mike could see where this was going and realized things could go downhill quickly. With the sheriff, plus three other deputies in town, winnings split five ways wouldn't add up to much.

"Well, Al, ah was plannin' to cut you een when the plan be all set. In fact, ah have about five hundred dollars set aside for you in ma room for you. I'll go get it."

"I'll go with you Mike."

"Sure, come along."

"Fishing under his mattress, he pulled up a wad of bills, here you are Al, five hundred dollars, just like ah said."

"Now that's right square of you, Mike. I'm thinking five hundred a day would cover the 'fines' a little more closely, don't cha think?"

As a gambler, Mike knew the odds on nearly every event that might take place. However, he never figured on a shake down by the sheriff. He knew when to hold them and he knew when to fold 'em. This hand he had to fold.

"Sure Al, five hundred es a good daily fine."

That night, Mike packed up and headed for Independence, Missouri. He had a full poke and a plan that worked.

112

He lasted two years in Independence until the sheriff caught on, and then he headed to Kansas City. Seemed wherever he went, the sheriff would catch on, sooner or later. He would also lose a player from time to time in a shootout. Still, the plan paid well.

By 1870 he moved into Wichita and ran the same scam, deputy during the day, collecting 'fines' at night. This time the scam came crashing down. For the first year his 'cheating fines' were working. A wild town, Wichita had rowdy saloons and raunchy brothels. He had experience as a deputy and was gladly hired on. He watched the card tables and had picked out cardsharps he felt would be easy pigeons themselves.

*****

Three card Monte involves three playing cards. Usually two black kings and one red ace, sometimes a red queen. It looks like the easiest game in the world to win, which is why a good cardsharp can make thousands of dollars. The dealer shows you all three cards. He then turns them over and moves them back and forth. You have to pick out which of the cards is the red ace. He, of course goes slowly the first couple of times so the 'sucker' can pick out the ace. The dealer also has two people working with him called 'Cappers'. They make bets and win money. The sucker sees how easy it is to win.

One particular cheat in town had a very smooth three card monte game. His cappers drew the people in. The dealer looked like he wanted to give away his money. He would lose several small bets to the 'cappers' and the rich suckers fell for the whole 'sure thing' game. The dealer let them win a few small bets but little by little he cleaned them out. He excelled at palming cards using a 'double lift' and tossing the second card. Even when the suckers were losing money, they were sure they could guess right. This guy made good money and after about a month of watching him, Mike cornered him with his offer.

"Y'all have a great scam goin' with your three card monte game. You are thee best card palmer ah have ever seen and your double lift is excellent. Half the time ah missed the shift. But here's the thing, cheatin's against thah law. If you want to keep playin' in thes town, you will need to pay a fine. Ah'm the one who collects thee fines. Your fine will be three hundret dollars per night.

He stared at Mike, never wavering, he had been at this game for many years, he knew the score.

"Sure," he said, "meet me tomorrow night in the alley

here by the saloon."

Running this scam for many years, Mike had never had any trouble. After all, being a deputy and the law, who would cause trouble? This time, Mike got too sure of himself. Mike forgot this man worked with two cappers and that is how Mike's scam ended.

The next night, Mike went to the alley way. From deep in the alley, Mike heard, "Over here deputy, I have your money."

Mike stepped off the wooden board walk and walked toward the man. The next morning, Mike woke up at the end of the alley by the trash cans. His coat, money, and weapons were gone. He had a raging headache and a blood crusted scalp. His ribs were sore and his muscles ached across his back. It took twenty minutes for him to get up and stagger to his room in a downtown boarding house.

As he cleaned himself up he wondered how stupid the card sharp could be. After all, Mike knew the man and where he gambled. He would go to the sheriff's office and tell the sheriff about the attacked and get a warrant for the man's arrest. An hour later he gave the sheriff his version of the attack.

"Shereff, last night ah was attacked and beat-ten and robbed. During my rounds, one of thee gamblers called me outside to tell me some-thing and ah was attacked from behind. Ah know who he ees so let's go arrest him."

"Mike, we aren't going to arrest no one. In fact, you're fired and you need to leave town. I suggest you head west to Colorado. Your scam is now well known, and staying in Kansas might not be a good idea."

"But Sheriff, what about thee guy who robbed me, what about him?"

"Oh, you mean my brother, he's okay, he wasn't hurt. If you go due west, get to a town called Marshallville and turn north, you can get to Denver in about three or four days. Be gone by noon tomorrow."

*****

Mike went back to his boarding house and packed. He backed into a scam and never saw it coming. The next morning he cleaned out his bank account, bought more weapons, then went by the livery and picked up his horses. He had two large bays and he switched off riding one and packing one. He packed his saddlebags with stock from the dry goods store and headed west.

He couldn't believe he got suckered. He, the con-man, with the sharp eye, walked right into the simplest con of all, the back alley. He got beat up and kicked out of town. Reliving the last night, he realized he let his guard down and lost his money, his guns, and staggered away with half a suit. With his chin on his chest, he slumped in his saddle, and let the horse find the trail.

He still had a lump on his head, and damage to his ego, as he rode away from Wichita. He knew his scamming days were over. After six years in Missouri and Kansas, too many people knew him and his seedy operation. People took to calling him 'Shady Mike'. He did not want to be a lawman; too much danger. He couldn't go back to New Orleans. Even with the war being over, there were still many southerners that would not let it rest. And there were probably a few confederate soldiers still looking for him. A check of the calendar put him at only thirty-five but the last thirteen years had been stressful. The last week had been agonizing. Change is not easy but he had to think of a new way to get money in his poke and food on his plate.

*****

A couple of days of dusty and dry trails later, Mike pulled into Marshallville. *It is an agreeable looking town*, he thought. The streets were laid out straight and wide. The river ran on the north side of town, and several buildings faced the main street and looked new. His jaw dropped when he saw a windmill pumping water into several covered tanks; tanks with spigots and overflow pipes leading to a small pond. He found the hotel and went in.

"Hello, sir. How may I help you?" The woman behind the desk gave him a big smile.

Used to flat faced men who usually just said, "room," the woman presented a nice surprise for Mike.

"Ah just arrived in town ma'am and ah would appreciate a room."

"Will you be staying more than one night," she asked.

"Ah don't know yet."

She turned the registry book around and asked Mike to sign in.

"Well, Mr. Hoz, enjoy your stay," she said after reading

his name. "We have a very good kitchen here or you can go to the River View café. It really doesn't have much of a view but the owner thought the name sounded good."

Again, used to grumbles, not pleasant conversation, Mike smiled at the clerk. An attractive woman came out of an office behind the check-in desk. She saw Mike and walked over.

"Hello sir," she said. "Are you checking in?"

"Yes ah am ma'am," said Mike.

"This is Mr. Hoz, Miss Kay " said the woman behind the desk. "Mr. Hoz, this is Mrs. Belle, she owns the hotel."

Mike immediately tipped his hat and looked into Mrs. Belle's eyes. He knew women appreciated a man who showed courtesy and paid attention to them.

"Please call me Kay," she said with a twinkle in her eyes, "are you here long?"

"Well ma'am, ah don't know, and you can call me Mike."

Kay took a map from behind the desk and spread it out on the desk. "OK Mike, let me show you a few places in town you might need to know."

Pointing at the map she said, "Over here is the livery, it's run by Nevada Slim." She gave a short laugh. "You'll see. This is Miss Kitty's bath house, it is a clean place and has hot water. Here is where Gentleman George runs a nice men's store. He's a pleasant man, you'll like him. You look like you appreciate fine clothes, and here is our favorite saloon, the Short Keg. The Short Keg is run by a couple of former marshals. And as you know, we have a good kitchen here as does the River View café. You can also get some food at the Short Keg. He has two women working the kitchen and it's reasonable food."

"Your friendliness is refreshin', Miss Kay, thank you." Mike tipped his hat and stood a little straighter.

He took his bags up to his room and unpacked. The room had a single bed, a wash stand with ewer and bowl, a mirror over a low dresser, one coat rack and a chair. It was clean with a single window looking out over the street. It even had a small circular rug in front of the wash stand.

He took off his boots, hung up his coat, beat the dust off his pants, layed on the bed, and closed his eyes for a nap. A few hours later, feeling a bit more refreshed, he washed up, went outside, and took his horses to the livery. He met Nevada Slim and realized why Miss Kay chuckled when she mentioned his name. Slim must have weighed three hundred pounds.

"Hi there, mister, name's Nevada Slim, what can I do you for?"

"Hello sir, ah've been on the road for couple of days and these two horses are friends of mine. Can you rub them down, giv'em a flick of hay, a scoop of grain, and a dry place to stay?"

"You've come to the right place, friend, and I'd take care of your friends like they was my friends," said Slim.

*****

Mike walked away feeling relaxed. He headed for the bath house. His traveling days had been hot, the nights cold, and the ground rocky. He felt dusty and unclean, a kind of sticky feeling. He needed a soak and Miss Kay said there was hot water at the bathhouse.

"Hello sir, welcome. I'm Miss Kitty. The sign on the wall tells you what we offer."

The bath house occupied a large tent. The soap and lavender water gave it a clean, fresh smell. *It has a nice feel to it*. He saw the tubs and the privacy arrangement; another pleasant surprise for a small western town. Mike figured he would visit here often. He looked at the sign and decided he wanted the full service, first in a hot tub and lavender water later. He also noted the Fu King laundry sign and decided he would bring over some traveling clothes later.

"Well, Miss Kitty, ma name is Mike, and ah could use a hot tub of water and some soap, so, ah'll have your first in, one dollar special."

"Of course," said Miss Kitty. "I'll get it set up right away. We'll need a couple of minutes to get that water ready."

Two women were outside with large containers sitting on a wood stove.

"You run a nice place here ma'am," said Mike.

"Thank you."

"Ah can't help but notice you wear a pistol. Is the bath house business dangerous?"

"I expect courtesy in here. You see the other sign about expected behavior. I don't want some surly cowboy picking on me or my ladies. You'd be surprised how rowdy men can be, sitting naked in a tub. We also have a special time when only ladies can bathe, so I have to shoot peeping toms now and then," she said with a grin.

Smiling, Mike said, "Ah feel very safe now."

"Later you can bring over your laundry and I'll see that Wang gets them done. Are you staying at the hotel?"

"Yes ma'am, ah am."

"I'll see that Wang delivers them to your hotel."

"That's right nice of you ma'am, I'd 'preciate that."

While soaking, Mike thought about how friendly folks were in the town. He felt welcome. Done and dressed, and feeling renewed, Mike walked over to the men's store. On the way, he noticed shops were busy. People went about their business saying hello, and greeting one another.

123

"Welcome, mister, look around. I just got in some new fashions from back east. If spiffy is what you want, we can do it."

The shop had a rack of coats, shirts and pants. Hats, ties and boots lined the shelves. A large front window made the shop light and airy.

"This ees a nice shop. Y'all have a good selection for a small western town."

"Mah name's George, some call me Gentleman George. This here town is growin'. The Denver and Rio Grande is adding a spur in a couple of years. Denver's not far away and I'm able to get just about any fashion y'all might want."

"Ma name is Mike Hoz. Pleased to make your acquaintance mister, George. Right now ah'm just lookin' but may need somethin' later."

"What brings you to town? You're obviously not a rancher or farmer. Maybe you're an investment banker. We have one bank in town, maybe could use another."

"Ha, ha," said Mike. "Yes sir, that's what ah am, an investment banka. I bank the Faro table and ah look for investors."

"I thought you looked more like a dealer of sorts?"

"Years ago, ah did deal on river boats on the Mississip'. Recently ah was a deputy in a few cities in Missouri and Kansas. Ah had a few set-backs and decided to get out of thee peace keepin' business. Ridin' toward Denver brought me through here."

"Are you staying in Marshallville?"

"So far, ah like what ah see."

"Interesting, Mike. Ah carried a Tex-as ranger badge for years, but, ah suffered a setback myself, got out of the peace keeping business, and found this little ol' town, and decided to stay. After supper, meet me at the Short Keg, and ah'll introduce you to a couple friends. Miss Kay is a friend of mine at the hotel, she can tell you how to get there."

Mike had supper at the hotel. He saw Kay Belle and commented on the cleanliness of the hotel and how good the food tasted from the kitchen. She bought him a glass of wine and thanked him for his gracious comments. She gave him directions to the Short Keg.

The Short Keg looked like many saloons Mike had seen over the years. It had a long bar with a boot rail and brass spittoons. A mirror behind the bar, oil lights, and pictures on the walls brightened up the look. The floor looked to be a rubbed fir, and a chandelier hung over the gaming tables giving the saloon a bright and almost cheerful look. There were two faro tables, some poker tables, a three card monte game, and one roulette wheel. The tables were busy, everyone seemed to have beer or a whiskey glass in hand. A few cowboys were standing at the bar, boot on the rail, looking around. Mike sensed something missing, but couldn't quite figure out what it might be.

Mike watched the Faro and Poker tables for several minutes. He needed to size up the players and dealers. He might decide to play Poker or Faro later and he wanted to know if the game was straight or crooked. He could play either way.

Twenty minutes later Gentleman George strolled in. "Hey Mike," said George walking over with a hand extended.

"Evening mister George, how are you'all?'

"Step o'er to the bar and meet ma friends and soon to be your friends, also. Mike, this bartender owns the place, his name is Ken Knight but we like to call him Short Keg, like the name of the saloon and maybe because he is a little short and shaped like a keg. This is his crazy friend named George but we call him Sundowner, sometimes 'Crazy' Sundowner'."

As they stood shaking hands Mike said, "Is it a tradition hare in the west that all men hav a second name? We have a Gentleman George, a Sundowner, and a Short Keg. Maybe ah need a crazy second name?"

"Boys, Mike here, worked as a deputy for the past few years in Missouri and Kansas. Mike, Short Keg, and Crazy Sundowner were marshals at one time. They had a setback, got out of the peace keeping business, found Marshallville and decided to stay. Now they just want peace."

"Ah," said Mike. "We are like cousins or mon frere."

"Maybe so," said George. "And there are more former law dogs around. We could start a law gang of our own 'cept none of us wants to get back in the law business again. We like a peaceful life, and a peaceful town. Sometimes we have to lend a helping hand to keep it that way."

"I like my saloon," said Ken. "Ol Sundowner and I run a clean saloon. No upstairs ladies but a good kitchen, some good whiskey, and a few gaming tables. We get a good crowd. No stampeding cows for sure."

"That's it, Ah knew something was different, no ladies."

"No ladies saves us a lot of problems," said Ken. "We have some ladies in the kitchen and they take care of food and cleaning the tables. The girls make a good sandwich, and some hot chili. They get tips and the men keep their hands off. There are more saloons down the street with girls, and a more rowdy crowd. As the town gets bigger, and the train gets here, more trouble will also get here."

"What do you think of the place?" asked Sundowner.

"Ah like it. It doesn't look like many of the saloons in Wichita or Hays, Kansas. Those places had shootouts every night. Every morning another dead body lay face down in the alley. I had a fear ah might get shot by mistake."

"Every now and then we have a sore loser that tries to make trouble, but I keep my shotgun in plain sight, and Sundowner carries his Navy Colt out in the open," said Ken

"Ken," said Mike. "You do have a couple of cardsharps

at the poker table and your Faro dealer knows how to fix a shoe, and the three card monte dealer knows how to throw a second. That may be why you have some sore losers. The thing is, if you know how to play, and read other players, you don't have to cheat."

Eye brows suddenly raised, Ken looked startled. "I run a clean game here."

"I travelled as a professional gambler for years, Ken. Ah'm one of thee best cardsharps in the country. Ah learned in New Or-leans and played the river boats for years. You know that deputies don't make much money, ah made extra money on illegal gambling fines. Ah can spot a cheat very quickly. Ah can make sure your games are honest, or mostly honest."

"If you decide to stay a while, you can have a job here. I can let you run a Faro table, rent free, if you watch the other tables to make sure they are fair."

Surprised by how quickly he liked the town and the people in it, Mike smiled to himself. He knew he had to change his old ways, scamming and cheating might get him killed. Running a table in a saloon, that didn't have someone getting shot every hour, appealed to him. As a skilled card player, he could make a good living and have some friends in the bargain.

"Deal," said Mike

"Deal," said Ken

Chapter 8

Molly and Short Keg

The sun had been up for an hour. After working day and night for years keeping the peace, Ken felt it might be his duty to sleep in now and then. He enjoyed the idea that the morning should be spent stretching, brushing then ambling down for breakfast. While some of the rowdier saloons stayed open all night, the Short Keg closed at two a.m. and didn't open until ten a.m. Most of the trouble, and shooting took place after two in the morning. Drunks were easier to roll late at night. Ken wanted no part of that.

Entering the kitchen and seeing Molly, Ken smiled. "Hi Molly, I could use a cup of coffee and some breakfast."

"Oh, hi Mr. Knight, comin' right up."

"Please call me Ken. It's been a few months now, we're friends. How are you getting along?" He sat at the large oak kitchen table.

Molly, pulled out a frying pan from the shelf and put it on the stove. "Oh, I know it's Ken, but, I want ta pay you respect, you saved ma life Mr. Knight, uh I mean Ken. I don't know how I can ever repay you."

"Payment is not necessary, seeing you safe and happy is enough. You've worked hard and the kitchen is doing a good business. We may have to offer up a few more meals on the menu."

"Me and Mary were talking bout maybe we could, someday, open up our own café. Not right now course, but in a year or two. We need to learn more bout cookin' and orderin' and such."

"Talk to Matilda Arthur, she's a good cook and knows the business. She can get you started in the right direction, and she is a nice lady."

"I like kitchen work better'an bedroom work. I never felt safe there, but, here I do, it's such a relief."

"What got you into the prostitution business, Molly?" He wasn't sure he should be asking, but he wanted to know more about Molly.

"Ten kids, a petty thief for a pa, and a mama who didn't know nothin'"

Molly put a few chunks of wood into the cook stove. A coffee pot sat on one of the four burners. She threw a slab of bacon in the pan.

"What do you mean, ten kids?"

"That's how many were in my family. Ma just kept havin' kids. My pa didn't work much, stole things now and then, usually got caught. Drank when he had a dollar. We had a garden and some chickens, but that don't feed twelve folk." Molly poured a cup of coffee and stood across from Ken. The smell of bacon drifted through the kitchen.

"Ladies from the church would bring us stuff. Never had no shoes; had some patched dresses. We'd steal eggs from the neighbors. We stole clothes offin clothes lines. Ma would cut'em up and resew stuff so's no one could tell them were their clothes. We'd do odd jobs around town. Sweep out the church, shovel stalls, run errands, not nearly enuff. We went to school some, but, pa thought it silly for girls to get learnin'. At fourteen, he told me I had ta pay for my food and room. There was no food for me or my two older brothers, only some for the young'uns. For two years I tried workin' wherever, I could. My younger brothers and sisters were always hungry, and a mite sick most times. The only job I could get that made nuff money was upstairs at the saloon. I did what I had to do, I didn't like it much, but after a while, I just smiled and did my job."

Molly started to sniffle. Her chest heaved up and down, then she cried. She wiped her eyes and looked away from Ken. She absent mindedly dropped her arms and nervously wiped her hands on her apron. "I was able ta give ma some money so my younger sisters didn't have to work in no saloon."

Ken stood up and walked toward Molly. He put his hands on her shoulders. Almost in a whisper he said, "You were very brave. You did what you had to do, you should feel good about helping your sisters."

Molly put her hands on his, then placed a kiss on the backs of his hands. "Thank you so much." She peered at him curiously through tear-filled eyes. Then she asked him a question that surprised him. "Why don't you have girls working upstairs like other saloons and bawdy houses. We were ready workin' but you let us go."

Ken looked long and hard at Molly. He had held his story inside for many years.

"I just don't think it is right; women shouldn't have to sell themselves." He sat back down at the table and sipped his coffee.

Molly saw a struggle on his face. She was young, but had more experience than anyone her age should have had. She knew there was more. "Why," she said. "Why do you care?"

"What does it matter? Why do you care?"

The bacon started to pop grease in the air. She slid the pan off the hot burner to a cool spot and set aside a couple of eggs.

She turned to Ken, her voice low, "Because I care about you."

Ken lifted his brow in surprise. He had only known Molly for a few months. She had been a hard worker. She took her work seriously, and always had a smile for him. He did enjoy seeing her each day. Running a saloon was a tense business, but seeing her brightened his mood. At past forty he knew he was too old for her. He should end the conversation, before it went any further, and get ready for his day.

She put her hands on his shoulders, bent over, and

kissed him on the cheek. It was all he could do not to grab her and kiss her back. But he held off. Being a sheriff for many years had toughened him against feelings; too many bad things happened to good people.

"My mother was a whore," he said matter of fact.

Molly took her hands off his shoulders and covered her mouth, reeling in shock. He said it so coldly. It sounded like he just called her a whore.

"She was a working girl, a painted lady. She struggled to survive, her dad died, mother took to drink. There was nothing else for her, but saloon work." He took a sip of coffee, swallowed slowly, not sure if he should go on.

"There were two men that ran the place. One was mean, one was not nice, but he wasn't mean. If a girl got pregnant, and many did, the mean one would punch her in the belly each day until she miscarried. She then had the day off, without pay, and had to be back to work the next day. Lucky for me, my mother didn't show for months."

Ken saw the horrified look on Molly's face; he continued in a strained voice. "There was a minister in town who'd take the girls until they delivered. He and his wife felt it was their duty to put the fear of the devil into the girls. 'Sinner' and 'Jezebel' were names they were often called. They also worked the girls, while they were there, doing housework and laundry. When finished in the house they had to clean and sweep out the church. The girls lived in a storeroom in the back of the house. There was an old mattress and one blanket. They also had to pay rent for the room."

He finished his coffee, put the cup down and stood. Tapping a knuckle on the wood, not looking at Molly as he spoke, "A doctor'd come in for the delivery. He took great pleasure in touching their bodies, and rubbin' them during and after delivery. One week after delivery, they had to go back to work. After working all day or night, they came back to the house, and tended their baby in the store room. During the day, the babies lay on the mattress with no care. It's a wonder I survived."

This was taking an emotional toll on Ken. He had never told this story to anyone. Aware of a connection with Molly, he felt a need to open up more about himself.

"Ken, I didn't know. I'm sorry, you don't have to say no more. I should never've asked. I just wanted to know more about you." She hugged him tightly.

He stepped back, "She came back every night, my mother came back every night. When I was old enough, I had to do chores around the house and church. I guess I was fortunate they let me stay. The minister and his wife also felt it was their duty to put the fear of the devil in me. I often saw a switch, and a stick come my way. A few other pregnant girls came and went. Their babies usually died. My mother had two more pregnancies that failed. When I was older and living elsewhere, I would see her whenever I could. She was getting used up. They actually kicked her out of the whore house cause she was too old, didn't make enough money."

Molly thought about her own mother and how she was being slowly used up by a bum husband and too many kids to feed. Her mom wasn't a prostitute, but the end looked the same.

"I ran away when I was twelve and worked at a ranch outside of town. When my mother was kicked out of the saloon I was sixteen. The ranch owners let me build a small cabin on the ranch; my mother and I lived there until she died. She was dead at 40. We had four years together, and I swore I'd always do what I could for all women, mothers or, or whoever needed help. That is one reason I became a marshal."

Molly cried softly. She looked at Ken with sorrow in her eyes. Here stood this man, this tough, strong, man, with a heart full of compassion. She vowed to herself that she too would do whatever she could do for any woman, or child that needed help. She also knew she had feelings for Mr. Knight.

Ken poured himself another cup of coffee, turned and went out to the front room of the saloon, sat down at a table and drank his coffee. Molly finished cooking the bacon and a couple of eggs. She put them on a plate walked out of the kitchen and set them on the table in front of Ken. She sat in a chair next to him, looked in his eyes and said, "I love you."

His heart jumped, but his brain went numb. Hearing a woman, a young, attractive woman, say she loved him was the furthest thing from his mind. He figured romance to be on the down side of the hill, pretty much out of sight. This would take some time for his mind to wrap itself around what he just heard.

Chapter 9

The Medicine Show

Wiping down his counter, Buzzard Cooper looked out the front window of his store to a slow, motionless Saturday. The noon day meal passed, some town's folk were going about the afternoon, poking around the shops. He watched some of the younger boys, in dirty shorts, running around barefooted playing tag, while a few of the older boys were throwing rocks at a neighbor's cat. The mercantile had made a batch of ice cream, and two families were lounging on benches, pushed up against the storefront, in the shade of the store overhang, digging into the bowls of cold delight, then licking the spoon. Coop liked Saturday mornings.

The drum beats broke the lazy air and attracted attention all along Main Street. A fancy painted, large medicine wagon, with a beautiful set of four black horses, plumes attached to their heads, moved slowly down the street. A colorful picture of stars, and a full moon, covered the side of a medicine wagon. Boldly written, under the picture, gold letters announced the name of Dr. Moon.

Behind the wagon walked a man, dressed in brightly colored silks. He held a small drum in one hand while beating it with a drumstick held in the other hand. The man chanted, "Over the stars, coming soon, follow me, meet Doctor Moon, Over the stars, coming soon, follow me, meet Doctor Moon."

More intriguing, a beautiful woman, in a silk, short, bolero type top, with a bare midriff, billowing silk pants and long black hair, walked barefoot in front of the drum man. She shook and beat a tambourine, swaying her hips, and shaking her hair. A large, bald man, with a gold earring drove the wagon.

The two families looked up from their ice cream and stared. Townsfolk were coming out of all the shops to see why there were drums playing in the middle of the street. The wagon continued down the street a couple of blocks, turned left at the corner, and headed for the park. The drum continued to beat as the silken beauty, shook her tambourine, and waved at the crowd.

The kids stopped playing tag and followed the procession down the street. Dogs ran alongside the wagon—but not too close—barking and snapping. Curiosity had the men and women stepping from the boardwalk into the street to follow the parade. Doctor Moon's wagon and show passed several saloons on the way. Ken, Molly, Mary, Sundowner and Mike looked out the door.

"I wanna go," said Molly.

They followed along to see what might happen. Kay Belle stepped out of her hotel and joined the crowd.

Several men came out of the other saloons, drinks in hand, lined the boardwalk, hooted and hollered at the beautiful woman in silk. Fortunately, the kids and women could not hear the plainly crude shouts.

The wagon pulled into the park, and set up right in the middle. The drummer, beating faster, chanted, "Over the stars, coming soon, come and meet, Doctor Moon." The drummer finished beating with a flurry and put his drum down.

The large, bald man with the gold earring unhitched the horses, locked the wheels, and set up a picket line for the horses. Doctor Moon opened the doors on the back of the wagon, stepped down a short ladder, and waved to a growing crowd. He stood tall but thin. He wore a long, black, frock coat. He had on black and white striped pants, a large red cravat, and a black derby hat placed squarely on his head. The hat shaded his eyes giving him a mysterious look. He quickly set up a table, and produced dozens of bottles of his special elixir.

Most of the people had never seen a medicine show before, and were walking back and forth, trying to get a good view. The drum beater pulled a large dagger from a bag. An uneasy mumble groaned from the crowd as the knife appeared. He lifted the dagger up, tilted his head back, and slowly swallowed the knife. First, with a little scream, the crowd held its' breath until he pulled out the knife. All at once, they let their breath out and cheered. He put the knife away and pulled out a sword. The crowd gasped, he held up the sword and waved.

"Oh my gosh," said Molly," "is he really gonna stick that sword down his throat?"

"How can he do that?" asked Mary.

"I can't even watch." Kay Belle turned her head.

The woman in silk started beating her tambourine, and the man slowly raised the sword. He opened his mouth, tipped his head back, and placed the sword in his mouth. The sword slowly slid down his throat. Suddenly it seemed to stick, several women in the crowd screamed. The young boys cheered. He lifted up slightly and then slid the sword down to the hilt. The tambourine shook quickly in anticipation, and the man pulled the sword out.

"Is that a trace of blood on the sword," Ken asked Mike.

A huge burst of applause roared from the crowd. The man bowed and put the sword away. He then took out three large knives from his bag and began to juggle them. Throwing up one, catching another while the first one was in the air. These were large knives, maybe twelve inches long. More people cheered and the crowd grew. All the time, Dr. Moon is waving, pointing, and charging up the crowd. Done juggling the knives, he took out an apple, threw it in the air and whipping a knife through the air, he sliced the apple in half. Another cheer and a round of applause followed.

The large, bald man stepped up, and the man in silk stepped back. He lit a torch and stuck it in a holder in the ground. He took a small torch, lit it from the torch, tipped his head back, and blew into the flame. The flames shot out about three feet. The crowd cheered. Next he stuck the flame in his mouth, closed his lips, pulled the torch out, the flame gone. The crowd clapped and cheered. Doctor Moon stepped forward, clapping his hands. He pointed at the big man, and the big man took a bow. The lady in silk, walked through the crowd with her tambourine to collect money.

"Please show your appreciation," Doctor Moon shouted, "show your appreciation."

The lady in silk bounced the tambourine whenever a coin was dropped in. It made music, and encouraged others in the crowd to drop in a coin. Doctor Moon stepped up on a low wooden stool.

"How are you'all feeling today? Are you'all full of pep and energy or are you feelin' a bit sluggish like a pig slogging through the mud. Are ya ready to tackle your chores, or are you ready to set a spell and rub your achin' feet? What's your belly sayin' to ya, you know it talks to ya. It tells you iffin its workin or iffin it ain't workin' Is it grumblin' and growlin'? Is your back getting' ya down."

Doctor Moon flannel mouthed the crowd another ten minutes listing all the aliments a body might have. By the time he finished talking about aches and pains, most of the people were feeling a 'might poorly and achey'.

Then, finally he said, "I've got just the right thing to cure all those ills. It's a sci-en-tif-ic form-u-la given to me by a man I met in New Orlee-ans. A man from Egypt. Yep, that's right, the land of the ancient Pyra-mids. It is a spe-chial drink used by the kings of Egypt and the doctors that created 3000-year-old mummies.

"I don'em a favor, I saved his life from sum of them French bullies in New Orlee-ans. It's a dangerous place, but my friend here (he points to the big, bald guy) 'Bullman' and I saved 'em. He was so grateful, he shared the 3000-year old, sci-en-tif ic form-u-la with me. He swore me to secrecy bout the form-u-la, so I cain't tell ya what's in it, but, this here elixir will cure those ills your body been tellin' you bout."

A few of the men shouted that they sure could use a batch of that elixir.

"You men better warn your woman folk before you go to bed, that you took a healthy dose of Doctor Moon's elixir. She need be prepared. Now, this bottle costs me a lot of money for the special ingredients, but you folk look friendly, and I like you, so today, and today only, I will sell you a bottle for only two dollars. I know two dollars sounds like a lot, but how much money can you put on your health? Plus, you are savin' twice that amount, but hurry, I only have 40 bottles left. Those folks in Denver bought up bout 200 bottles. I have to get several special ingred-ients to make a new batch. I'll have to go to New York and send to Egypt for part of this here magic form-u-la. I'm on my way now. I'm only here one more day. We will have another show morrow bout noon, so tell your friends to come watch."

The beautiful woman in blowing silks stepped up next to Dr. Moon.

"This here, lovely lady is Selma. She is descended from some of the most famous gypsies in the world. This mystic woman in silks has special talents; she can read the future. She has some special cards, 200 years old, handed down to her from her great, great, grandmother. Will you live a long life? Will you find gold or silver in the mountains? Will you be lucky in love? Selma can look into your future. For 50 cents, you can know what is coming. You hold the cards. You shuffle the cards. Then Selma reads what the cards say. We have a tent for private readings. We don't want no one else to interfere with your special touchins that control the cards. We don't want no one else list-nin' to your future."

The men lined up, and the forty bottles sold out in

twenty minutes. A fight almost broke out between some men that didn't get a bottle and ones that did. Doctor Moon said he would look around in his medicine wagon to see if any of the special makins' might still be on one of his shelves, stuck in the back. He might have some more tomorrow. Several women lulled around the tent waiting for a chance for a card reading. All in all, the medicine show went very well.

"That guy has a great act," said Mike. "And they call me 'Shady'. Ole, Doctor Moon is like triple shady."

"I think I can whip up some magic elixir myself," said Ken. "Enough whiskey, a little honey, some hot peppers, and tobacco squeezins', and it'll have those aches and pains gone in no time, especially when you pass out."

"I enjoyed the show," said Molly. "I never seen nothin' like that before. He swallowed a sword. Maybe I have Selma read my cards."

"Molly," said Ken, "I can tell you your future. You work hard, you don't cheat, you'll be happy."

"Ken," said Molly with half a smile, "are you sayin' you gonna make me happy?"

Shrugging, Ken suggested they get back to the Short Keg.

*****

"C'mon boys, that gypsy woman said tonight is ma lucky night and the Jack is ma lucky card. Let's visit the faro table at the Short Keg. Time ta get rich," said the young, grinning cowboy.

A couple of quick wins, a few drinks and the grinning cowboy started whooping it up. A few hours later, he stood drunk, broke, and awfully mad.

"That bitch lied to me and she's gonna get it good," he mumbled.

Storming out of the short Keg, he stumbled to the park. The dark night lay still and quiet. The moon shone enough for him to see the wagon. Staggering up and down the wagon, he started shouting "I want my money back. That the 'Shalera' girl lied to me, and I'm gonna pay her good." He pulled his gun and put two holes high up on the wagon. A dark shadow slipped around the wagon. Before the cowboy could fire a third shot, a knife found its mark.

He felt a sharp pain in his back, confused, he tried to

reach over his shoulder to his back. Waving his gun in the air, he turned around, and another knife found its target. The man dropped his gun and looked down at a knife sticking out of his chest. With a soft, gurgling sound, he dropped to the ground.

"Damn it, Selma, I told you, do not tell those cowboys it is their lucky day. Never say anything about cards. Tell them they will live a long and happy life. Tell them they will meet and fall in love with a pretty girl. Tell them to stay away from bulls, but do not mention the word 'lucky'. Now I have to plug up two more holes in the wagon. This is the third time this has happened. One of these days, I'm going to get shot. Start packing and I will go see the sheriff," said Doctor Moon, dropping his down home, folksy twang.

Walking back to the wagon with Cal, Doctor Moon explained what happened. "Weel sher-ef, dis cowboy started to a shootin' my wagon. He sure was drunk. I donna know why he be shootin' that way, but my man had ta stop 'em. We don't have no shootin' guns. We all very scrared." He showed Cal the man's gun and the two bullet holes in the wagon.

"I heard about this guy from the faro dealer at the Short Keg," said Cal. "I can see it was self-defense, but he had a few friends that may want some sort a revenge. I suggest you light outa town as soon as you can. I'll get this guy over to Hitch's funeral parlor. I'll keep it quiet until tomorrow. I guess there won't be a show tomorrow," said Cal.

The next morning, the park was empty. A few people walked by the park on their way to church, and looked puzzled when they saw the wagon gone.

*****

1871: Some rich investors from Denver bought an entire block on 4th street. Three story homes, on double lots, were built, thus establishing a rich district in town. Another investor built a three story hotel and resort out by the mineral springs. A three story, brick court house, now stood on the corner of 2nd and B Street. Shops lined most of Main Street down to the saloon, prostitute and gambling section of town. The industrial zone had several businesses including a brewery.

A newspaper office opened up, the Marshallville Gazette. News, fliers, announcements and opinion stories were printed twice a week.

The population hit 1200 and six more saloons opened up. A theater was under construction. The sheriff added a second deputy, an ex-cavalryman. A one man sanitation department opened. The man vigorously enforced the privy and human waste regulations, and made sure the food scraps were emptied. Dusty usually took care of that. Once a week, the sanitation department hired teenagers to pick up litter around town, and shovel the larger piles of animal waste. The waste was taken to the farms for fertilizer. The kids made twenty cents an hour; they were happy.

The town was getting a reputation as a clean, orderly town with a mineral spring resort. English, French, and German accents were heard often.

Chapter 10

Buzzard and Sally

"Mr. Cooper, what brings you into the shop today? You looking for a new dress or some material for a tablecloth?" asked Sally, the shop owner.

With a twist on his lips, Coop skipped right over that question. He knew why he had come into the store. He had a personal mission on his mind.

"Please Sally, call me Coop, or call me Buzzard."

"Buzzard? Why would I call you Buzzard?"

"That's what my friends call me sometime."

Sally frowned in puzzlement. "Am I your friend?"

"I've stopped in to say hello many times. I've always taken your order myself, friendly like, when you came into my store. We've swapped smiles many times, so ya, we're friends. I think that maybe we could take a step up, and maybe step out."

"Mr. Cooper, Buzzard, what are you saying?"

Buzzard struggled with this whole conversation. Talking to ladies didn't fit his style. He tried courting a few times in the past, but it never amounted to anything. Now he was determined to take the necessary steps. He liked Sally, and he thought she liked him. He knew you couldn't break a horse sittin on a fence, so he shrugged his shoulders, let out a puff of air and blurted out his question.

"Sally, there's a dance at the town hall on Saturday and if you're willin', I'd like to take you."

Sally liked Coop, and now she actually liked calling him Buzzard, it sounded cute. She had hoped he would finally do something. She figured she might have to be the one to get this wagon rolling. She had gone to his store a lot more times than needed. She could have done all her shopping at one time, but, she only bought a few things at a time so she could see him more often. She had smiled her best smile several times. *Well*, she thought, *he's finally catching on.*

"My-o-my, Mr. Buzzard, it's about time you figured on 'stepping' up, and I'd be happy to step out with you."

Coop's eyebrows raised in surprise. What had she meant, it's about time? He let that sink in a bit then broke into a smile. She *wanted* him to ask her out. Then the next realization struck and he muttered, "Uh, Sally, I don't rightly know how to dance."

Sally first saw the surprised look on his face, then the smile. The dance would be a good opportunity to get to know one another better. Apparently it just dawned on him that he couldn't dance. She giggled inside about his dilemma.

"It is as easy as counting to two and knowing your left foot from your right."

All balled up, he absent-mindedly reached up and scratched his head.

"OK, let's try this, count to two."

"One, two," he said

"Okay, now say one, two quickly, then say one, two, slowly. So it's one, two, then oooone, twooo, then one, two, then oooone, twooo. That's the rhythm," she said.

He tried. It actually took a few tries and a few prompts, but he got it.

"Now the hard part, you have to move your feet when you count. Start with your left foot"

Coop was getting frustrated. He came over to ask her to the dance, forgetting he didn't know how to dance, and now he was getting a lesson he hadn't asked for. On the other hand, she said '*yes*', and wanted to spend time with him. Being with Sally was exciting, even if it came to counting one and two.

"Buzzard, just walk, one, left foot, two, right foot, one, left foot, two, right foot."

"I'm trying, but my feet aren't listen' too good."

"Now you're doing it, now you are walking and counting. Just one more part. When you get this, you'll be dancing."

Feeling doubtful Coop said, "OK, now what?"

"Remember when you counted one, two, quickly, then

slowly? That is how you are going to move your feet; quick, quick, slow, slow. left, right, leeft, riiight, left, right, leeeft, riiiight. Try it."

For someone who has never danced, moving your feet in any kind of rhythmic motion is like walking with your feet tied together. Coop tried and almost tripped.

"What the shhh...oh, excuse me. I didn't men to swear."

"I've heard the word 'shit' before. I use it myself sometimes."

"How about the word 'damn'," he blurted out before thinking.

"That one too and a few others, but right now lets' work on dancing."

Right in the middle of the lesson, two ladies walked into the dress shop talking to each other. They abruptly stopped and looked at Coop.

Quickly, Sally said, "So, Mr. Cooper, when you get some of that fabric I ordered, let me know, and work on that project we discussed."

Catching on, Coop said, "Should be about a week, I'll let you know." He turned, tipped his hat to the ladies, and walked out.

*****

Walking into the hardware store that afternoon, looking for nails, Slim saw Coop sliding around the store. "Hey Coop, what are you doing," asked Slim.

"What does it look like I'm doing, I'm counting to two and moving my feet."

"Oh, that's what I thought," snickered Slim. "Where'd you keep your nails, I've a few boards need'en to be nailed up. It's almost closing time, meet you at the Short Keg, and you can show me how ta count and move my feet at the same time." He chuckled.

Chapter 11

The Dance

Barbara Franks, Angela Miles and Matilda Burns set up the town hall for the dance. They moved the benches and tables along the walls to open up the floor.

"Barbara, help me move the speakers' podium back and cover it. That will leave the stage open for some music folk. Plus, let's add a few more oil lights along the walls to give light for dancing", said Matilda. "Angela, will you set a table for food, add some benches, and bales of hay outside for seating."

The town hall was large by small town standards. The city council had allotted the money to build it so the community could enjoy activities such as a dance, sewing Bees, charity auctions, and other group meetings. All the town's official business offices were there also.

Dances are a big deal in a western town. It is time to

relax, listen to music, meet people, and have fun. Most times, work took up six or seven days a week, often from sunup to sundown. If you are farming or ranching there are chores every day; cows or chickens never take the weekend off. Spending even two hours, not thinking about those chores, makes for a purely, delightful time.

Seeing neighbors and friends is a treat. You might not see other town folk but once every week or two, and then it is usually passing in the street with a wave and a "Hi", or in church on Sundays, if you can break away from ranch or farm work. At a dance, you can relax, and talk for hours; in between dances that is. This is also 'gossip' heaven. Items that have been saved up for weeks come spilling out like lava.

"You know Matilda, what I like best about these dances is to see the young, single men and single women make contact."

"I agree," said Angela. "Watching them flirting, smiling, and dancing, is so romantic. A dance is like a big group date. Little by little, boys and girls, men and women, find who may be of interest, and might rate a courtin' call."

"What I enjoy is seeing all the folks with a musical

instrument showing up to play," said Barbara. "My favorites are the fiddle and accordion. Also throw in a drum, a guitar, a harmonica, and the dance is on. Hopefully we get a waltz, a lively jig, and a polka. That is all you need to have most everyone enjoy the dance."

Food and drink always come to a dance. The women from the local farms, and from town, all bring a basket with whatever they can afford to bring. A table is set up, and the baskets are emptied. Fruit, pies, breads, jams, meats, pickles; potato and bean salads, appeared like magic. Men bring their flasks, and homemade wines. A few of the saloon owners bring beer, and some whiskey.

*****

The August night turned out to be warm and Mayor Marshall, and the city council members were out welcoming the people as they arrived. Several musicians gathered to work out a band or two. If you have enough players, they can take turns, and play all night. This night, the Marshallville town dance would be in full swing.

"Mr. Mayor, we are especially lucky tonight," said Harold the marching band leader. "We have some new band members from Germany and they can pound out some great Polkas; one man even has a tuba. Two other new players are from Louisiana and can fiddle a lively tune that will have every foot in the building stomping the floor."

"That is great Harold. Music really gets people happy."

The fourteen children of the six original families now ranged from thirteen to twenty, except Francie who was eight and little Jane Marshall who was three. Counting kids from the town and surrounding farms, there were about thirty young adults and teenagers mingling, wandering, and talking in groups. Several hours were available, so each boy and girl had chances to see many prospects before making an initial pick.

Coop and Sally arrived in a buggy and joined the crowd. The Gentry brothers were there, as was Ginger. Ken, Molly and Mary were there along with Miss Kitty. Slim and shady Mike, Gentleman George and Kay (the hotel owner) stood together watching the fun. Sheriff Cal and his deputy showed up to make sure the dance stayed peaceful.

The music started and hooping and hollering competed with the music. Some of the ranch hands, and farm boys hadn't been to a dance in years. As it turned out, most of the young adults didn't know how to dance, but they managed to turn, and hop, and walk in circles just fine. The older boys went right for the cutest girls, and twirled them around the floor. The girls were thrilled that the older boys were interested. The younger boys and girls, ten to thirteen, stood around in groups, giggling and laughing. A few of the young city boys had on their best bib and tucker and strutted around the hall.

Most of the married men went for the food and drink while the wives formed hen parties, and chattered like magpies; so much gossip, so little time. The men meanwhile were comparing homemade wine and makins'

"Look at the Gentry brothers makin' mash with some of the single ladies," Slim pointed to Mike. "They sure look spruced up a bit with a clean shirt, and a brushed up hat."

"You look quite handsome tonight Mr. Cooper," cooed Sally. "I like your coat and that tie looks good on you."

For his part, Coop felt a little uncomfortable dressed as a dude, but was pleased to have Sally by his side. He had been practicing his one, two, dance, and willing to try if it made Sally happy.

*****

When the fiddlers took a break, the Polka band set up. Otto and his family were from Germany. Otto loved Polka music. He brought his tuba, and accordion, all the way from Germany. Otto and his wife Olga had three daughters, Helga, twenty-five, Hedwig, twenty-three, and Hilde, twenty-one. Otto played the tuba and his wife played the accordion. Otto and Olga took the stage along with a few of the town marching band members, and played some rousing Polka music. The three daughters were big girls, still single, and looking for an American husband. They had their hair in braids, wore Bavarian style blouses, and large billowy skirts. They all wore smiles and clapped and swayed to the music. Several of the big farm boys had taken notice, and seemed to be getting up their courage to say 'howdy'.

Helga spotted Nevada Slim. She could not take her eyes off him. Finally, she went to him, took him by his hands and said, "I'm Helga, we dance."

Slim stood 6' 8" and weighed 300 pounds. Helga stood 6' and weighed 180 pounds; they looked like a couple made for each other. Taken completely by surprise, Slim half stood and half moved his feet. Helga had a large body, a pretty face with blonde hair, and blue eyes. She was quite attractive and quite strong.

"Hey, I don't rightly know how ta dance, complained Slim.

"Das okay, I vill show you", grinned Helga.

When she tugged, slim started moving. Helga lifted her right foot and stomped down, did a one, two, three and spun Slim around. Slim had never done a Polka before. He tried to hop, but his feet stuck to the ground. Much like an avalanche, once his upper body started to move, and his lower body didn't, there was no stopping the fall. The two of them tumbled and rolled to the ground. When they finally stopped rolling, Slim lay on his back and Helga lay flat on top of him. They were a little stunned and didn't move for several seconds.

Then Helga looked into Slims' eyes and said, "Das is gut, I like."

She rolled off and they struggled to get up. Several people watching the show, applauded. Helga took Slim's hand, and walked him out to the table with the food. She picked up a bottle of beer, opened the top and handed it to him.

"My papa, brewd dis, ist gut."

"Hey Slim," yelled Mike, "I didn't know you could

165

Polka."

"Ha, ha, you should try it sometime. Maybe Helga's sister can show you how."

All in all, they looked like a cute couple, time would tell.

"Ken," Molly said, "I never had a nice dress like this before, neither has Mary. You're kind, thank You."

"Molly, you and Mary deserve something nice now and then, you both look sweet."

"Thank you again," said Mary and she wandered into the hall, sat against the wall and listened to the music with a smile.

"I never been to no dance before neither," said Molly. "This is wonderful. People seem so happy. I'm happy to be here with you Ken. I ain't never learned to dance. Ken, can you teach me?"

"Not me, Molly, I can't dance either."

"Sally might help you," said Coop. "She showed me

some. I might even try to do some one, two step, tonight."

"I can help you Molly if you like," said Sally. "Moving to music makes life easier to live."

"I want ta learn this Polka dance. People are just flyin' around the room, jumpin' and laughin'. I want to jump and laugh," said Molly.

"I think we could do that Molly. When Mr. Short Keg here gives you a day off, come see me at the dress shop."

Molly turned, hugged Ken's shoulder and said, "Oh, Ken, will you do the Polka with me someday?"

Seeing how happy and excited she was, he had to say, "Sure, someday."

She threw her arms around his neck and kissed his cheek, then she turned, watched, and swayed with the music.

Ken felt froggy about Molly, and he didn't know which way to jump. He had only been in town a few months, found a killer, and started a business. He wanted to get used to some peace and quiet, and lay low for a while. Now a beautiful young girl was setting her cap toward him. She said she loved him and he was pretty sure he was feeling the same. He had spent a lot of years learning the law, but now he felt like a fish out of water. He had closed one chapter of his life, and now a new chapter opened. At times it seemed like a new book opened. Could a normal life be possible? He'd like to find out.

"There's John Marshall," said Coop to Ken. "Looks like he's drawing a lot of attention from some single ladies. Is that Miss Kitty talking to him?"

"It does look like Miss Kitty. It has been almost three years since Jane died, and he may be ready for a lady's company, plus, having little Jane with him attracts a lot of women," said Ken. "And, little Jane could use a woman's touch around the house. Many of his wife's friends have helped John take care of little Jane, but a woman in the house is best. At least that's what I hear; never had one myself."

Molly looked at him, smiled and hugged him again.

Finally, the Polka was over and a fiddle, guitar and wash board started to play.

"Well, Mr. Buzzard, are you ready to dance?" asked Sally.

"When it comes right down to it, I ain't ready, but I'm willin', let's go," grinned Coop.

It was an exercise in stops, starts, and stops and starts. The quick, quick, slow, slow was more like a quick, shuffle, slow, stop, shuffle. Coop hit the rhythm a couple of steps, then his eyes dulled over and the brain sputtered.

"OK Coop, you tried," Sally smiled and shook her head. "Do this instead, walk. That's right, walk, left, right, left, right. Go slowly and we can move around the room with the music."

Holding Sally's hand and having a hand on her waist put a big grin on Coop's face.

"I'm mighty proud being with you tonight," said Coop.

"Me too." Sally gave him a tight hug.

It was a beautiful night with plenty of food, music, and laughter. Most people were hesitant to leave. There were a few hugs and kisses, and promises of future meetings. One attractive lady (might have been Miss Kitty) helped Marshall straighten up for the evening. They walked away together.

Chapter 12

Wild Shot

"Hey, did ya hear the news, Reeves?" Ben shouted. "Did you hear the news bout that Reb General Lee? He surrendered."

"What? When was dat?"

"I dunno, five, six days ago, maybe."

"Oh man, I dun kilt five more of them Johnny Rebs after the war was over, damn."

"Heck, you are the best sniper in the troop. What you gonna do now Reeves?"

"Well, there ain't no work in the south fo a black boy wearing blue unions, and not much goings on in the way of job openings in the East either, so I guess I'll head West. I hear tell of a cavalry outfit in Colorado, since my only job fo past few years is soldiering, I best head that way.

In 1866, Reeves joined the 9th cavalry Buffalo soldier unit in Colorado territory. Two years later he mustered out reasoning it wasn't right fighting and enslaving the Redman, after fighting for years to free the Black man. Losing his thirteen dollars a month pay check put a feeling of urgency, in his empty gut, to find some work. Drifting around a few tent towns that had sprung up around some mining claims in the mountains, he hooked up with a couple of prospectors working a stream using a sluice box. *Your color don't matter much if there's hard shoveling to do*, he thought. Putting a big ache in his back, even with some dust in his poke, meant ditching the sluice box.

One never knows when a chance meeting can turn your life on a dime. Providence smiled on ole Reeves one day. While leaning on a bar made of some long planks resting on a couple of barrels in a tent saloon, his old union buddy, Ben, saw him.

"Hey Reeves, come on over here," and waved him to his table. Ben and a couple other union boys were talking to some buckskinned trappers. The trappers eyed him cautiously. "Grab a chair, you might want to hear what dees trappers was a sayin'."

One grizzly old boy spoke up, "These boys were asking bout trappin' and I was tellin' them the beaver's runnin' mighty thin in the streams, but Buffalo hides was sellin' good. Plus, thars millions of them shaggies standin' round for the takin'."

"Say, Reeves, you still got that Sharps 50 you had in the war? Oh Reeves here was our best sniper. I'll bet he could knock down a few of them buffs. Reeves, this here trapper fella is lookin' for a partner to go buffalo huntin'."

"Names Alfred Packer," the trapper said. "You any good with that Sharps, we can make some money." Reeves thought bout the irony (he didn't know it was called irony) of going from Buffalo soldier to Buffalo hunter, and gave a little snort, with a head shake, about the humor.

"Let's get us some hides," Reeves agreed.

Reeves teamed up with Packer, also known as Skinner. With his last dollars, and a bag of dust he panned out of a stream, he bought a wagon, two yoke of oxen, and with his Sharps, he and Skinner went hunting. Working primarily in New Mexico, they sighted large herds of the American Bison. The Sharps is a powerful rifle. Reeves would set up on the side

172

of a hill, position his Sharps on a tripod, and drop bison after
bison. He did have a few mishaps while adjusting his rear sight
and Skinner got to calling him 'Wild Shot.' Once he missed so
badly he hit one big bull in the rear and it took off running,
taking the herd with him. They had to pack up, and chase down
the herd again; Skinner wasn't too happy.

On another occasion things went terribly wrong
(reinforcing the name 'Wild Shot'). Firing at a large male bull,
the bullet glanced off the bull's head, knocking him out, but
not killing him. When Skinner grabbed a leg to start skinning,
the bull sat up snorted and glared at Skinner. Yelling "Shit"
and soiling his pants, Skinner took off running with the bull on
his tail. Just as the bull was about to stick a horn up Skinner's
butt, the bull stepped into a prairie dog hole, stumbled and fell
on his face. Stunned, the bull got up, shook his head, forgot
what he was doing, and trotted back to the herd. Skinner was
spittin' mad, cussed, and yelled at Reeves about another wild
shot, screw-up.

"Working ten and twelve hours a day is wearin me
down purty thin," groaned Skinner.

"We got ta skin and scrap, and dry out the hides or they
no good, we got no money" said Reeves. "Being poor sure is

unhandy."

They used their horses to pull hides, but it was still hot, gritty and smelly. Dried buffalo blood and greasy fat, caked their hands. They'd have to take a day off now and then just to rest their hands. They weren't big on bathing, but the smell from the hides got them looking for a river.

"I smell like a god damned buff," said Skinner. "We got ta scrub up a bit in a river or one of them buffs think me kin."

While drying the hides they would 'jerk' some buffalo meat for eating later. Buffalo steaks were a nightly meal.

After several months of work, they had a wagon full of rich buffalo hides. With hides stacked several feet high on their wagon, and two yoke of oxen doing the pulling, they rambled by Marshallville on their way to Denver.

"Look at dat town, Skinner. Saloons, stores, a hotel, and a bath house; we got to come back after we sell the hides."

A few weeks later, hides, oxen, and wagon sold, they rode their newly purchased horses back to Marshallville. The bath house was the first place they entered.

*****

"We better soap up at the bath house, Skinner, folks don't cotton ta no smelly, dusty, roadies. I remember seein' a yung cowboy steppin' to a saloon after a month on the trail, gettin throad right back out the door by a couple of men trying to enjoy a beer. 'We don't need no foul-smellin', grubby looking, stank weed standing next to us having a beer', they yelled. So we'll scrub our hides, pick up a few new duds, get us a beer, and make ourselves ta home."

"I don't know, Wild Shot, I'm more ta home in a stream somewhere than indoors at some fancy, dancy, soapy, bath house."

"Give it a shot, Skinner, ya won't believe how a long soak in hot water make ya feel. You can skip the lavender water if ya want."

The boys met Miss Kitty and her two lady friend helpers. Both the boys reckonned it felt funny being naked in a tub, indoors, with women folk close by. Both boys agreed, however, it was right smart feeling, soaking in the hot water.

Cleaned up with the dollar special for Wild Shot, and

the fifty cent special for Skinner, the boys went to the River View café for supper. After chowing down on the two dollar steak supper, with all the fixins', the boys patted their full bellies and went to the Short Keg for a beer.

Over the beer, Wild Shot made an observation to Skinner. "You know, I like dis town, and I don't like killin' and skinnin'. Let's take stock of this town for a while and see what comes up."

"I'm not real used to being round town folk," replied Skinner, "but, I'm also bout done with skinnin', and sleepin' in the cold. Maybe I could find us a cabin just outside of town for us ta hole up, whilst we look things over."

They made friends with the owner of the bar, a man named Ken, while having a couple of beers. Chatting with Ken about the cavalry, buffalo hides and looking for work, Ken made mention that the town lacked a good barber and tanner.

"You know, Wild Shot," he said, "with your skill at skinning hides, you should be able to skin a few whiskers off a man's face without hurting anyone. And Skinner, tanning those buff hides is good business. You could set up a shop on Corral Street. Head over to the land office tomorrow, and meet up

176

with John Marshall. He's the mayor and knows all about the town and buildings."

Wild Shot and Skinner found a spot outside of town to toss a bedroll. The next morning after a slab of bacon, and coffee, they went to the real estate office, and found John Marshall.

"Welcome to Marshallville, name's Marshall, what can I do for you?"

"Lookin fo a store fo a barber shop, a cabin on skirts of town and a lot for tanning hides," said Wild Shot.

Marshall took out his town map and pointed to a spot. "Got just the place for the barber shop and the rent is cheap. Also, got a tanning shop over by the woodlot. There is an abandoned log cabin just west of town. An old miner stayed there, but he's gone, no one been there for months. It's yours' for the taking."

"Thanks Mr. Marshall, that's right friendly, ain't it Skinner. I believe I'm gonna like this town."

Wild Shot found the small shop and put out his barber sign. Skinner found a shop by the wood lot, suitable for tanning.

They found the abandoned cabin, spent a few days cleaning, chinking up the cracks, and set up a stove. The one room cabin had two rickety beds. They bought the makings for two decent beds, and picked up two more blankets from the dry goods store. They bought a few shingles from Phil Franks carpenter shop and tightened up the roof. They had to dig, and build a new privy.

They settled in to the cabin, sharpened their blades, and opened their shops for business. It wasn't long before Wild Shot and Skinner had established a steady clientele.

Sheriff Cal and one of his deputies, Dead Eye Kid, went by the barber shop to say hello, and welcome them to town.

The Gentry brothers, in town for supplies, paid a visit to the barber shop. Walking in Van said, "Short Keg told us to stop by and say hello. My brother and I could use a shave. Ranching keeps us busy, and a fresh shave has a way of making a guy feel good. Ken said if you could shave 1000 buffs, you could probably a shave a man OK"

"Sit right here in ma chair. Ma name's wild Shot. I'll have that chin clean as a whistle afore you can blink your eye."

After his shave, Van invited Wild Shot and Skinner out to the ranch for a bar-b-que. Wild Shot showed off his skills with his Sharps, bringing down a big elk. Skinner skinned and quartered it, and cut off a few steaks. They had a good meal of elk steak, and beans at the ranch that day. Life was pretty good for the boys.

While Wild Shot and Skinner were at the ranch, they met two ex-lawmen visiting Van and John. They were bounty hunters, but they too were looking over Marshallville as a place to retire. One, named Levi, carried a sawed off shotgun as his weapon of choice. "Don't need to aim much," he quipped. He had it rigged across his back like a quiver of arrows. He was right quick about its draw. The other man carried two guns. One gun was set up for cross draw, the other sat on his left hip. Not surprising, his name was Lefty.

"Watch this," Lefty said. He popped the cross draw gun out with his right hand, caught it with his left hand, and shot it. "Confuse the rowdy folks," he smiled.

As they left, Wild Shot and skinner thanked the brothers. "Y'all come in fo a free skinning, ah mean shave." Wild Shot laughed.

Chapter 13

Kidnapping the Banker

Cal poured a cup of coffee and put the old banged up coffee pot back on the stove. He returned to his chair, sat and put his feet on the desk. He wondered if the creak he heard was the chair or his back. Looking at some wanted posters, the deputy talked about the coming day's events. Suddenly the door to the jailhouse swung open and Maggie, the banker's wife, ran in, breathing hard. Her eyes were wide with fear.

"Whoa, slow down, take a breath, Maggie, what's wrong?" Cal set down his coffee, stood and held a hand out.

"My husband's gone," she gasped, "and the bank's been robbed. I woke up this morning like I usually do, at sun up. Ben was gone. I thought he must have gone to the bank early to work on the audit. It's the time of year when he makes a report to the other owners. I figured he didn't want to wake me, and tip-toed out of the house. I got dressed, and went to the bank with a freshly made cup of coffee. That was when I saw the safe open and everything gone." She sobbed, wringing her hands and wiping her eyes with a hanky she gripped between her fingers. "Ben was gone too!"

"You think that was about an hour after sun up?"

"Yes, the sky glowed but I felt a chill in the air."

"That gives them at least a three-hour head start, maybe more. You go on home, and try not to worry. I'll get up a posse. We'll track'em, and bring Ben back."

"Thank you Sheriff." Twisting her hanky, she hurried out of the door.

Cal and his deputy, shrugged on their coats, and headed for the Short Keg looking for Ken.

"Ken, there's been a robbery in the bank. I'm getting Wild shot and Skinner and those bounty hunters at the Gentry's ranch and lightin' out after the robbers. It appears they kidnapped Ben so we got to hurry. Will you check out the bank, then close it up and locked it? We'll ride over and round up Wild Shot and Skinner."

"Sure thing." Ken was thinking he was glad someone

else had to get up, sit leather, and run down men with guns.

Cal headed to Wild Shot's cabin. Banging on the door he yelled, "Hey boys I need your help." The door opened wide. Wild Shot stepped out with Skinner standing behind him, each holding a cup of coffee.

"What's up, Sheriff," asked Wild Shot.

"I'm forming a posse and I need your help. I need a tracker and someone who can take the long-range shot. Some outlaws, I think it was the Chambers gang, robbed the bank, and took the banker hostage. I'll deputize you boys, and you can keep the reward money. If it is them Chambers boys, there's a five-hundred dollar reward on their heads."

Skinner's and Wild Shot's eyes widened the size of silver dollars at the mention of a reward.

"They got three or four hour jump on us, so, get a wiggle on." Cal headed back to his horse as he spoke.

Nodding their chins up and down like fleas jumping off a dog, they gathered up their kits, and joined the sheriff. The three of them took off for the Gentry's ranch.

As they rode into the front yard, two men came out of the ranch house. Behind them, Ginger stood on the porch, shading her eyes with one hand.

"Levi and Lefty, I'm forming a posse to go after the Chambers gang, and I need your help. With you two, Skinner and Wild shot, we should be able to catch them, and bring them back. They have the banker as a hostage. Will you help?"

"We're with you, Sheriff, how do we find them?"

"Skinner here is a tracker, so he'll look for a trail coming out of town, let's go."

It didn't take long to get into town. As they approached the bank, Skinner told them to stay back as he dismounted and cast for tracks. After scanning the area around the bank, Skinner found some fresh tracks behind the building.

"Look here, Sheriff, one of them horses has a chipped shoe leavin' a simple to follow track, and I see five sets of fresh tracks. There must be four of 'em with the banker."

They followed Skinner from the back of the bank as he walked quickly along behind the buildings, then out to the main road.

"They went ta the main road to hide their trail in amongst all them other tracks made yesterday, but they didn't count on having a chipped shoe markin' their way."

They followed the tracks out of town for a few miles then the trail turned north toward the mountains. Soon the trail went cold, too many rocks, limbs, and washed out stream beds to find that chipped shoe. The men spread out, walking their horses looking for any fresh tracks. Occasionally they found a trace that kept them heading north into the mountains, but the hours slowly drifted by.

Hiding in an old miner's cabin, the gang figured they could hold up for a week to let things cool down, before drifting into Denver. Tucked away in a natural crevice, near a small stream with several dogwoods growing nearby, the cabin was virtually invisible. They had stored some food and blankets in the cabin, and now with a hostage, they felt safe; they had not counted on the return of the miner.

Skagway had worked the streams around the foothills for many years. He built his cabin as a place to rest up after several weeks shaking a gold pan. No one had ever invaded his cabin before, so he was a bunch put out seeing squatters making themselves at home.

184

He approached the cabin, shouting, "Get out of my cabin, you're in ma place, now skeedadle."

The robbers looked out the door, seeing the old man, they told him to skeedadle, and sent a .44 round near his feet to emphasize their words. The old man saw the dirt kick up by his feet, shouted an obscenity, turned tail, and headed downhill. As it turned out, as Skagway headed downhill, the sheriff and posse were headed uphill. Happy to see the sheriff, he blurted out his story of invasion. The sheriff was equally as happy to see Skagway because the trail had gotten lost in the tumbled rocks and dried runoff beds. Skagway told them where to find the cabin, and how to injun up quietly to surround the place.

An hour later, the sheriff and his men took up their positions around the cabin. Wild Shot found a place facing the cabin door, laid his Sharps across a tree branch, and sighted in the big gun.

"Come out with your hands up," shouted Cal, and fired a shot into the roof. After some shuffling and shouting, one robber came out of the door with the banker held in front of him, gun to his head.

"Back off, Sheriff or the banker gets a trip to the holy land." He pushed out four or five feet, and shuffled sideways toward the horses. The other three men ran out of the cabin and made a dash for the horses. Wild Shot focused in for a head shot. When the other men made a break, the man with Ben stopped for just a second, and looked away. It was an easy shot for a bison hunter who had been sighting in shots five times farther than this one. The robber blew backwards, gun flying in the air. Ben's knees buckled, and he fell. The other three spurred their horses in a panic and took off out the back. Levi's shotgun emptied one saddle. Lefty's bullet hit one of the men, causing him to fling backwards, but did not knock him off his horse.

The gang members had planned an escape route, and the two were off before anyone could get to the horses and follow. Cal and Wild Shot ran up to the fallen banker, helped him to his feet, and into the cabin. Levi and Lefty followed them. With dark rolling in, Cal, the posse, and the banker settled in for the night. The thieves had left plenty of stores, so the posse started a fire in the stove, ate, and bunked in until day break.

An hour or so down the road, the wounded robber called out to his buddy, "Stop and help me bind up this wound."

Looking at the wound, the man shook his head. "You're on your own, you'll just slow me down."

There was a lot of cursing and yelling, but with a gun pointed at the wounded man's head, he gulped down his anger.

"Hide yourself, I'll leave you a few bucks, but I'm riding out of here. You're bleeding too badly to keep up."

With that, the last man took off through the woods. The wounded man tied off the bleeding with his bandana. Looking around for a place to hide, he found a carved out area under a large boulder. He shooed away his horse and struggled to drag some downed branches in front of the depression. Angry and hurting, he curled up for the night.

The lone robber figured he would travel through the night and work his way into Denver. Riding under a moonless night, he continued heading carefully downhill. Things seemed to be going according to plan until his horse stepped in some loose gravel, lost its balance, and rolled over. They both slid down and to the left. Unknowingly, they had been walking along the side of a steep ravine. The horse recovered his footing, but the man went over the side. He tumbled into and over several large rocks, knocking him unconscious. Eventually, he hit the bottom of the ravine. His slide down caused several loose rocks and stones to follow his path downward, covering him under two feet of dust and boulders. He lay there and died, covered from sight. His horse slowly walked away from the edge, found a flat area with some trees, and stayed for the night.

The posse found both horses the next morning. One had the money in the saddle bags draped across the saddle, the other, casually eating grass. They did not find either man. Puzzled, they ended their search after an hour or so and headed home with the banker, and two dead men tied to their horses. When they hit town, Cal took the dead men to the undertaker, Everett Mitch. Hungry, he bought his posse some breakfast in the Short Keg.

"Did you get them," asked Ken as the ladies served breakfast.

"Funny thing," said Cal, "got two of them, lost the other two. Can't figure where they went, but we got Frank and most of the money."

"Thanks, boys," he said to Wild Shot and skinner. "I hope I can count on you again if need be."

"Well," replied Skinner finishing his third cup of

coffee, "just don't forget that reward money, I don't work for free ya know. Plus, I do work as a guide sometimes, if ya hear of any folks needs a guide, you let me know."

Chapter 14

Hannah Calder

"George, what do you know about that newspaper lady?" Shady Mike asked, while he poked around the new outfits Gentleman George had just unpacked for his men's clothing store.

"Shady, y'all seem to be takin' a trunk load of interest in that lady editor."

"No, what you talking bout? She's new in town and I jest like to know about folks in town."

George stacked up a couple more shirts, turned and chuckled, "There's a new lady over at the dress shop, but y'all haven't asked bout her. There's a lady cook at the River View café, but y'all haven't asked bout her either." Pointing across the street he continued, "There's a new lady working the desk at the hotel, but y'all haven't asked bout her. But that newspaper lady is the one you're askin' about so…"

"It's jest that she's kind of a mys-tery. One day she shows up in a wag-on, driven by a man, with a prin-tine press, and all the makins' of a news-pa-peer, rents a store, and two blinks later she starts postin' news. May-be Slim knows more about her. She has her team and wag-on at his place. It's after working time, so he's maybe over to the Short Keg by now. I'll buy him a drink and see what he knows."

George finished sortin' and stackin' the new arrivals, set out the price tags, got his coat, and locked the door. He and Shady headed to the saloon. Nevada Slim and Ken each had a beer in hand. Slim slapped the bar, finished a laugh and took a slug out of his glass of beer.

"Hey Slim," George called out, "what do y'all know about that newspaper lady. I think Shady here might be interested. You have her rig to your place, did she say anything?"

Setting his beer down, Slim turned. "Hey boys, come over and bend an elbow, I was just telling Ken a joke about a dude, a cactus, and a snake. The newspaper lady huh, all I know is she come in from Topeka. She seen a flier sent out by our mayor, she figured it needed a newspaper. Right smart name, "The Marshallville Gazette", don't ya think? Her name

191

is Hannah Calder, she come in with her brother-in-law, and that's all I know. She's a handsome woman, tall, dark hair, curves in all the right places far as I can see. She don't seem to cotton to no men, busy woman. She's staying at the hotel right now, so you might ask Kay what she knows since she owns the place. Maybe even ask John Marshall, she rented one of his shops."

"She does a good job of printing," Short Keg added. "She printed up that poster I put over in the window. See, I put, 'buy two beers and the third one is half price,' pretty catchy uh? I figure a little advertising might bring in more customers."

"Good thinking, Ken, then you'll have to hire some good looking women to serve all those extra customers, might spruce up the place a bit," offered George.

"Come on George," said Slim, "if this place gets too fancy, I'd have to go somewheres else. Course a piano player couldn't hurt this place none."

"You know having a newspaper in town might just smartin' you boys up a bit," chuckled Short Keg. "Did you see the headlines in today's paper? Some guy named Jesse James and his gang been robbing banks. They held up a bank in

Missouri getting $15,000. That's more 'an a cowboy makes in his whole life time. Then there was a train robbery over in Ohio; who'd try such a thing? How do you stop a train and rob it? I can tell you, I'm done with bank robbers. I chased more than I care to think about. It seems like you catch one, and two more show up. I think I'll just read about them and not chase them. Hey, here comes ole Buzzard, bout time he closed up shop, it's way after his work day."

Coop walked over to the bar, put a foot on the rail, tipped his hat back and announced, Hey, I just got in a can opener. You can stock up on them airtights, and with my can opener, you can take food home, and eat whenever you want. I also got in a shipment of condensed milk from Borden. But," he said with some wonderment, "the big news is one of my freight haulers, a bull whacker named Whip Lash, told me about a new invention he saw at the Majestic hotel in Denver. It's the darndest thing; I may have to carry one in my store. Dang if a guy didn't invent a coffee percolator."

"What the heck are you talking bout?" said Slim. "A coffee what?"

"A percolator, Slim. The way I was told, you put coffee in this here basket with a stem and put it on the stove. The

193

boiling water rises up the stem, and spills over the coffee, and drips down in the pot. You just keep boilin' the water till the coffee gets as strong as you want. It has a glass bubble on top so you can see the color of the coffee. "

"Well what's wrong with just throwin' a hand full of coffee in the pot and boiling it like we always done? I don't think I need some new-fangled thing to make my coffee."

"The difference is the basket keeps the grounds out of the water, and out of your cup. Ain't you tired of spittin' out those grounds in the bottom of your cup?"

"Well dang if that don't put a ring around your tail. Next thing you know there'll be coffee saloons where people sit around drinking coffee."

"I'll admit," said Shady, "I actually put a dollop of honey in my coffee, cuts the bitterness a bit."

"Well of course you do you fancy, dancy cardsharp," said Slim with a twinkle in his eye.

*****

"Hey Ken, remember the soiled dove Kathy, that was working

here when you took over? She was gonna look for a rich man or sumptin', well apparently she did find a rich friend," said Coop

"How so, Coop?"

"She opened a dance hall down by the lucky lady. They sell drinks for fifty cents, and dances for twenty-five cents. Plus every half hour or so there's a singing act. The place is always crowded. Maybe you could have a few women dancers here, liven up the place?"

"She was a right smart girl as I recall, but how do you know this. You been learning to dance?"

"It's an ad in the Gazette. See it's right here."

Coop showed Ken and the other fellows the paper. The ad read, 'Come dance, meet Roxie, Ruby, Jackie, and Louise.' Under the top line it said 'Drinks 50 cents, dance 25 cents, and songs for your pleasure for free. Open 2 pm to 2 am at Kathy's Kantina. Dance lessons, one hour, noon to 1:00, $1.00.

"Those four ladies used to work as prostitutes at the Lucky Lady, but now they just dance with the men, and make more money," said Coop.

"I'll bet that place will be chuck full of men, twelve hours straight. Most these cowboys, and single men, ain't danced with a woman in years. She said she was gonna get outa the sex business, good for her," said Ken. "Hey, Coop, weren't you takin some dance lessons yourself?"

"I was, but not with those sportin' ladies. Maybe you can learn to do the Polka and go dancin' with Molly."

"Hey boys, looks like a fancy palaver at the bar," said Wild Shot, coming through the bat doors wiping his brow. "Another hot one today, time for a beer. You know some day some guy needs to invent something that blows cold air thru the window."

"It's mister 'shave and a haircut' guy," said George. "If I read that poster in your window right, you're chargin' twenty five cents for a shave. At those prices you'll be rich in no time."

"Twenty-five cents is cheap fo the job I do. First I wraps a hot towel round the face. While the towel softens up the whiskers, I hone my blade to the sharpest edge you'll ever see. I lather my brush with a special soap I get from Denver; cain't get it in this town. Hey Coop, how bout getting' some of that fancy soap from France in yo store? My blade cuts those whiskers slick as sliding on ice. Then I slap on some lavender water to finish the job, and the customer walks out rubbin his chin with a smile on his face. A lotta single guys come in right fo courtin' a friendly lady. Yes sir, twenty five cents is cheap. Throw in a haircut fo another twenty five cents and a man just rightly feels handsome."

"Speaking of things in my store, I got in some new cowboy hats made by a guy named Stetson. A right smart looking hat any cowboy would like. They're five bucks, but well worth it. Come over tomorrow and take a look. I can order more if you like. Shady, you cut a swell, you might like one."

"Hey, Slim," said Ken, "I never did hear how you stepped into a lawman's boots then stepped out again."

"Well, I was working foundry in Omaha. As a railway stop it attracted a lot of trouble makers. The local police took a look at my size and asked me to join the force. After five years of the heat and stink of the smeltin' process, I quit and joined the force. They wanted me to break up fights. Just lookin' at me stopped a lot of fights. But then a lot of drunks didn't pay me no never mind and kept a swingin' and wrestlin' and throwin' chairs and I took some lumps. After seven years of

197

being in the middle of flyin' fists, I shucked my badge and looked elsewhere for adventure."

"Don't blame you one bit, but why 'Nevada Slim?' I get the slim part, but why not 'Okie' Slim?"

"That's a good one Ken. Omaha had a lot of people movin' west. I heard a lot of folk talk about minin' in Nevada and I had set my mind to goin'. I talked about it for a couple of years and the other cops got to calling me Nevada. I hooked up with a wagon train and started on way to being a rich miner. The train stopped here for supplies, I looked around and liked what I saw in this town. It needed a blacksmith so I figured set up shop, fill up my poke a bit then poke around Nevada a bit later. Now I look to be staying here a long while."

The guys hung out for a while longer, had a nice steak with the fixins. Mary and Molly came out to say "Hi" and asked how they liked the food.

"Felt like lickin' that plate clean," said Slim. "You ladies smartin' this place right up."

It was a solid friendship the ex-lawmen had formed. They looked forward to meeting at the short Keg and swapping jokes and stories. Ken usually threw in a free beer and made sure everyone felt welcome. You could find four or five of them, around a table nearly every day about sundown. The mayor and councilmen joined them now and then.

Shady went to work at the Faro table, Ken and Sundowner stepped behind the bar, and the boys headed home.

The next day, Shady wandered over to the hotel and looked for Kay. The hotel had been built by Bill Williams and Mike Miles when the town was first founded. It was the first big building in Marshallville. It held a café, dry goods store, bar and hotel. While just a basic design, with basic decorations, it got the town started. It made money for the town and brought travelers into Marshallville. It served its purpose well for two years.

A gold miner bought the place for his wife, Kay Belle, (at a nice profit for the city treasury). He had struck gold at Pike's Peak, took his money, and moved to Denver. He met Kay there, where she managed a small hotel. He bought the hotel, and they married. A few years later, the Cherry Creek flood damaged the area near the hotel, and business slowed while people tried to rebuild. Kay saw an ad in the Rocky Mountain News for Marshallville. The mayor, John Marshall, told of a wonderful new town, and its potential, and invited people to come see for themselves. She grabbed her husband, and took a trip. They actually stayed in the rooms upstairs. She loved the small town feel, so they sold the hotel in Denver, and bought the Marshallville hotel.

She had a good eye for color and décor. They turned the dry goods section into a sitting room and enlarged café. She remodeled the building into a pleasantly, fashionable building, upstairs and down. They serve drinks with supper, but also added in a nice selection of wine. Unfortunately, her husband fell ill and died. Unbeknownst to people at the time, Mercury was a poisonous element. He had handled a lot of Mercury while in the gold business, and that took its toll.

Kay stood at the front desk explaining to a middle-aged woman the duties of the desk clerk. The woman, tall, wearing a high buttoned light brown suit, hair put up in a bun, looked very official.

"When someone comes up to the desk, you ask, 'May I help you?' If he asks for a room, you ask 'how many nights?' Make him sign his name in the register. You look at the name and always refer to him as mister and his last name. Rooms are three dollars a night, including breakfast; always collect in advance. If anyone argues, just tell them it is company policy."

Kay was an attractive woman, short but full-figured with blonde hair. The few gray hairs mixed well with blonde and added a certain wise and regal look. She had sparkling blue eyes and a smile that could melt a man's heart in two beats. She may be a widow, but there was still a glint in her eye, and she did not mind flirting a bit. She saw Mike approach, finished with the new desk clerk, and turned to him.

"Hi Mike, good to see you." She smiled. "What brings you in this morning?"

Tipping his hat he said, "Hello Mrs. Belle, you're looking well today. Ah have a question for you'all if you have a few minutes."

"Sure Mike, come back to the office."

A few feet back of the check in desk, a heavy oak door lead into her office. Tidy and neat, the office had a feminine touch. Lace curtains covered the window and a round blue and red checked rug sat on the floor in front of a solid oak desk. There were two high-back chairs opposite the desk, and Mike took one while Kay sat in a sturdy leather chair behind her desk.

"What's up, Mike?"

"Well, I'm afraid curiosi-tee has gotten the best of me, ma'am. I'm not the gossipy type, but between you and me, what do you know about zee newspaper lady?"

"Why Mike, do I detect more than a passing interest? What are your intentions Mr. Hoz," she said with a smile and tongue in cheek.

"Like I said, curiosi-tee got me wonderin'. She is a little mysterious. She rolls into town one day with a man driving her wag-on, and then she sets up her own news-pa-per. Nevada Slim says she's in from Topeka, and her name is Hannah Calder. She is printing posters for people around town, and puts out an interes-ting pa-per. Zee man she came in with, helped her set up the equipment, but now she runs zee place by herself. So, what do you know?"

"You're right, she is an interesting woman. We had supper together the other night, and I got to know her somewhat. I'll tell you what I know only because I am concerned about her safety. Her father ran a newspaper in Illinois. She learned the business from him. I don't know if you ever heard of the 'Bandits of the Prairie', you were only about ten at the time. In much of Illinois, bandit gangs roomed the area. I'm from that area and remember it well. Even some of the township and state officers were bandits. After years of trouble, some citizens formed a vigilante group known as regulators. Some of these groups also became 'lynching clubs'. Hannah told me her father got mixed up in the trouble. Her dad had published a lot of news naming some town officials as bandits. As a young girl when this started, she grew up tough. She can handle a gun, and did so on a few occasions. What worries me is her father was killed, shot in the back, after some of these stories ran in the paper. After her father's death, she, and an uncle moved to Topeka, Kansas."

"Does anyone one know who did the killin'?"

"No, not specifically, but everyone knew it was one of the bandits so they moved out of town. They opened up another newspaper, and the uncle kept printing stories about corrupt politicians. A few years later, the uncle hired a young man as co-editor, eventually he and Hannah were married. They printed several stories taking the position of anti-slavery. It was during the war and Kansas was in the middle of the being a slave or no-slave state. Pro-slavery folk damaged the paper a few times. Her uncle was found dead one morning in the office with a deep gash on his head. It looked like maybe he had fallen off a ladder onto his heavy desk. She never believed it."

"Printin' the newspaper seems to be a ver-y dan-ger-ous buisness, no?"

"Yes, but the big story, and maybe why she may be in trouble, was a story on corruption by the US senator. When the town sold bonds to build a new state capitol, the senator was involved with the construction company. In 1866 they laid a cornerstone for the building. A year later the stone crumbled because of faulty material. They printed a story about bribery, cost cutting, and cheap materials. The story pointed fingers at the senator. There were investigations, but nothing could be proven. Over the next two years, she and her husband unearthed many corrupt officials, and printed stories about vote buying, and shady deals at the state house. They were warned, anonymously, many times, but kept up the investigations. One night her husband was shot in the back, just like her father had been. She may still be in danger if she knows anything about those officials. There may also be relatives seeking revenge about her uncles' or husbands' postings."

"You are right, she may be in dan-ger. I am sure, certain high officials do not want their names flapping in zee wind. So," he said with a sly smile, "I should maybe, keep out the eye on her."

*****

Mike headed over to the Marshallville Gazette. He walked in to say hello to Mrs. Calder, but to his surprise, Van Gentry stood there flirting around with a smile on his face. Shady could feel the blood rise in his face as he tried to look casual.

"Hey Shady," Van said, "come on in. Hannah was showing me how a printing press works."

Mike immediately became aware that Van called her by her first name.

"What are you up to, Shady?" asked Van.

"I jest came over to wel-come Mrs. Calder to town, introduce myself, and tell her how much I enjoy reading the paper." Looking at Calder, holding out his hand, he said, "My name is Mike Hoz."

Calder took his hand. "Pleased to meet you Mister Hoz, and thank you for the compliment. Mr. Gentry was filling me in on his ranch, some of his friends, and the town history. It is a comfort to know many of our town's citizens are retired lawmen. I have met Mayor John Marshall and the rest of the city council. I met Mr. Cooper, Mr. George, Mr. Knight and Sundowner at the Short Keg. I printed some posters for them, and for the Short Keg, along with some for the barber shop. I look forward to meeting the other ex-lawmen soon. Perhaps someday you will tell me why they call you 'Shady'?"

"Oh, zee boys have a sad sense of humor, as you'll likely find out."

"The stage has rolled in and I need to check the mail," said Hannah. "There are stories coming in from Denver, plus our little town is plenty active. Seems the 'Ladies Society for a Sober Town' are complaining about a few of the saloons on the South side of town. They are starting a petition for a 10 p.m. curfew on all the drinking halls in town. They want me to do a story about their cause and mention some upcoming meetings."

Looking out the window Mrs. Calder grimaced and nearly shouted, "I hate to see that, what can we do?"

Mike and Van looked out the window in time to see a wagon load of women, 'sportin women,' some say, heading toward the south end of town.

"They are being used up in the brothels and saloons."

"That's a true story Mrs. Calder but it ain't against the law," Van said. "Wherever you find men, drink and money, you find women close by. Some got nothing else, sure ain't a decent way to make a livin.'"

"Someday, I will start a home for those women and figure a way for them to make a decent living."

"Well Mrs. Calder, it is a pleasure to meet you, we'll let you get back to work. Van, let's go chat with Short Keg."

Van hesitated to go. He wanted to flirt a little longer, but not wanting to be too obvious he said, "Sure."

On the way to the Short Keg, Mike told Van about the bribes and corruption in Topeka and Hannah Calder's connection. "We need to watch for any strangers that might be taking a special interest in the paper. It may be nothing any more, but let's keep her safe." Van shook his head and agreed.

*****

Nearly every night at the Short Keg saw crowds of men having a good time, drinking, laughing, and looking for a big score at the Faro tables. A few players would object loudly to a losing streak, but Mike settled them down by offering to buy them a drink. They grumbled, but took the drink.

Faro was strictly a game of luck, no thinking involved;

maybe that was why it was so popular. The betting lay out is a suit of cards, usually spades, from Ace to King printed on a cloth covered board. Players put money on any card. The first card the dealer (or bank) turned up was a losing card (suits do not matter only the face). The dealer then takes any money placed on that card. The second card turned up is a winning card. Any money on that card is paid by the dealer. If both cards turned up are the same, a pair of fives for example, the dealer takes half the bet from the five. That is supposed to be the only advantage the dealer has. Mike got his nickname 'Shady' for a reason. Besides rigging 'fines' for cheating in many towns, he was able to 'shade' the odds in his favor without being too obvious. For one thing, a pair seemed to turn up a lot more than usual. He also knew how players might try to cheat. He made it very clear to anyone who sat at his table, if he caught someone trying to cheat, he would take their bet, and the cheat got run out of the saloon. Mike had two helpers (bouncers actually) standing on either end of the table. Both were large, both wore a brace of guns, butt first in plain view. Neither was an ex-lawman, both were ex-cons. Having done prison time, both carried a menacing look that said, 'don't try nothin'.

There were plenty of gamblers in town so a second Faro table, run by a woman named 'Poker Alice', sat near the back of the short Keg. Attractive with a loose fitting blouse, most men didn't seem to mind losing their money to her. They also assumed a woman didn't cheat. Yet, as some people pointed out, she made a good living night after night.

The Short Keg had a friendlier feel than the other saloons on the south end of town. There were no upstairs ladies; Ken did not deal in women. The more 'upstanding' residents in town frequented the place for drinks, conversation, and gambling, while the rowdies generally hit the ones a few blocks further south.

Two of three strangers drinking at the bar decided to play Faro at Mike's table. They were a rough looking pair. Card after card, the two men seemed to be on the losing end of the deal. There were over ten players at the table making it lively and loud. The strangers were at either end of the table. They both put up a large bet then 'coppered' the bets. (Putting a piece of copper on the bet reversed the action on the bet). Attached to the copper piece was a thin horse hair. If the card played was a winner, the copper coin stayed on the pile of chips. If the card played was a loser, the horse hair could be pulled, tacking the copper off the chips, making it a winning bet. With eight or ten other players at the table placing bets, losing bets, winning bets, swearing loudly at cards, swapping out a 'copper' might go un-noticed.

Mike knew about the horse hair coppering trick; he had done it several times himself. Any time someone coppered a bet, he became alert to the bet. He also signaled his 'helpers' to watch the action. Right on cue, when Mike turned up a losing card for one of the coppered bets, the stranger yanked the copper changing the bet from a loser to a winner.

Mike stopped the game and looked at each man. "You boys are strangers in town, where you'all from?"

"Kansas, now pay up the bet."

"I ask because I have zee rule here you might not know, coming from Kansas and all. Zee rule is if I catch you cheating, I take zee money and you get thrown out."

"What's that got to do with us," one man said looking nervous.

"Well, one of you tried to cheat by pul-ling zee copper off your bet. Now, ah'm going to take both your bets, and you two are get-ting thrown out."

As both men reached for their pistols, each heard a

210

clicking noise behind their heads that sounded a lot like a
hammer being pulled back to full cock. Mike's helpers had
moved behind them when Mike had started talking. The two
men froze in their tracks. Mike took the money, and his helpers
nudged the men toward the door. These were men who did not
take kindly to being 'nudged'. As they went out the door, out
of sight, they drew their guns and came back in looking for
Mike. Mike's helpers, backs to the door coming back toward
the table, didn't see them come back in. After years of
sheriffing and double dealing himself, he knew the looks on the
stranger's faces meant trouble. He stood ready, guns out.

As the two men came back, Mike shot one in the arm,
and the other in the side. Both men fell to the floor dropping
their guns, and twenty other patrons ducked as well. Mike spun
on the third man still standing at the bar. "Leave zee guns on
zee floor and take your friends to zee doc. He is open all night,
there across zee street."

"You'll be sorry," he shouted as he helped his friends to
the door and toward Doc's.

Seconds later, drinking, talking and gambling, returned
to normal like a shoot-out was business as usual.

The next morning, more like noon, after breakfast Mike

went to Doc's. "Just a couple of flesh wounds," Doc said, "they said you took their money and that you should pay the bill. A dollar a piece please." Doc held out his hand.

Mike handed over two dollars with a chuckle. "You eva seen them boys before?"

"Nope, but a rough looking bunch."

"A bunch?"

"Yeah, four men altogether, two wounded, two not. Couldn't tell where they was from, but they looked to be traveling for days, still dusty and smelly. They were none too happy bout being shot, but one said, 'We'll get her anyway'."

"Get her?"

"That's what he said."

*****

Two days later, Hannah sat at her desk working late. She heard a loud bang as the back door blew inward, and four men came rushing in. Hannah went for the gun she had in the desk drawer. Before she could aim the gun, the biggest one grabbed her, squeezed her arm, and her gun fell harmlessly to the floor.

"You shouldn't've printed those lies in your paper, now you're goin' ta retire from the printin' business." He squeezed even tighter, a grimace covered Hannah's face.

A second man kicked over a tray of letters, scattering them over the floor. A third man dumped ink and broke all the bottles resting on the shelves.

"Where's the list of names you have, we need it," he growled, as he lifted her out of her chair sticking his face into hers.

While the second man started breaking up the press, and smashing plates, the fourth man tore open the drawers in Calder's desk, throwing the drawers and contents on to the floor. Rummaging through the papers he said, "Here it is, and Senator Meadows will love this."

"Hobble your lip, no names," the first man snapped.

While they were wrecking the place, Hannah tried to break away but the grip on her arm tightened. He spun her around, slapped her hard, and she went down.

"Let's go darling," he said, "you need to take a ride."
He dragged her out the back door. In the dark, they rode away.
No one saw a thing.

The next morning, after breakfast with Lefty and Levi,
Mike walked over to the newspaper office to talk more with
Hannah. Lefty and Levi sat drinking a second cup of coffee. He
immediately saw the mess, went inside, and noticed Hannah
was gone. He ran out to the street and saw Lefty and Levi
leaving the diner. He called out and when they came over, he
showed them the mess.

"Hannah is missing," he said. "let's find her."

They swung by the sheriff's office, grabbed Cal, then
picked up Skinner and started tracking. Skinner picked up the
trail quickly from behind the office. Five fresh tracks headed
out of town. Urgency gripped the men as they spurred down
the road. They found her unconscious in a ditch about four
miles from town. She had bruises, a bloody lip, and looked like
she had been dragged along the ground. Gently Mike lifted her
and set her in front of him on his saddle, holding her steady.
They rode carefully back to town and went directly to the doc's
office, he carried her in.

"Wait outside til I tell you OK," said Doc. "She needs a little time. When she's ready I'll give you a shout out."

A half hour later Hannah opened her eyes, blinking at the light. Doc had her cuts and scratches bandaged up by then.

"How ya feelin' Hannah?" asked the doc.

"I hurt all over," she cried.

"Can you sit up? I have some men outside, waitin' to see you."

The doc helped Hannah sit up against a pillow. She closed her eyes for a few seconds, took a deep breath and said, "OK."

The doc's office was small so Mike and Cal came in first, while the other men stayed outside. The mayor, John Marshall, had heard about the kidnapping and joined the other men outside.

"Hi Hannah," Mike said. "I'm sure glad we found you alive. Do you know who did this to you?"

Through a swollen lip she muttered, "Yesh. Senator

Meadows sent sum men from Kansis. In Kansis, my uncle, husbund and I had prin-ted several names of town officials who had been pawrt of a corrupt business deal." She sighed, took a couple of deep breaths and continued. "After my uncle and husbund were killed, I left town quickly, but with a list of the rest of the names of people involved with constructshion fraud. Meadows' name was nex. I heard one of the men say 'Senator Meadows will like dis'. They threatened to kill me if I ever prin-ted any more information about the bisness dealings in Topeka."

Cal said he would put out a warrant for their arrest. Mike went outside, looked at Lefty and Levi and said, "Boys, interested in visiting Topeka?" Seeing Hannah, they quickly nodded. "Let's get loaded up." Facing in the room, Mike said, "Hannah, you won't have any more trouble from Topeka."

"Tanks," she said trying to talk and smile through a swollen lip.

John Marshall entered the room with a frown on his face. "Hope you feel better, Hannah. We need people like you in Marshallville. Get well soon."

216

Chapter 15

Gang Trouble

Walking into the dry goods store, Van Gentry brushed the dust off his pants and looked around.

"Hi Coop, time again to pick up supplies. Anything good happen these days that I ain't heard about?"

"Had some miners in the other day loading up supplies to last a month. They was flush, paid with gold dust, had a nice pouch full. If I was a young man again, I might go throw a few pan fulls' myself."

"Yah, Coop, you old buzzard, you're just getting old, older every day, and don't you love it. You got no time or inclination for any gold pannin'. Come on out to the ranch Sunday, bring some of those old peace keepers with ya. We'll throw some venison on the grill, maybe have a little shootin' contest. I'm meeting John oer the Short Keg, close up early and have a beer, it's a hot one today."

On the way to the Short Keg, Van saw Shady Mike come out of the men's store with a new frock coat, vest and tie, all black as usual. He wondered how many black coats, did Mike need. A former deputy, now a Faro dealer in the short Keg, calling him 'Shady' was a compliment.

"Hey Shady," Van yelled, "grab George and come over for a beer. Slim, Buzzard, and John and I are ready to swap some stories."

Short Keg brought over several beers, sat down, held his mug up with a "Cheers." They all took a gulp and smacked their lips. "Something about a beer, on a hot day, with friends, sends a satisfying feeling through a fellow," sighed Ken.

"Where's Cal?" asked Coop.

"He and his deputy headed down the street looking into some trouble," said Short Keg.

"Glad it was him and not me," said Coop. "Trouble will always come a visitin', no need to go lookin' for it."

"Seemed a couple of miners got way-laid and lost their gold dust pouches. And it seemed that a couple of drifters were suddenly buying beer, and gambling with a couple of pouches of gold dust."

"Wow," said Shady, "even 'moi' could figure out that one."

Three men pushed the bat wing doors opened and walked heavily to the bar. They were tough looking men, dusty, road weary, and each had a '64 colt sitting butt forward style.

"Where's the bartender," one man groused, "how's a man supposed to kill his thirst without a bartender." He looked over at the men having a beer and yelled, "Hey old men, where's the bartender, we need a drink."

Short Keg stood up. "I'll be right with you boys."

"Well, hurry it up, I don't like to be made waitin'." One of the other men chimed in, "Dang old man, move it."

Short Keg slowly moved behind the bar, with a hint of a limp in one ankle.

"Ease up boys, you'll live longer."

"Ain't your business how long I live, your business is to get a bottle and some glasses over here now," growled the first man.

Short Keg put three glasses on the bar and holding a bottle he said, "That'll be three dollars for the bottle."

"We'll pay ya after we drink and where are the girls?" He leered around the saloon.

Just then Miss Kitty walked in. "Hi boys, it's hot out and I need a beer." Women, other than working women, didn't usually come into a saloon, but Miss Kitty was just one of the boys when it came to swapping stories and havin' a beer now and then.

The loud mouth stranger grabbed her. "Now here's a right purty gal, I'll take her."

Miss Kitty carried a small, six shot, .22 pistol tucked under her vest. She pulled it, tucked it under his chin and tersely whispered, "I've got six lead beans in this barrel, and unless you feel like eating a few, you'll get your arm off me."

He laughed, squeezed her tighter and huffed a bit. "Come on darling, you won't shoot your new boyfriend would you?"

"No," she replied, and pulled the gun back, and shot a hole in the brim of his hat, then tucked the gun back under his chin. "No, not yet."

Visibly shaken, he shoved her away and shouted, "Bitch, I'll get up for that." Van let out a whoop followed closely by a chorus of laughter from the other men.

The tall, angry man started to pull his gun when he heard the sound of a shotgun being dropped on the bar. "I think you boys ought to head further downtown," suggested Short Keg. The angry man's interest in drawing his gun changed quickly.

"Let's get out of here," he grumbled, and the three toughs headed for the door, but not before kicking over a couple of chairs.

"Those three boys look like trouble," Coop stated, "we better warn Cal to be on the alert."

Looking out the window, John noticed two more rough looking men joining with the three leaving the saloon. "It appears a small gang of men rode in together, and they look like they legged hard and long, let's get back to the ranch Van, we can warn Slim to keep an eye out on the way. You'all come out to the ranch this Sunday, we have fresh venison we can throw on the fire."

They pushed their way out of the door and headed for the livery.

"That big ol' boy didn't much cotton to you Miss Kitty, after you put a hole in his hat," mentioned Shady Mike.

"That bunch is trouble", she replied, "we all better keep an eye out. Well, where's my beer, it's still hot out."

The rowdies headed to the rougher south side of town. They found a loud saloon with a piano player, card games, and women. They spent the next several hours drinking, gambling, and spending time with the upstairs ladies. Later that night the five toughs were sittin' at a table having another drink.

"I'll get that bitch for shootin' my hat," bragged the big tough, "and those old men thought they were so smart, we should teach them a real lesson in manners too."

"Hey boss," whispered one of the men, "we're a little short on money so how bout we rob the bank first thing in the morning, then shoot up the saloon, and send a few balls into the bath house on the way out, that'll fix 'em." The big guy said, "Oh ya," and the other men grinned and nodded their heads in agreement.

*****

Standing at one end, Dusty leaned heavily on the bar. He was tipsy as usual, but Ken walked down to see how he was doing.

Dusty had come into town with a wagon train. As it neared town his right front wheel dropped suddenly into a pothole. The wheel snapped, jolting the wagon sharply to the right, throwing Dusty's pregnant wife off the seat on to the ground. She hit hard, breaking her neck. He was devastated. They had been trying for years to have a baby, and they were headed west for a new life. In a lightning second, all that ended.

He had the wheel repaired, left the train, and parked the wagon near a drop out camp. He buried his wife in the Marshallville cemetery. She and Jane Marshall were the first two graves in the cemetery.

He sold nearly everything, but two mules, his wagon, his clothes, and cooking gear. He drank himself drunk every night trying to forget, trying not to think about his wife.

Early on, the people of Marshallville had a garbage and scavenger problem. A city ordinance was passed requiring that any building serving food had to have a trough out back for all food scraps. The trough had to be emptied at least once a week and taken a few miles outside of town. When farms sprang up and pigs were being raised, the pig farmers would bring a wagon into town, and shovel up the scraps for hog slop. Nobody liked the job. Dusty needed money for drink so he hired out to shovel slop. The farmers were happy to let someone else do the dirty work. Dusty used his team of mules, and borrowed a small wagon from the pig farmers.

Dusty drank most of the night, then staggered out to his wagon and flopped down for the night. Around noon the next day he'd come to, have some coffee and bacon at his camp, team up his 'slop wagon', shovel the troughs, and head for the pig farms. The farmers paid him a few dollars, some bacon, potatoes, coffee, and feed for his mules. Back to his wagon, he'd stake out his team, and sleep some more. Evening time, he'd have some bacon, and potatoes, walk back into town, drink to a stupor, and stagger back to his wagon. He was young, but he was aging fast.

224

"Hey Dusty, how are you tonight," asked Ken. "Can I get you a sandwich? You look a little pale."

Dusty looked up, stared at Ken over an empty glass, and attempted a smile.

"Shord Keg," he slurred, "I've been some down on my luck, but you've always been right by me."

Dusty leaned in toward Ken and put his hand up to his face and waved him closer and whispered, "I wash down at da Bufflo Girl saloon and dees guys was drinkin' and talkin' loud and angry bout sumpin. I heard dem say bout robbin' bank and shootin you. They probably shoot me for tell'n' you but you my friend."

"You sure about that Dusty," said Ken

Barely able to pronounce his words, Dusty went on, "I worry bout you, you my friend. I at next table, ma head down, I think I fall sleep, but then I hear man say rob bank, and shoot old men at Short Keg, and sassy bitch morrow so I come tell you."

"Hey George," said Ken, "help ole Dusty back to his wagon then hurry back, we've got trouble." Looking over at a table close by, "Hey Slim, Coop," Ken waved his friends over to the bar.

"What's up Ken?" asked Slim.

"We got trouble. Remember those guys in here earlier, that grabbed Miss Kitty. Dusty over heard them planning to rob the bank then shoot up the Short Keg, and then Miss Kitty, tomorrow."

"We knew they looked like trouble," said Coop, "we need to tell Cal. I'll run over to the jailhouse, Slim, round up George and Miss Kitty. Come back here with them. Ken, better tell Shady what's going on."

*****

"I'm going to need your help friends," said Cal. "I know you were looking for some peace and quiet. You all got good reasons for staying out of gun play but my deputy is out of town, and I can't take on those boys by myself."

"Can't we just get zee drop on them at zee saloon, then throw them in zee jail?" said Mike, patting his gun.

"Mike, I'd like to, but we gotta catch them breaking the

law. We've nothing to hold them on, only the word of the town drunk. We need to face them coming out of the bank."

"Ya sure we cain't jest shoot them, and say it was an ac-ci-dent?"

"Can I count on you tomorrow? I will deputize you so's it's all legal. We'll keep an eye on the bank, and when they make their move, we make our move."

"Peace and quiet comes at a price, boys, you know that," nodded Ken. "Not sure I want to be a deputy again, but they'd be coming for us, so we better go at them first. They won't expect us to take a hand, so we have an advantage."

"I'm not a boy, but count me in," said Miss Kitty.

"Well?" said Cal.

They all shook their heads yes, and in unison said, "We'll be there."

A quiet, breezy, morning started the day. The bank hours on Saturday were 10:00 to noon. The town woke up slowly after Friday night. Most of the shops opened by 9:00, or after, and a few shoppers were making the rounds to the grocery store or hardware store, but in no rush. Dogs were lounging in the shade. A few chickens were scratching, and pecking near the corner of Main and A street. A cat stalked something under the boardwalk.

The rowdies were hung over, and that made them even madder. They grumbled about waiting until 10:00 to rob the bank. That didn't stop'em from having another drink or two.

"They'll be people walkin' and gettin' in the way," said one man. "We mightin' have ta shoot one or two ta get'em moving."

They packed up their rolls and headed for the bank. Coop saw them and knew the play. He stuck his head in the Short Keg, and yelled, "strap up boys, here they come," and went for the sheriff's office.

Shady Mike went to the café, rounded up George, and Miss Kitty. Coop picked up Slim after alerting Cal. Each strapped on a holster, checked the loads in their guns, and made their way toward the bank.

"We've done this many times over the years," waved Ken, "let's hope this is the last. With five bad guys, and only one of Cal, we need to suck it up."

Two of the men stayed outside holding the horses while three of the rowdies went inside for the robbery. As they came out of the bank, Cal was standing there facing the bank, and on either side stood, Gentleman George, Buzzard Cooper, Nevada Slim, Short Keg, Shady Mike, and Miss Kitty. The former lawmen didn't look like much trouble. A little gray, a little overweight, a saggy chin or two, but there they stood. The young rowdies started laughing when they saw the bunch of old men standing in the street with guns on their hips. The sight of Miss Kitty wearing a hog leg high on her hip produced a chorus of cat calls; Miss Kitty did not smile.

"Hey old men," one of them shouted, "better head home and sit down before you fall down."

"Hey, there's that witchy woman," yelled the big guy, "I need to put a bullet in her hat."

The townsfolk saw what was coming, ran, and ducked as fast as they could.

The men all laughed. The young toughs did not realize that a man, or woman, who could live long enough to retire from peace keeping had to be fast, and accurate with a gun. A little gray hair just made them less tolerant of stupid behavior. The robbers were still laughing when they started to draw their

229

guns. They figured a shot or two would scare the old men away.

It wasn't pretty. When the smoke cleared there were five empty saddles, and five 'not so tough' men lying on the ground. They weren't dead but they were shot up pretty good. Several holes had blood oozing out, and mixing with the dust in the street. The old peacekeepers just shook their heads, and breathed out an air of disgust.

"Something about the younger generation," said Coop, "they don't rightly respect their elders."

"Or a lady," added Miss Kitty.

They stripped the rowdies of their guns and weapons while they lay in the street moaning and coughing. Miss Kitty picked up the bank money and took it back to the bank. The tellers were peeking up over the counter not knowing the score. They were grinning happy to see Miss Kitty.

The town doc walked over with a few men, and loaded the shot-up men into a wagon, and headed for the jail. After they were bunked into the old adobe jailhouse, the doc started to patch them up.

"You don't have to be too careful bout pullin' the slugs," mentioned Cal.

He had been an army doc, and he knew plenty bout pullin' slugs. "These boys'll be able to stand trial in a week or so," said doc.

The ex-lawmen headed back to their stores, hung up their guns, and went to the Short Keg for a beer, and a bunch of back-slapping. On the way over, they got some cheers, and hand clapping from some of the town folk. The mayor met them saying the beer was on him.

"Mayor, I could use a few more deputies. We can't keep calling on a bunch of old men, and a lady, to keep things peaceful like."

"Next council meeting, we will add that to the city budget," echoed the Mayor.

Life has a way of dealing aces or jokers. Quick judgements when you don't know the territory has a way of blowing back in your face. Those rowdies found out judging men you don't know can bring you a lot of sorrow.

Chapter 16

Miss Kitty and Kay Belle

"Hi Miss Kitty," said Kay Belle, "looking for some supper?"

"I am, I like dining in your hotel now and then, makes me feel special."

"Good timing, I am just about to have supper myself, join me please. We need to get to know each other better."

"Thank you, Kay, we do need to be better friends."

"Watching you at the shoot-out at the bank makes me want to know more about you. I have seen a lot of crazy things in my life, but never a woman, standing in the street, sending lead into a bunch of robbers. Let's have supper, and we can swap stories about our lives."

The hotel and restaurant had been remodeled and now gave a warm and inviting feel. The entryway opened to a nice sitting area. The carved, dark wood, check-in desk sat near the end of the entryway. One side of the sitting area had high backed chairs and small end tables, with a crystal ornament of some kind sitting in the middle of the tables. There were several oil lamps on the walls, giving it a light airy feel. The owner's office set behind the check-in desk. The stairway to the upstairs rooms was right of the desk. Rugs on the floor gave a quiet, soft feeling. A large opening with draped curtains led into the restaurant. Several tables were placed around the room, all with white tablecloths bordered with blue stitching, and place settings for two and four.

The restaurant had a nice menu and a variety of wines to go with the food. The waitress was dressed in a white dress and white apron. She added a sense of style to the room. The chairs had upright backs with soft, deep seats. Four other tables had guests seated waiting for supper. It was a pleasant evening and both ladies seemed comfortable with each other. Kay ordered soup and salad as did Miss Kitty. They started with a bold red wine, sat across from each other, and smiled.

"You start," said Kay. "I heard about your husband being killed and you were his deputy, but what came before all that?"

"Seems we both lost a husband, Kay, almost makes us sisters, feels nice. I didn't have any sisters, but I had six older brothers. We lived on a farm so my parents figured the more kids, the better. We were all two years apart. When I was born I had two, four, six, eight, ten, and twelve-year-old brothers. We all had hand me down clothes, mostly coveralls, except the older brother, Bob. By the time I got any clothes, they were pretty worn. Plus, they were all boy's clothes. No one knew I was a girl til I was six. I didn't get my first dress til I was ten. I had a short haircut, so if we were all lined up we looked like seven boys."

"That was a lot like me," said Kay, "except I was the oldest kid of five girls. Seemed like I was always helping mom take care of the younger kids. I learned to make clothes as soon as I could sew. Fortunately, being the oldest, I got the clothes first"

"Sounds like you grew up being a girl," said Miss Kitty. "My brothers treated me like a younger brother, not a girl. We wrestled, jumped in the mud, and threw rocks. I didn't know I was a girl. I just didn't have a hangy down thing, and I had to squat to pee."

"You are certainly a beautiful woman now. Where did

you live?"

Miss Kitty smiled. "Thank you. You're a lovely woman too." She took a sip of wine. "We lived on a farm, so we all had daily chores. At two, I collected the eggs. I learned to fight the rooster when I went in the coop, he was a mean one. I had scratches on my arms until I took in a big wooden spoon." Waving her hand up and down she said, "A few whacks in the head and he let me alone. Each year I had more chores, that's how I grew up."

"No wonder you're so tough. But with a name like Kitty, people must have known you were a girl. What happened when you were six for people to know you were a girl?"

"My real name is Danielle, but my brothers called me Danny, everyone called me Danny. My husband Todd called me Danny. Miss Kitty is a nickname I picked up when I got married cause I 'adopted' every stray cat in town." Smiling and looking wistful, she said, "Todd thought the name was cute and started calling me Miss Kitty. He made me feel special so I took the name of Miss Kitty after he died. I go by Miss Kitty to remember Todd.

What happened at six is a funny story. It was my first

year in school. One day at lunch, some of the first grade boys found an ant hill. Three of the boys started to pee on the hill. They yelled at me to pee on the ants, too. So, I pulled down my coveralls, squatted over the hill and peed."

Mouth wide open, Kay sputtered, "You did what?"

Laughing, Kitty went on, "The three boys stood there with their mouths opened. A minute later one of the boys started yelling, 'That boy doesn't have a pecker, that boy doesn't have a pecker'. I stood up, pulled my coveralls up and stared at the boy."

Kay Belle almost spit out her wine. "I'm seeing this in my head." She started coughing, she was laughing so much.

"One of the older boys came up to the boy, called him stupid and told him I was a girl not a boy. The boy was a little slow, one of the other kids said he couldn't teach a hen to cluck, that was kinda mean but true. Then the teacher called us in from lunch."

Wiping her mouth with a napkin, Kay waved a hand to get some time to catch her breath. A few seconds later she said, "go ahead."

"After school, we went out to play and I went to play with the boys like I always did. That boy who thought I was boy without a pecker came up to me, told me to go play with the girls and pushed me down. When my brothers pushed me, it was fight on. I jumped up, charged him, knocked him down, and started pounding him. Well, he started gasping and turning blue. I didn't know at the time that he had asthma. I didn't even know what asthma was."

Kay raised her eyes in shock. She again waved her hand for some time while laughing and trying to catch her breath. Miss Kitty also started laughing because Kay was laughing. Some of the other diners turned to see why all the noise.

"I was suddenly yanked by the back of the neck of my shirt and thrown backwards on the ground. This ten-year-old boy yells at me to leave his brother alone and kicks me. If he had just saved his brother, we'd be done, but when he kicked me, it was round two. Like before, I jumped up and charged him. He was big, and he knocked me down, and laughed. He didn't know my brothers were also at school. My ten-year-old brother charged him and knocked him down. The boy's twelve-year-old brother knocked my brother down. Then my twelve-year-old brother knocked the other boy down. In five minutes there was a full blown riot goin' on in the school yard."

Kay nearly spit out her wine again. She slapped the table, gulped the wine, and grinned from ear to ear. "Stop, stop, for a minute, I can't breathe," Kay gasped.

Taking another sip of wine, Miss Kitty waited for a signal to go ahead. "Half of the kids were crying, but half of the kids were cheering. The teacher, Miss Halverson, comes out of the school house screaming to stop fighting. No one paid her any attention, probably because most of the kids were having too much fun. She was a big woman and didn't cotton to no disobedience. She started grabbing boys and tossing them like flapping chickens. That ended the fighting, and everyone knew I was a girl."

"My husband woulda called that a son-of-a-bitch stew fight. Everyone got thrown in, the pot got stirred, and fists flew. Could'a been some hair pulling, and biting goin' on too, he'd say."

Miss Kitty nodded, "After the fight, I was sorta stuck round my school yard games. The boys didn't want to play with me. Not because I was a girl, they didn't want my brothers to hammer on them if I got hurt. The girls were doing sissy things, and I didn't share their dolly dancing. Course, my brothers had no problem pulling tricks on me."

"We sure had a much different growin' up time," said Kay. "With four younger sisters we played dolls, learned to cook and sew. The only time we threw rocks was at a chicken trying to peck at us. Course, sisters did some fighting, but that meant yelling and crying, not punching and hitting."

Kitty finished her soup and commended Kay for its taste.

"I brought a cook with me from Denver. I was spoiled a bit by good food when I was married. My husband took good care of me. I can't imagine having six brothers, living on a farm; how did you meet other people?"

"My brothers had friends in town, and some would come to the ranch and hang out. When we'd lose a chicken or eggs, we always had a little varmine, huntin' party. I was shooting like the boys, in fact, I was hittin' more'an they were. Then it happened. When I was fourteen, one boy that palled around with my brothers struck me in the heart. His name was Todd and he was eighteen. I couldn't take my eyes offin' him. As far as he was concerned, I was a little sister. If he was anything like my brothers, he'd be married in a couple of years, and be havin' babies."

"We might need another bottle of wine before we finish

239

this story," said Kay. She waved the waitress over and ordered another bottle. "Living in town with five girls, boys were always hanging around like bees around a patch of flowers. My mother tried to tell us girls about boys and the trouble they could cause. It was a losing battle, there was no shortage of the male persuasion floating around. What happened with Todd?"

"There was a dance in town for the 4th of July that year, and the whole family went. Well, I see him dancing with Becky Jane. That put me in a pissy mood for a month. I reckoned they'd get married, and I'd have a broken heart, and never find love again. When I turned 16, I didn't look like no one's baby sister. I popped out curves and bumps where a woman should have curves and bumps. Todd was 20, but he didn't get married to Becky Jane. And when he came out to pal with my brothers, he didn't look at me like a baby sister anymore."

Tipping her head back with a smile, Kay went on, "At sixteen, I didn't look like anyone's baby sister either. I had many beaus', but none of them really stuck. At the dances, I was the one the other girls were jealous of. Then what happened?"

"His dad was the sheriff in town, and Todd his deputy.

When he came to hang out with my brothers, he brought his holster and pistol. He favored the 1851 Navy Colt .44 caliber with the seven inch barrel. They set up pie tins, and took practice. I wasn't about to sit around moon eyed, so I joined them. Right off, I was hittin pretty good. Two years later, I was eighteen and we got married, I even wore a dress. We were able to rent a small house in town, that made me very happy."

"You were lucky; not so with me. I just didn't pick'em right," said Kay gulping down her third glass of wine.

"Those boys you met, didn't know a jewel from a rock," said Kitty raising her glass to Kay. "Todd was a deputy, and I started walking around town with him, in my levi pants, no more coveralls, and not in a dress either. We talked about the town, the people, and where trouble might start. We also talked about where we might want to go on a picnic."

"I grew up in the Denver area," said Kay. "My dad was a gold miner, first at Pike's Peak, then around Denver. It was a wild time, with miners coming and going. We ran a rooming house, and it was loaded with rough and ready men. Like I said, with five girls, men were hanging around sniffing the wildflowers. I just naturally fell for the men who wouldn't be branded. Later, I managed a small hotel. I did keep a pocket revolver but never had to use it."

"Can't be too careful, Kay. Four years after we married, Todd's dad had a heart attack, and had to step down from action. Todd became the sheriff. We were a team. We played together, worked together, did everything together so I became his deputy. It might sound dangerous, but a sheriff does a lot more than shoot people. As a deputy, I collected fines and taxes, inspected buildings, posted bulletins, and shuffled all the legal paper. And, I also walked the town with Todd."

"I heard it was some angry drunk, shot Todd in the back. Then you put two in his chest."

Trying to keep from tearing up Miss Kitty nodded, took a quick breathe and went on. "The town hired another sheriff, and I quit the law business. I went to the family farm for a year or two trying to get over losing Todd. An old friend stopped by the farm to see how I was gettin on. He mentioned Marshallville as a place I might want to make home, and here I am. I was fed up with Kansas and bad asses, excuse my language, but too many drunks was actin' worse than any vermine we had on the farm. I was ready for some peace and quiet."

"How did you go from rough and ready deputy to running a bath house?"

"Dirt under my nails, dirt in my hair, dirt on my clothes, I guess my woman side finally come out. I still wear pants but I also like to spruce up a bit, and be genteel. Bout once a week, after closing, I sit in a hot tub, and relax. You can get cleaned all over if you know what I mean. Hey, you should come over one day, and have a soak. With no one around, it feels good. Once in awhile I see a naked man, but I had six older brothers so nothing new. I seen more peckers than a chicken rancher."

Kay gagged on her wine and let out a big laugh, coughed and waved her napkin up and down. "Kitty, you are a funny lady, I love it."

Leaning in close to Kay, Kitty spoke in a hushed tone. "Besides, seeing a naked man now and then don't hurt nobody."

Kay responded with a big grin and a knowing look. "Honey, you are a woman after my heart. I look forward to getting to know you better."

"Todd and I did our share of fooling around. I was married at eighteen but we sparked and spooned a bit when I was seventeen. Those sparks flew for eight years. We didn't have any kids, don't know why. It's been four years since Todd was killed. I'm starting to feel an aching in my heart, and other parts."

"I know what you mean," said Kay. "Having a man around has its' advantages. I think I might have someone in mind for myself, we'll see."

"I was thinking that John Marshall might be available. He's a handsome man, and seems kind. He has a daughter that needs a mama. His wife died about three or four years ago, he may be ready. I'm not sure how I go about seeing if he is interested," said Kitty.

"Well now Kitty, we'll have to put our heads together and come up with a plan."

"Kay, I hope you don't mind my asking but what happened with your husband? I heard he was sick."

"As I said, good men and me never took hold. But Al was different. He was older but kind. He made me feel loved and safe. He was a gold miner, and cashed out pretty good from the mines. People thought I was a gold digger because I married him, but I loved him. After the Cherry Creek flood in

'64, I wanted somewhere safe. About five years later, I saw a flier that John Marshall had posted in the Denver paper, so I grabbed Al, and we came down here. We bought the old hotel, and fancied it up a bit."

"You did a nice job on this hotel. Like I said, I like to eat here now and then because the food is good and it feels warm. So what happened to Al?"

"Al was feelin' poorly for the last year or so. The doctor said something bout handlin' mercury in the gold process or something, I didn't understand, but it proved to be deadly. When he died there were a lot of rumors about me, but I didn't care. He was a good man, and we had a good marriage for a few years. I love this hotel, and I have money in the bank. If you want, you can come live here, no charge. It would be good to have a friend close by."

Miss Kitty sat back, put her hand over her mouth, and with a barely audible voice said, "Really? I have the old lawmen in town as friends, but I don't have a lady friend. Someone I can talk to like sister to sister. I really feel easy with you. I don't want to put you out, I can pay some."

"I'll make you a deal. I'll send some hotel guest over for a free bath, and you can stay here for free."

245

"Deal," said Miss Kitty.

"Then it is settled," said Kay, "pick any room you like and no charge."

The salad showed up, their wine glasses were filled, they clinked glasses and with a smile, then set to eating.

Chapter 17

Gentry Brothers Ranch

A bright Sunday and round fluffy clouds floated calmly over the bar-b-que going full on at the Gentry brothers' ranch. There was meat on the grill, beans in the pot, and biscuits in the Dutch oven. Ken handed out some bottled beer and, laughing, George started the story-telling.

"When ah was living in Texas we had a Mexican family next door. Those folks could roast chilies that would melt paint off a barn. Ah'd been in the rangers a couple of years, and we had some rookie recruits over to ma house for a meetin'. They were young but makin' an effort to look mature and tough. I brought out the chili, but warned them that it was very hot, and they should go easy. Of course, I made it sound like they'd be babies if they didn't grab a big mouth full. One big bite and those boys turned red, their eyes watered, and they were sucking air like there was none left in the state. The whole time, they're trying to be tough."

"You're a cruel man George, then what happened?" Van said with half a smile.

"Without even asking to be excused, they headed for the water bucket outside. Those boys had the runs for two days."

"I had a crazy one a couple of years ago," said Coop. "We had a trouble maker in town who drank too much, but thought he was a tough guy. I made him a visitor to the jail house a few times, and he was mad bout that, kept saying one day he was goin' to get even. So, one day I'm walkin' toward the saloon, and he steps out, and sees me. Steeled by a few drinks, he immediately yells, 'OK Sheriff, it's you and me, draw.' I yell, wait, let's go in the street so we don't shoot anyone else. He thinks a moment, and says 'OK'. He turns to walk off the boardwalk into the street. I can't believe he fell for that. I quickly step toward him figuring I'll whack him in the head, and be done with it. He turns, and sees me coming, and quickly reaches for his gun. Well, he pulls the trigger before he ever gets the gun out of the holster, and shoots himself in the foot. He starts hopping up and down, and I figure that would be the end of it. He looks at me even madder and while hopping up and down, he tries to draw again. But this time he gets the gun barely out of the holster. I step at him so he pulls the trigger too soon again, and shoots himself in the knee. At that point the gun flies out of his hand, and he falls backward. When the gun hits, it goes off, and puts a hole in his hand. Now I think it is really over, but he looks at me again, and with even more determination, he rolls over to get his gun."

"You really brought the beast out in this guy, Coop," said Ken, "what'd you do to him?"

"Nothing special as I recall, but now I have a decision to make. Do I stand there, and see how many more times this guy can shoot himself, or do I do something cause next time he might miss himself, and go bout hittin' me. I decide I've had enough fun, and I step over and pick up his gun. Now, I wonder, what should I do. He is bleeding out his boot, out his leg, out his hand, and he's still cussing me out. I'm thinkin' I could let him bleed until he passes out, or I could help him get to the doc's office. I tried to keep from laughing, but that was the strangest thing I had ever seen."

"That does beat the band all right," pointed out Slim.

"Fortunately, the doc heard the gun fire, and he came over carrying his bag. I told Doc when he got the bleeding stopped, I would take the guy to jail. Attempted murder should get him a few years in the state pen. So, I have a prisoner in jail, who tried to shoot me, he has three wounds, and I never fired a shot. But a month later, I'm in church and get shot twice. That is when I turned in my badge and headed home."

"Funny and ironic story Buzzard," said Ken. "Goes to show ya, life is strange. Sundowner and I are in a cattle stampede, and now we own a saloon. He wanted to be here today, but someone had to watch the store."

"OK, enough stories for now," said Van. "Let's have a little shooting contest. Everyone throw a dollar in the pot, and winner take all. We have eight shooters so we'll draw numbers. Number one will shoot against number two, three against four and so on. I'll set up two tin plates on a rail by the corral. We'll get back twenty feet. This is a draw out of the holster contest. I'll yell ready, wait a few seconds, and then yell 'go'. The fastest one to hit the plate wins. You get one shot only. The rest of us will judge who hit first. If you both miss, you take one more shot. Of course, if one hits, and one misses, the hit wins. The four winners will draw numbers again, shoot off, and then the two winners will shoot to see who wins the money, and title of best shooter in town."

"OK, Van, sounds like you figure to win a few dollars," laughed Coop.

An hour after the shooting contest, Miss Kitty remarked, "What a great day. Sunshine, good friends, good food, and I won eight bucks. Goes to show, fast is fine but accuracy is final."

"Have to give you that, Kitty," said Slim. "You darn near hit every shot."

"Thanks Slim, but we need a little more from you. We need the whole story. We're all friends here, we've been telling our stories, so now, give it to us straight, how'd you lose half an ear?"

"What, you don't think it was bitten off by a cougar," he chuckled. "All right, I'm a little embarrassed by it, but we're all friends here, and lord willing, and the creek don't rise, we will be for a long time. This story stays here, I don't want to lose my rep with the town folk."

"Just tell us the story," chimed in several voices.

"So, the police in Omaha hired me on account as I was so big. I usually had to break up fights in the saloons or hotels or where ever, before someone pulled a gun, or there was too much damage being done. After getting pounded a few times, being in the middle of a fight, I developed a system. If a brawl

251

was going on, I moved to the guy on the edge of the fight, grabbed him by the collar, and tossed him head first on the floor. Then I moved to the next guy on the edge, and tossed him head first too. Pretty soon I got to the last two guys. Usually, I could just bounce a couple of heads together and be done with it. Another policeman would cuff the guys I threw on the floor. Once in a while some big fella would come at me and I'd have to bear wrestle him to the ground and smack him good. I took my lumps but aren't too many cowboys my size."

"One night I'm called over to the saloon about a fight. I walk in expecting to see a brawl or three or four cowboys swinging at each other. I see some busted chairs and a table knocked over and three guys on the floor. Standing by the bar, having a glass of wine, is this regular looking guy maybe five and a half feet tall about 140 pounds. (I find out later he is a Frenchman). I look around and ask, 'what's going on.' The bartender points at this guy and says' he's the trouble. Apparently he was challenging anyone to a fight, offered $10 to anyone who could beat him. Put the money on the bar. After he whipped three guys, business stopped, and he wouldn't leave. I looked at the guy again, and asked the bartender if he's kidding. The bartender gets real testy, and tells me to get that feller out of the saloon. I don't understand what's going on so I say to the fella, let's go. I walk toward him to take his arm, and escort him out."

"So far Slim, not much of a story. What's this little guy got to do with your ear," said Miss Kitty.

"I know, I know, let me finish. I walk toward him, and the next thing I know, he is runnin' at me, leaps, and kicks me in the face with his boot. I stagger back, and he spins, and whips his foot into my shin, almost breaks my leg, and I almost go down. Before I can do anything he leaps again, and kicks me in the stomach. Finally, I catch my breath, and start after him. Well, he comes running at me again, leaps, and kicks straight at my face, but, I turn my head, and he still whacks me good on the said of my head."

Taking his hat off and rubbing the side of his head, Slim gives an 'ouch' look and continues.

"People in the saloon are watching this little guy kick my ass. I'm gettin' mighty embarrassed. I start for him again, I see him run and leap, but this time I shoot a big right hitting the bottom of his foot. His leg crumbles, he flips over, and lands on the floor. His leg is bent in the wrong direction, and he screams, what apparently was a stream of profanity in French. Well, I know a broke leg when I sees one, so I bend down to tell him I'm going to straighten his leg. When I bend over, he grabs me, and bites off half my ear. I grab the little son-of-bitch and head butt him. His eyes roll back, his lids close, and he lays flat on the floor, out like a light. Since he's out, I go ahead and straighten his leg. I didn't get it real straight, but, good enough. I carried him back to the jail, and had the doc come over and splint it solid."

"You're right, Slim, if I was there, I'd be splittin' my side watchin' y'all gettin' whipped by a guy half your size," said George.

"He left town a few days later, when he could sort of walk, after paying a fine for damages. I don't think he'll be leapin,' and kickin' much with that leg no more. But really, after bustin' big guys, and breakin' up brawls, I nearly get whooped by some scrawny, leapin', dip shit, and lose half my ear. I know trouble will come to visit, but I don't need to give it place to sit down, so that's when I shed in my badge, and landed in Marshallville. Now, promise that story don't leave here."

"Well, you did break his leg Slim, and knocked him out cold; that's still a good way to end a fight. So, we won't ever mention the first part of the story," said Miss Kitty.

Chapter 18

George and Kay

George had seen Kay at the hotel, he liked what he saw, and figured he would go in for supper. His plan was eventually she would see him and be interested. One night, intrigued, she introduced herself.

"Hello, my name is Kay Belle. I own the hotel. I've seen you in here for supper a few times, welcome."

He quickly stood. "Hello ma'am, ma name is George Kay. Ah own the men's store down the street. Ah'm new here, and this here looked more civilized than the other cafes in town." He smiled slyly.

Kay recognized flirting instantly. She had been courted many times over the years. She had been married once. Her husband, a little scruffy, had been a gentleman to her with a kind heart, and she had fallen for him. He hadn't been her first lover, but he treated her right, and she loved him for it. He had died a year earlier. Many men had smiled at her, hoping for more, but she ignored them. Here was George, well dressed, polite, with a well-trimmed beard. She had not immediately ignored him.

"Thanks," she said, "if there are any complaints, see me personally."

George came in for supper two or three times a week. Kay greeted him each time. It had been a long time since she enjoyed a man's company. A few gray hairs, streaked through her head, had not dimmed her desires, and she found herself feeling a little warmer around George. First, they took a walk to the city park. Then they went for a buggy ride in the country. Next, they shared a bottle of wine one evening. Then another evening, a bottle of wine led to a conversation into the night. Finally, the wine and conversation led behind closed doors.

"George, you're in for supper again, nice to see you," said Kay Belle.

"Well ma'am, Ah heard you had a good kitchen here at the hotel." George politely stood up.

"Oh, we do, is that why you come in here so often?"

"Well, there might be another reason. There is an attractive, charmin' woman seen here on occasion."

"Oh my, Mister Kay, I do admire a well-dressed man with a nicely trimmed beard. Do you know anyone like that?"

"I think I saw a man like that coming out of your office t'other day."

"Shush up, someone might hear you."

"You don't suppose people've noticed I come here a lot. The boys at the Short Keg tell me ah should rest at home more at night and not risk anymore back injuries." He held his lower back and arched in feigned pain.

Kay looked aghast and shook a finger at George. "Ha, I can see I'm going to have to wash some mouths out with soap."

"Sit and join me for supper, please. I've an idea for a picnic out of town. Do you like picnics?"

Sweeping a chair back, she folded her dress in front of her and lightly settled onto a cushioned seat. George waited for her to sit before taking his seat.

"It's about time you took me out somewhere. Our evening walks are nice, but, a picnic out of town sounds delightful. What do you have in mind?"

Looking around the dining room at the other patrons, leaning in close, he lowered his voice. "You know people be talking if they see us going out of town."

She stared at him with a sly smile. He liked that about her.

"I'm long past worrying what people might think. They already think I'm a gold digger, because of my late husband. Besides, the people I care about know who and what I am. And that includes those ex-lawmen friends of yours and the families that founded this town. So, tell me your idea."

"You're going to think ah'm a 'devious' man tryin' to take advantage of a young widow lady but…"

Kay quickly held her hand to her mouth in mocked shock, "Ha, that's what I like about you, go on." She grinned.

"Well, bout an hour outside of town, there're some mineral springs, warm pools of water that are supposed to have healin' effects. So you see, ah'm just thinking bout your health

when ah suggest we take a picnic, possibly a bottle of wine, on
some sunny day, and soak in a warm pool of water, healin'
water."

A smile reached from ear to ear. "That's mighty
thoughtful of you George, how could I resist an offer that
might actually be good for me? I'll pack a lunch, when should
we go?"

"Ah think next Sunday bout ten am. Most town folk
will be in church or sleeping in. Ah'll have Slim set up a buggy
for us, and we can think good thoughts on the way out of
town." George gave that sly smile again and Kay nearly melted
away.

*****

Sunday came as a clear, warm, summer day, a slight breeze
cooled their faces. Wearing a sporty outfit, no coat or tie, but a
nice vest and a three button shirt, George looked snappy. Kay
had on a colorful spring dress, a bonnet, and ankle laced shoes.

Slim had a buggy with a pair of matched roans set for
them at the livery. She put the basket behind the seat, and
George helped her up. With the picnic basket, and a bottle of
wine, they set out for the springs, giggling like two teenagers

on a first date.

About an hour later they came across a small stream flowing out of a pile of boulders facing a narrow canyon surrounded by evergreens. The sides of the canyon had a red hue, giving off a warm glow. It was a beautiful spot, and Kay took a deep breath and gave George a tight hug. They took the basket and wine and walked to the edge of the pool where the water flowed out of the rocks.

"Ah have a confession to make," said George with a chuckle. "Ah didn't bring no water bathing suit."

Kay put her hand to her mouth in mock surprise. "I have a confession to make also, I didn't bring a bathing suit either. What shall we do?" She batted her eyelashes.

It didn't take them long to lay their clothes to one side and step into the water. George could not help but admire Kay's figure. Short but with curves in all the right places, time had not affected her body much, and George felt a stirring in his loins. It had been a long time since he had felt this way.

His mind raced back over the years he spent enforcing the law, never knowing if one day would be his last, never feeling like he could fall in love and live a peaceful and safe life. But, here he sat on the edge of something that might resemble happiness. He watched her put her hair in a bun on top of her head.

She turned and looked straight at George, eyeing him from head to foot. It had been a long time since she had felt aroused and a warm feeling draped over her, surprising her. She smiled.

He was still in decent shape and puffed out his chest a bit. Seeing her stare at him with what looked like a gleam in her eye, kicked the stirring up a step. He quickly stepped into the water before it was too obvious that he was firming up. The warm water did feel good. Looking straight into her eyes, he drifted over to Kay, caught up in the moment that took his breath, he reached out, took her by the shoulders, and pulled her close.

The warm water, the affectionate embrace, passionate kisses, had a noticeable effect. Kay became aware of George's excitement. She rewarded him with a firm grip and a tug. *It had been a long time*, she thought, *since she felt this rush going through her body*. She was going to play this hand to the end. Several more minutes of splashing around, each receiving desired rewards, and both blew a sigh of relief. They climbed out of the pool, and lay in the sun on a large flat rock. Neither one scrambled for their clothes.

"This is what Eden must be like," said George.

"I think there is an apple in the lunch basket," said Kay.

"You're a little vixen aren't you, and that is one of the things ah like about you."

Getting up and slipping on some bloomers, Kay opened the picnic basket, set out a tablecloth, and took out the lunch. George threw on the bottoms of a union suit and opened the wine.

"George," she said, "we may have to make this official some time. If we got married, my name would be 'Kay Kay'. No rush though, I don't need to lose another husband. How many more shoot-outs will you be in, Mister Kay?"

"Ah think, besides you bein' a beautiful woman, y'all are very wise, and ah don't plan on any more shoot-outs. Ah do like the train we're on. It may come to a station some time, but for now, let's enjoy the ride."

They ate lunch, drank wine, kissed, and touched a bit

more. George let the past disappear and the present take over. Kay slipped out of her bloomers and laid back on a warm rock, George dropped his bottoms, covered her, and pressed into her with a firm intention to please.

"Ah could stay here for the next ye-ar and ne'er get tired of bein' with you." He breathed lightly as he spoke.

"I agree, but your old buddies at the Short Keg would send out a search party and we don't have enough food or wine for that bunch."

Slowly they packed up and headed for town. "Have you ever caught yourself dreamin' and hopin' it was real when you woke up?" sighed Kay.

George cracked a grin. "Ah think ah just did."

*****

1872: Marshallville incorporates. The courthouse is busy with new lawyers in town. A second newspaper opens. A hospital is built and a second doctor joins Dr. Barry. Cindy Davis is still the expectant mothers' choice. Population nears 1500, plus hundreds of rail workers are showing up ahead of the train spur and its station. Railroad graders are stretching and leveling the line to Marshallville. Wagon loads of rail ties are brought in daily as the line approaches town. Rails are being pounded into the ties covering a couple of miles a day. Railmen camps are set up, and moved daily, including food tents, liquor tents, and of course, women tents. Wagons for supplies are coming into town disturbing the quiet pulse of the town, but huge sales help the shopkeepers, and the city purse is bulging. There are now several saloons, open all night. The theater is finished and traveling shows are there every week. The sheriff has three deputies that are ex-cavalry, and tough lawmen. With prosperity comes many problems and the entertainment section of town is open 24 hours a day.

The town is four years old and experiencing some growing pains, but it is still the envy of many western towns. It is a wonderful place for families. There are parks, schools, churches, a marching band, and family activities every month. If the town was human, it would be a strong, healthy teenager with a great future.

Chapter 19

Boot Hill Bryce

"Well, I'll be higgledy piggledy," said Slim. "Do I hear some pi-ano music?" he asked Short Keg. "Almost wants to make me dance a jig or two. What's up?" He nodded toward the piano.

"You remember, Slim, when you suggested I get a piano player for the saloon? Might perk up the place, you said. Well, this fellow comes in one day, sees the old thing over in the corner, sits down and starts bangin' on the keys. At first I thought he was mad at something, but I guess he was warming up the keys, and his fingers. Next thing I know he is cranking out tunes like a regular music man. He started out with "Beautiful Dreamer", went to "Camptown Races", then pounded out "Tramp, Tramp, Tramp." I bought him a beer, said it was on the house, he thanked me then dropped his nose down and slid up and down those keys like they was long lost friends. A while later, he comes over with his beer and asks if I was looking for a piano player. I told him I would put out a tip jar, back him for a few drinks, and toss in a meal day if he wanted the job."

Tipping his hat and scratching his head, Slim goes on, "Don't he look familiar to you Kenny? I seen him somewhere before. Maybe Coop will recognize him."

Piano music floated through the air as Coop pushed through the bat wings and into what might have been his second home. The music put a smile on his face, and he saw Slim and Short Keg standing at the bar. The Gentry boys were right behind him, slapping dust off their clothes. "Old Dan Tucker," "Buffalo Gals", and "Jimmy Crack Corn" were some familiar tunes that filled the air.

He put a boot on the rail, an elbow on the bar and turned his head slightly to hear the music. "Pour me a tall one," said Coop, echoed by the Gentrys. "And where'd the skinny piano player come from? He sounds good. Those old tunes bring back memories. What's his name, Kenny?"

"I don't actually know, haven't talked with him. He's doin' a little practicing, be back this evenin'. It'll be a real surprise to the folks tonight. There's somthing about an old piano tune that can liven up a dull evening."

"Coop, does that guy look familiar?" asked Slim. "He reminds me of someone. This guy's a little skinny and ragged, but he's got a familiar look."

"Well, I'll be damned," says Coop, " that there is Boot Hill Bryce. I ain't seen him in four or five years. He's a bunch skinnier and more worn down than I remember. He sheriffed a bit in Texas then on up to Arizona territory. "

"You called him Boot Hill Bryce, why?" asked Kenny.

"It's kind of a nasty story. Seems he went after outlaws with a vengeance, he usually brought'em back dead. Sent'em right to 'Boot Hill.' I'll tell you one thing, outlaws started to give him a wide berth. I heard he had some trouble, but don't rightly know what happened. To look at him, it must have been a heap of trouble. Gentleman George rangered down in Texas same time as Bryce, he may know more about him."

Dapper as usual, even on a hot summer day, Gentleman George slipped into the short Keg and waved at the boys.

"Dang George, you must be roasting potatoes in that suit," said Slim, "don't know how you seem to stay so cool."

Sitting at a table close to the bar, George unbuttoned his

coat and looked at Slim. "Ah have to look good if Ah want to sell clothes to the courtin', and strutin' boys in town. That goes for those "city slickers" coming in on the train also. There's a new class of dandies in town now. Also coming in on the train are gamblers, takers, and con men. Don't like to see those leeches taking up residence, but they pay cash for a slick look."

"Hey George," says Coop, "what do you know about the new piano player?"

"Let me get a beer first. It is a hot day, and this vest tends to hold the heat in."

Holding his beer, George turned to look at the piano player. He squinted his eyes, his facial expression turned flat, and then eyes opened wide, and he muttered something under his breath. He immediately walked over to the man plinking out the tunes.

"Boot hill Bryce, is that you," George shouted. "Man ah thought you were a goner. You're looking like a beat up old pair of pants, but you're alive."

Bryce looked up and for the first time a smile crossed his face. He stood up and slapped both arms around George and hugged him like a long lost cousin.

"Hey boys, this is an old friend. We used to hunt outlaws down Texas way. And ah'll tell ya, after the war, we had a state full of outlaws. Ol Bryce here put a bunch six feet under."

"Good to see you George. Glad to see you're still alive too," said Bryce.

"Yea, we both got shot up pretty good. Last I heard you got married and moved to Arizona, then met up with some serious trouble."

"Picked up four pieces of lead and three months in bed, but I don't like to talk about it. Heard you picked up some lead yourself, down by the border."

"Same story as you, pieces of lead and months in bed. Still got the lead in ma back. You play piano, I sell snappy clothes. Come on in ta the store soon, I'll get you lookin' like a regular guy, not like a guy slept in his clothes for a week. We can catch up on history."

George headed back to Coop, Slim and the Gentrys. Bryce headed back to the kitchen for a meal.

"So what's the story George?" Coop asked. "Looks like

you two were old pals."

"We stood for law in Texas for a few years then he got married and moved to Arizona territory. Ah heard he had some trouble, but don't rightly know the whole story. Lefty and Levi did some bounty huntin' out that way, they may know more. They're due in town soon for some supplies, maybe they can fill in the holes."

That night, the saloon was packed. Shady Mike dealt Faro at one table, Poker Alice at another. The tables were jammed, drinks were flowing, and the piano man banged out spirited tunes to the crowd's delight. Bryce's jar overflowed, and Short Keg kept his beer mug full.

Quick Cal stepped in, surveyed the place, and dragged back a chair at the table with Lefty, Levi and the Gentry brothers.

"So Sheriff," said Van, "looks like the railroad crowd is lightin' up the south end of town. How many deputies you have now?"

"Three, but that ain't hardly enough. Seems like a new saloon opens up every week." With frustration in his voice, he said, "Mitch's funeral parlor is busy day and night. I swear we find a new body lying in an alley every morning. Good thing we're near a sawmill and lumber yard. Building coffins everyday uses a lot of wood." He waved his hand around. "This place here is packed but it's downright peaceful compared to saloons in the south end of town." Leaning forward, with fists on the table, Cal went on. "There's a nasty element growing in the "Buffalo Horn" and "Lucky Lady" saloons. A lot of hard cases seem to hanging around those places. I feel sorry for many of those rail workers. Their pay just slips in and out of their hands like water."

"Hey Cal," asks John, "do you know the piano player?"

Looking over his shoulder, Cal said, "Well John, I do know him, it's Boot Hill Bryce and it's a shame he went from a mighty tough lawman to a bar room piano player. He did rightly earn his nickname, he put several outlaws six feet under. He never hesitated to shoot first, and sort things out later."

"It's a shame what happened to him and his wife," said Levi.

"That's the truth," said Lefty.

"What did happen?" asked John

271

A loud argument, glass breaking, chairs sliding, and two men flopping on the floor interrupted the conversation.

Cal started to get up, but Van said, "Relax Cal, Short Keg has bouncers to take care of those boys. He liked the way Shady Mike hired a couple of ex-cons to watch his Faro table, so, he got up a couple himself. The ex-cons were happy to get a job, and happy to bust some heads, and get paid for it. Short Keg told them they could rough up the trouble makers a bit, but not to do any serious damage. Just seeing them boys keeps a lot of tempers from heatin' up, Levi, back to your story."

"The story goes like this." He pointed a finger in Van's direction. "Bryce was leading a posse, chasing some horse thieves. The thieves pulled up behind some trees, and bushwacked the posse. Bryce killed one of the gang, but two of his deputies went down. The thieves took off, but Bryce stayed back to help his men. Turned out the one Bryce killed was brother to the gang leader. One of the deputies died, the other patched up OK, but by then the trail was cold. In the dead man's saddle bags he found a name, and some old wanted posters, so he knew who the gang was. He put out new wanted posters, dead or alive."

"I remember that fracas," said Lefty. "Levi and I were

looking for that gang ourselves. There was big money on their heads from other jobs too, but we could not sniff out their trail"

"Anyways," Taking a sip of beer, Levi went on, "a few weeks later, Bryce and his new bride were headed for church in a buckboard. Suddenly, from behind some trees, those same outlaws come riding right at them firing away. Bryce and his wife didn't have a chance. His wife was killed right off. Bryce should have been sent to boot hill himself. He took three pieces of lead straight to his arms and chest. As he slumped over, the leader pulled up to the buckboard and yelled, 'This is for my brother,' and shot Bryce point blank. He then laughed, long and hard, along with the other three guys, and rode off. The buckboard horses took off for town."

Van shook his head in disbelief and looked over at Boot Hill playing the piano. He was banging out an old war tune recognized by many of the men in the bar.

"That was a couple of years ago, and here he is playing piano in the Short Keg. He's a long way from the Northern territory."

"How'd he go from being shot up to playing Piano," asked John.

Lefty spoke up, "Well as I said, Levi and I went looking for those boys, but they lit out of state, and we lost them. Ol Booty took three months to heal up enough to walk around town. It was a pitiful sight. He spent most of his time drinking, and sleeping at the cemetery near his wife's grave. Many a morning we went to the cemetery, picked him up, and hauled him home only to find him passed out again at the cemetery the next day. He was living up to his name, Boot Hill Bryce, but in a bad way. "

Bryce finished a song, stood up arched his back, stretched his fingers and walked over to the bar. "A shot of your finest, and a beer please, Short Keg." He waved at Cal, downed his shot, and followed that with a gulp of beer.

"Hey Boot Hill," called Cal, "come over for a minute."

Bryce took his beer, pulled up a chair, and slouched at the table.

"Do you know all the boys?" said Cal. "This here is John and his brother Van Gentry. Ex-law men, they have a ranch out of town. Been here about four years. These guys here are Lefty and Levi, also ex-lawmen, now in the business of bringin' wanted folk in to face justice, for a price of course."

"Hi John, Van. I know Lefty and Levi from up north Arizona way. When I got laid up they tried to chase down those bastards, and then sorta looked after me a bit. Hi boys, real good to see ya, been awhile."

"So Bryce, when you were sheriffin'," said Levi, "I never knew you to play the piano."

Bryce turned his eyes down, took a deep breath, hesitated for a second and said, "It's a hard story to tell, but here I am, and I need to get past, the past. And we are all friends here so I'll tell my tale while I finish this here beer. Lefty and Levi know I was tore up pretty good after being ambushed, and my wife being killed. But, I knew she'd want me to get straight, and move on. She was always singing around the place. We had an old pump organ in the house, and she loved to play those old Steven Foster songs. She would get me over to the organ now and then, and take my finger, and plunk out a simple melody."

"For months after the ambush, while drinking, I would sit at the organ remembering those happy times. I would try to remember the notes she showed me, and eventually, I learned a few songs. And, unbeknownst to me, I actually had a knack for music. It eventually cleared my head enough to sorta straighten out. I had to leave town, shake loose some of those memories, so I wandered a bit."

"Looks like you went through a lot of towns trying to shake those memories loose," Levi pointed out.

"One place had an old New Orleans piano man that commiserated with me, and we drank, and played piano for months. He showed me a lot about music. It was an old piano that finally got me up enough to begin an odd travel path. When I hit a new town, I'd look for a saloon with a piano. I'd play for drinks, and tips and when I got tired of the town, I'd move on to the next one. Playing the piano keeps me going. I kinda like it here so maybe I'll stay awhile."

All the guys at the table sat quietly for a moment, perhaps thinking about their own journey. Almost in unison they slapped Bryce on the back and welcomed him to town.

*****

"There you go Bryce," said George, "a decent set of clothes makes you look like a new man."

"Thanks George, I'm beginning to feel like a new man. I may look for a place to stay of my own. Sleeping in a room over the barroom is getting a bit stale. A few more months of good tips, and I am on my way. See you tonight George?"

"Maybe not tonight, there's a little lady over ta the hotel that needs my attention."

At the Short Keg, Bryce shouted out, "Hey Kenny, looks like another good Friday night for the Short Keg. I better pound out a few good war songs to get the crowd drinking and excited. That ole piano is missing a few hammers so a few notes never make it out of the box, but, no one seems to care."

Four men, strangers, cautiously came through the doors, eyes swept the room under beat and dusty hats, and moved to an empty table. There were three bartenders working that night, and one came over to the table. "What you having gents?"

One of the men started to laugh and said to his friends, "He called us 'gents', ain't that a funny one."

They all snorted out a chuckle and ordered drinks. A few shots, and a few beers later, the men got a little loud, and start telling crude stories to each other, all the time laughing and guffawing. Most of the other men in the saloon ignored them, and did their own talkin' and gamblin'.

Bryce stopped playing the piano and slowly turned toward the men. He stared. He listened carefully. He tilted his head as if to hear better. Their laughing continued, and he frowned, then turned angry.

Shaking, he walked over to Short Keg and says, "Kenny, back my play."

The owner of the Short Keg immediately recognized the seriousness in Bryce's face and tone. He grabbed his shotgun.

Bryce pulled his seven inch barrel Colt from under his coat. He walked to the table and fired two quick shots into their drinks. The wooden table splintered, the glasses jumped, the bottles tipped over, and the startled men let out a flurry of obscenities. Bryce pistol whipped the man on the right and jammed the barrel of his gun into the temple of the man on the left. Everyone in the saloon suddenly stopped mid-sentence. The place was absolutely quiet and several men automatically ducked.

"What's goin' on," the man yelled, "we just got into town. We ain't hankerin' for no trouble but ifin' you want some"....his voice trails off as Bryce stared hard in his face.

With teeth bared Bryce said, "Remember two years ago, northern Arizona territory, a man and a woman in a buckboard?"

Blood drained from the man's face as the situation became clear. "Don't know what you're talkin bout," choked the man, hardly breathing. A third man, realizing the play reached for his gun. Two clicks of a shotgun behind his head froze the action.

"Stand easy friend," said Short Keg.

The fourth man knew what was coming. As he moved his hand toward his gun, Bryce whipped his gun around, and put a hole through the man's hand. Blood flew and the man screamed, "Damn you, you busted my hand good."

"Don't matter, you'll be hanging soon," said Bryce.

With the gun moved from his temple, the first man tried to pull his gun. Bryce jammed the colt back in the side of his head. "Dead or alive, you choose."

Hearing the shots, the sheriff busted through the doors, gun pulled, and looked around. Seeing Short Keg and Bryce, he made his way to the table.

"You boys look mighty serious, what's up?"

"These are the men who killed my wife, shot me in cold blood, and left me for dead. But, I ain't dead am I boys? I recognized their laugh. I've played it over and over in my head for years. I'm sure you have posters on them. I'll be glad to help you get them to jail."

More yellin, and more obscenities, but with Cal, Bryce, and a shotgun toting bartender, the gang ended up on the inside of the bars looking out.

Two weeks later, the circuit judge found them guilty and ordered death by hanging.

One morning at breakfast, at the Short Keg, Ken said, "Well Bryce, do ya feel any different now that there's an ending or such to what happened over in the territory?"

"I do feel calm, Ken. I'll never forget that day, and I'll never forget my wife, but puttin' those guys away lightens the load a bit."

"One good thing," said Ken, "you collected a bunch of money on those guys, what are you going to do now?"

With a little smile he said, "For now, I am staying at Dinah's boarding house over on Second Street. The place is clean and the food is good. There's a nice privy out back, and I am finally out of this noisy room over the bar. Next week, I'm heading up to Denver, and haulin' back a new piano for the Short Keg. That old one is missing a few pads and keys, and I plan to be playing here for some time, so I want it to sound good."

Ken nodded, squeezed Bryce's shoulder and toned, "I'd be proud to have you sharin' this space."

*****

The late afternoon found many of the old law dogs at the Short Keg. They often finished the day over a beer before supper. They had their regular table, and Ken and Sundowner would usually join them. Even Mary and Molly would peek out from the kitchen and say "Hi." They always had some chili waiting if needed.

Joking and story telling kept the group laughing and in good spirits. It was a good group of men and the brotherhood was obvious. The Gentrys dropped in every couple of weeks. Shady Mike would show some card tricks, and always dazzled them with 'find the queen' in three card monte. Coop usually brought in the latest edition of the Gazette, and announced the latest news.

Looking at the paper Coop reads out loud, "Seems a woman named Susan B. Anthony voted for Grant for president."

"Women can't vote," said George.

"True enough," said Coop. "She was fined $100 for an illegal vote. Miss Anthony feels women should have the right to vote and is leading an equal rights association. She is quoted as saying, 'Men have their rights, nothing more; women have their rights and nothing less.'"

"She may be right," said Ken.

"What's next," said Mike, "A woman goin' ta run for pre-si-dent?"

"Funny you should mention that," said Coop, "there's also a story in the Gazette bout a woman named Woodhull running for president. She's runnin' agin Grant. That's got to be a crazy idea. Who'd vote for a woman?"

"It's crazy times these days for sure," said Slim. "Some women will put a spoke in it, just to mess things up."

"Any of you boys ever ride a stagecoach," asked Coop.

"Ah did once," said Mike, "one of zee worst tree days in my life. Ah was used to ridin' zee rivair boat not bouncing on zee rocky road. I could not deal cards for a week."

"Well, this here story says people can go crazy on the stage. It was reported that during one trip across southern Arizona territory, a passenger suddenly jumped from the stage and ran off screaming into the desert. They don't rightly know where he went."

"I've been in the southern Arizona desert," said Bryce, "And I felt like screaming myself, even without a stagecoach ride."

"Do they have a story in there bout George and Kay, or Coop and Sally," asked Sundowner.

"That's a story yet to be told," chimed George and Coop in unison.

*****

1873: El Paso County is growing, home to several farming communities, and a few small towns. Marshallville is the largest town in the county, and may become the county seat. A political presence is an important issue in town. Competing politicians are forming parties. City elections, and county elections are in the spotlight. Colorado may become a state in the next few years, and politicians in Denver and Marshallville are lining up support.

The railroad spur is complete with its own station. Population is about 3000. The railroad brought in hundreds of people, mostly men, and a lot of liquor.

Mail order buildings come in on the train. A complete catalog of different homes made of brick or wood is available, and the housing section of town seems to grow overnight.

Tourists are a familiar sight, and two more hotels are opened up. Several rich investors are building homes. Touring acting companies play each week at the new theater. A new French restaurant is opened near the posh homes district adding elegance to the booming city. Families are moving in, opening many shops, and business is booming. The town has established a three man sanitation department. There is now a brick fire station, a fire chief, and uniforms for the volunteer firemen. A large marching band has formed, and they too have uniforms. Law and order has become an issue with hundreds of new comers brought in by railroad. Construction crews, saloon workers, gamblers, and prostitutes are a common sight.

The hardware store now carries wallpaper, window screens, can openers, Arbuckles, glass windows, linoleum, Chiclets gum, along with all the regular tools, nails, ropes and wire.

The town is maturing into an active place to live with schools, theater, music, shops, parks, families, and a large community pride.

However, a menacing presence has come into town; his name is David Kelly. Kelly is from New York. He appears to have a large number of men working for him, and he runs three saloons. His gambling, prostitution, and liquor sales, bring in a lot of money. He is interested in money, power, and perhaps taking over the town.

Chapter 20

City Council January 1873

"Mayor, I think the violence in the south end of town is getting out of hand. Since the train station was built, trouble has grown immensely. I am proposing a city ordinance that might help cut down those troubling numbers."

"What do you suggest Mr. Miles. This council would love to hear any suggestion that can bring our city back to some kind of civility."

"Mr. Mayor, when we first settled this town it was an active community, but a respectful one. It took a few years of steady growth to gain a busy, but peaceful population. With the lumbermen and miners, we had some wild times, but always under control. Since the railroad came to town, the population has mushroomed, and so has the violence. We set up the zoning laws to keep the saloons, and brothels in the south end of town, but that end of town has expanded beyond our planning. Currently, saloons are open twenty-four hours a day.

I talked with councilman Franks, and we propose that any business that offers drinks, gambling, and prostitution be closed from 2:00 am to 8:00 am. Those times seem to be prime time for arguments, violence, and gun play. Maybe we won't find so many unconscious men lying in the streets and alleyways every morning, with that curfew in place."

"Mr. Miles, you are talking about over ten saloons. Cal, as sheriff, what is your opinion of Mr. Miles' proposal?"

"Mr. Mayor, that is a right smart idea. We do need to put a lid on that stew pot before it totally boils over. I also suggest that any violation of the ordinance result in immediate shut down for a week and a $5000.00 fine."

Standing up, David Kelly said, "Mr. Mayor."

"Yes, Mr. Kelly. What is your comment?"

"I pay my $300.00 per month tax on my saloons, and I need to be open as often as possible. Sure, sometimes some men get out of hand, but that's not my fault."

"Your concern is duly noted, Mr. Kelly, but the whole south end of town is becoming a danger, and the noise and gun play is starting to flow over to other parts of town."

"If there is no further discussion, let's take a vote. Members of the city council, how do you vote? All in favor say 'aye'. It appears all the councilmen are in favor of the proposal," said the Mayor. "Sheriff, please post the information on all the saloons in town."

"Mr. Mayor, I have an issue I would like the city council to address," said Hannah Calder.

"What is it Mrs. Calder?"

"Miss Kitty and I are concerned about the workin' girls in town. Maybe the council could consider regulating work conditions, maybe even limited hours. It can be a rough business, and we want the girls to be protected from harm. We also want an age limit of sixteen. No girls under sixteen should have to sell themselves. We want 'Cribs' to be outlawed."

"Mrs. Calder and Miss Kitty, I and the council members understand your concerns, and I believe we share your views. It does get a little touchy tellin' folk how to behave. I think we need to hear from the girls, and from their employers, before we can set limits. However, the city must protect its citizens, all of its citizens. We will act on this very soon. Perhaps you can interview some of the ladies for their ideas, and be here at the next council meeting. Thank you, ladies. If there is nothing else, the meeting is adjourned."

*****

May 1873: "Welcome, welcome," said Mayor John Marshall. "Welcome to a town hall meeting, and our new three story civic center. The old, single story courthouse, is currently a school and library. The courtroom and jail are on the second story, offices, and record storage is on the top level. Here, on the ground floor, you see a large city council and meeting room. It can hold over one hundred people. The fourth of July is two months from now. It will mark five years since the town was founded. We want to have a big celebration. That is why we are having a special meeting today. We will need a lot of help."

"But first, let me introduce the town council members. I think you know most of them, but here they are. Bill Williams, he is our vice mayor. Phil Franks, he is our town accountant and treasurer. Mike Miles is our building inspector. Darryl Burns and Ken West are the other councilmen."

A polite round of applause followed the introductions. "The town council has recommended a parade. It will start at

Avenue A and Main street, then go down Main three blocks, turn on D street, and over to the city park. Also recommended is a picnic in the park, a pie eating contest, a race track, and fireworks after dark; and of course a dance. The dance will be in the old court house. Set up will be at 6:00 p.m. Bring your musical instruments, food baskets, and the entire family is welcome. In a minute we will ask for more ideas and people to volunteer to help."

The crowd looked eager and excited by the announcement. A loud applause filled the room.

Marshall stood tall and proud. Only a few years ago his wife had died and he a small group of friends started the town. Now he looked out at a sea of happy faces. "Ken West is in charge of the fireworks. See Ken if you want to help, light up the sky."

An excited murmur rose from the crowd, especially from the kids in the room.

"Phil's wife, Kay, is heading up the decorations committee. If anyone can help with bunting, ribbons and other decorations, please see Kay. She likes' to say, 'the more helping hands, the easier the work.'"

"Darryl's wife, Matilda, is in charge of the pie eating contest, and Mike Miles's wife Angela is in charge of salads. Anyone who wants to volunteer for other side dishes, and maybe ice cream for the picnic, please talk to either one of those ladies."

"Miss Apple, our school teacher, will organize some kid activities. A three-legged race is always fun, and maybe an egg toss for a little excitement. If anyone else has some ideas or wants to volunteer to help, please see her."

"Mike, what can we do for a race track? I know a lot of people want to watch horse races."

"I have a couple of ideas. One is a short dash for the kids that have a horse. I know they love to kick dirt as fast as they can. We can use the road out of town on the south end. They would start out about two hundred yards from town, and race back to the edge of town. We can set up a finish line just before the last store on the south end, that's about where the theater is."

"That sounds great. I'm sure we can put together some prizes for those races, what else?"

"For the regular race, we use the same road on the south

end of town. About a half mile out is a rock outcropping about fifty feet in diameter. The start line would also be the finish line. That's the same line set up for the kids. The race would go out of town, around the rocks, circling around from the right, and back to the finish line. That would be about a mile, and that makes for a good race. We would need to have a race official standing on the rocks to make sure everyone went around the rocks from the right side, and back to town. I can take my oxen and grading equipment, and make an even track around the rocks. I can also touch up the road coming into town. It's a well-travelled road and there are a lot of wagon wheel ruts. I can knock them down a bit."

Marshall nodded in agreement. "Great idea."

"I think too, with the size of the road, a limit of six horses per race would be safest."

"Makes sense, thanks, Mike."

"Mister Mayor."

"Yes, Harold."

"The Marshallville marching band has been practicing and is in fine tune. We have music from George Root, John

Hewitt and Henry Tucker. We would like to lead the parade, then set up in the park in the band stand for music for the afternoon."

"That's a great idea, Harold. I've heard you practicing, and you sound good. I didn't know you had a brass tuba."

"I was very excited. A new family from Illinois moved in, and they had a tuba, and a coronet. Plus one of the German families has added their tuba. They joined us last week; really adds a nice punch to the band."

"Who can be in the parade?" asked a lady from the audience.

"Good question," said Marshall. "Anyone or any group that wants to march is welcome in the parade. Entry sheets are here at the main desk. Our secretary, Miss Taylor, has the forms. Tell us who you are, and have a banner made so people watching the parade know who you are. It might be good advertising for your group. I think the "Ladies for a Sober Town," might march. You can walk, ride a wagon, or ride horse-back. Our volunteer fire department will be marching with the new 'pumper' the town just bought. You can see any of the firemen if you want to volunteer for the fire department. The sheriff and his deputies will have a horse patrol also in the parade."

"Mr. Mayor"

"Yes, Mr. Jones."

"I saw a lady acrobat walk across a wire from building to building in Denver last week. Should I see if she would perform here? We can set up a wire for her, and I think she passes a plate for donations."

"That would certainly be a thrilling act. We have two months to organize so go up to Denver and see if she is available."

"Mr. Mayor, it's Dave Kelly, owner of the T-Hall saloon. I would like to set up some boxing matches on the fourth. I'll have the ring built and maintained. There is an empty lot next to my saloon, and I could set up there. I can also run the horse race betting, and the boxing matches betting. As mister Miles suggests, we can have six horses per race, and depending on the number of horses for the racing, I can set up the number of races."

John Marshall did not like David Kelly. He ran a rough saloon with rough bouncers. His saloons were the scene of a lot of trouble and gun play. He had suddenly become the owner of three saloons. The previous owners seemed to have disappeared. He had a gang of thugs around his places at all times. But, Marshall knew a lot of people would want to bet on the races, and matches, and the town did not want to run a betting service so someone else had to organize it.

"That's a big help Mr. Kelly, I'll have a deputy help watch the betting tables. We don't want anyone getting mad and trying to take back their bets."

"Mr. Mayor," said Councilman Arthur, "I will set up a fire pit for roasting hot dogs, and a grill for hamburgers. And I will donate ten pounds of hotdogs and ten pounds of hamburgers. The Gentry boys said they will also bring in some meat for the picnic."

"Excellent, thanks."

"Mr. Mayor," said Hans Haupt, "ma brewery ist gut, I ban bring zei kegs of bier too for picnic."

"That is very generous, Mr. Haupt, thank you."

"Mrs. Calder, I would like to see you about printing some posters and the signup sheets for the parade, perhaps tomorrow about ten, at your office?"

"That would be fine, Mr. Mayor, tomorrow at ten."

"That is it for today, folks. We will have parade forms here by next week. If you have any more ideas, or you want to volunteer, see Miss Taylor, our town secretary. We will meet next month to finalize the plans. I hope you are all as excited as I am, it will be a fine Fourth of July. Meeting adjourned."

The crowd buzzed with excitement, and a group formed around Miss Taylor.

*****

"Short Keg, set up six beers please, the town hall meeting went well and the mayor and councilmen are thirsty," said Marshall.

"Coming up John," said Ken, "looks like big doins' for the fourth."

"We are all excited," said Franks, "we sold several business and home lots these past few years. With the train coming in this year, the increased business licenses and property taxes are boosting the towns' economy. The population in town is nearly 3000. To think, five years ago, we were six wagons stopping for a baby."

"We didn't just stop after an easy wagon trip," said Ken, "we spent several months planning, two months of tragedy and danger on the road. Remember the lightning storm that burned up two wagons and killed two families?"

"And the buffalo stampede that crushed two more wagons right near us, and killed those two families," said Bill Williams.

"I think back about the accidental gunshot deaths, the river drownings, the Indian scare, and I am amazed, and thankful, that we made it this far," said Marshall. "Cheers and enjoy the beer."

Chapter 21

The Beginning of the Show Down

"Son," said Gentleman George, "y'all are in the wrong place, and in the wrong business. I don't need fire protection or any protection. I'm sorry y'all walked all the way over here for no reason. I strongly suggest y'all sign up for your own protection. If you ever come back here again, you're gonna need it. Take those two loafers outside and crawl back in your hole."

The man, looking grim faced, walked out of George's clothing store, and talked to his two friends standing by the door. George knew they would make a play to worry, or intimidate him. He expected all three to come storming in any minute threatening and yelling at him. George had a beautiful, hand tooled, double holster rig, with two ebony handled Walker Colts. These were very large and very heavy guns. They were built to take down a horse. Looking at even one of these resembled like looking into a canon. He stood to one side of the door, behind a rack of coats. Sure enough, the three hard cases barged in the door shouting obscenities. George stepped behind them, both guns leveled on their backs, and pulled back both hammers. Hearing the two clicks behind their back, the men froze.

"Ah told y'all if you came back, you would need protection yourself." George pistol whipped the "protection" man across the head, and he dropped to the floor.

"Turn around very slowly with your hands up." His voice sounded menacing so the other men raised their hands, and slowly turned around. Looking at a pair of seven inch Colts, aimed square at their chests, the men let out a gasp.

"These here Colts can put a hole in you large enough to see to the next town. If y'all ever come back again, we can maybe, try that out to see if I'm right. Now pick up your friend and get the hell out of my store."

The men dragged their friend out, stumbling down the wooden boardwalk. Out in the road, one of them yelled back, "You'll be sorry."

An ex-Texas ranger, George, a no-nonsense guy, stepped out of the door, and put a couple shots in the dirt by their feet. The two men dropped their buddy and took off.

Well aware of the 'protection' racket, George knew that to be the start of big trouble for the town.

Still fuming, he closed up shop and headed for the sheriff's office. "Cal", he said, swinging the jail house door wide open "looks like trouble is startin' to shadow the town. Three saddle bums come into my store trying to sell me protection. Ah wiped one and threw the other two out the door."

"You're the second person come in today with that complaint. The lady at the dress shop came in earlier today saying the same thing. She's a tough, hard case herself. She pulled out her six shot .22 and ran them off. Miss Kitty has one of those .22's also. Looks to be our lady folk come well heeled. I think they thought they could start with you clothing shop people thinking you might be the easiest ones." Chuckling, Call said, "They found out different."

"You need to get a hold of the others and warn them. I'll check around town to see how bad things are," said Cal.

Chapter 22

Protection

Black smoke came pouring out of the carpenter shop a few blocks north of the Short Keg. The volunteer fire department pumper's bells were clanging as four men pulled hard on the wagon, down Main Street, to the shop.

The four-man pumper had two men on each side. Two more men were dragging a hose from the town water tank to the inlet valve. Two other men were dragging a hose to be attached to the pumper's outlet valve. When the inlet and outlet hoses were attached, the men started pumping the handles on each side. One side pushed down while the other side flipped up. They had practiced their up and down timing and had an even tempo going.

Water came shooting out, but they could not save the shop, so all the effort went to keeping the fire from spreading. All the shops were made of wood, so a fire could spread quickly and destroy the town. It would not be the first time a town was destroyed by fire.

Coughing hard, the shop owner barely crawled out of the shop before the flames erupted. His breath made wheezing sounds as he tried to inhale. He also had a large bruise and cut across the back of his head. He hung on a horse rail a few feet away from his shop. The firemen worked quickly and hard to put out the flames. Many of the town folk joined the effort to keep the fire from spreading. When the people of this town saw something that needed to be done, they jumped in and got it done. Fortunately, the fire was contained to the one shop. Unfortunately, there was nothing left but a smoldering, wet mess.

It took a few hours to raked out and clear the building. Out back was a soggy pile of what had been tools, partially finished furniture, and a stockpile of finished wood. The sides of the adjoining shops were thoroughly brushed, scraped and wetted down to prevent any further damage.

"What happened Thumb Buster," asked the sheriff. Thumb Buster's real name was Dave but over the years he had managed to whack his thumbs a few times so his friends went to calling him 'Thumb Buster'.

"I....I don't rightly know," he said. "A piece of wood must have fallen on my head, and some tools must have fallen, throwing a spark or something."

"Dave," the sheriff said, "are you sure that's what happened? You weren't hit by that protection scam were you?"

"I... I don't know what you are talkin' bout, Sheriff. It was just some kinda accident. Now I need to get on home, and make sure my wife knows I'm OK."

The other shop keepers, with worried looks on their faces, were outside watching the cleanup. Cal immediately knew, from the looks on their faces, they had all been threatened. *I'll have to step up patrols*, he thought to himself. *These people need to know they're safe.*

Sunday mornings the Short Keg was usually closed till after church services. But this morning, several men were gathered behind closed doors.

Molly and Mary brought out a pot of coffee, mugs, buttered toast and jam and set them on the tables. After the men filled their mugs, gave a round of thanks, Short Keg spoke up. "Gentlemen, we've got trouble. He wears a black frock coat, a black hat, and runs a gang out of the T Hall saloon. He goes by the name, Dave Kelly, an Irishman from New York. Mike, what have you heard from the other Faro dealers in town?"

"Ah've talked to ah few of the dealers who work at the T Hall saloon. We often have breakfast over at thah Bison café early in the morning or late at night, whichever you'all prefer. Seems, this heah Mr. Kelly claims he's thah new ownah after thah old ownah suddenly disappeared. He says he bought thah saloon, and thah old owner left town with thah money; heading west it seems. Kelly now owns three saloons. He's also takin' ah major rake from the Faro dealahs, and they don't cotton to it one bit, so they are willing tah complain. When A'h say complain, A'h mean complain tah me in hushed tones; they don't want tah suddenly disappear eithah. There is also thah mention of several new, grizzly hombres hangin' around."

"What I really don't like," Miss Kitty said, "are the wagon loads of girls he brings in. They bathe at my place from time to time, and these girls are bruised and scared. They have no way out of town, so, they're stuck working upstairs nearly twelve hours a day. They were happy when the city council passed the ordinance closing saloon doors from two a.m. to eight a.m. But they tell me there are still a lot of "private" games going on late at night, and Mr. Kelly seems to be planning something big."

Van Gentry spoke up, "We've been missing cattle over the past few months, and I've a pretty good idea where they are. Skinner came out last week, and we caught up a trail. We're taking Wild Shot, Lefty and Levi out for a little huntin' party tomorrow night. Mr. Kelly's gang is due to lose a few members."

"Ah had to run off three of those bums t'other day," said George, "seems Mr. Kelly is running the fire protection scam. Thumb Buster had his place burn down. Cal talked to him, and he looked very nervous, and seemed worried about his house."

"Gentlemen," said Short Keg, "this looks a lot worse than I thought."

"Something else," said Coop, "Doc tells me a lot of guys are showing up barfing blood. Seems Mr. Kelly is cutting his booze with turpentine and gunpowder. He's running rot gut."

This time the sheriff spoke up, "Mr. Kelly and his gang appear to be settin' up to take over this town. Marshall laid out the town in fine order, set up parks, a school, and a good water supply. Why, all you boys settled here for well-deserved peace and quiet. Even with the railroad we prospered. Mr. Kelly saw a good thing and figured he could squeeze a lot of money out of this town. It won't be long before he swallows us up. Marshall came from back east; maybe he knows more about Mr. Kelly. I'll check with him later today."

"I've got an ideer," said Slim, "we cain't take them head on. We all came here to live out the rest of our time in peace and quiet. We aren't as young or as tough as we think, and sides, they got a bunch more guns than we got. I figure we need to whittle that gang down a bit, push up our odds a bit. There must be thirty or more of them guys. The Gentry brothers will start the whittle tomorrow, but here's another idea. I got a lot of freight haulers comin' thru the livery. They're haulin' a lot of liquor. Kelly has a warehouse back of his saloon, and them boys unload there. Then they stop at my place to rest up their teams, and grease up the wagons. Now, it don't take a New York banker to guess what might happen if that warehouse catches a spark or two with them kegs. I'll also suggest to the freight haulers that it would be in their best interests to lollygag a lot on their next trip here."

"Well boys," said the sheriff, "I'd better not hear any more plans. As Sheriff, I need to be able to stay in the dark in case anyone asks me what I know. You're right about one thing, we don't have the manpower to take them on head to head. A lot of people might hurt. Adios boys, I better head over to the church. We have a new preacher in town, and I'm told he carries a gun, and doesn't always preach forgiveness. Then I'll talk to Marshall about Kelly."

"Miss Calder may know a beet more about Kellay, she gets news from back east and may have a few ideahs about his plans," said Mike. "I'll have a talk with thah lady."

"Kenny," said Miss Kitty, "I have a few more ideas that might help whittle down the numbers a bit. We want that gang to be looking for greener pastures. My ladies know the cooks that serve up the food to that gang. If their drinks are gone, and their food ain't too good, don't matter how much money they get, they won't be happy."

"Even after some whittling," said Buzzard, "them boys will be heading our way, and we still need some manpower and a plan."

The men stood, nodded their heads in agreement, and planned their next meeting.

Ken looked at his friends and felt a sense of pride and

strength knowing he could count on every one of them for support. They were good men, Miss Kitty being one of them. Sundowner had been his friend for years but he had often felt alone with no real place to call home. After only a couple of years in Marshallville, he had a home, good friends, and a young woman who cared for him; he was not going to let that be destroyed by a worthless criminal gang.

After the men left the saloon, Molly approached Ken. "What's going ta happen? I worry about you. I like what we have and I don't want to lose you."

Looking at Molly, he knew this would be his last stop, there was only one way he would leave this town. Giving her a big hug he said, "I don't want to lose you either."

Chapter 23

Newspaper Office

Mike finished his breakfast, for Mike that was noon, and headed to the Marshallville Gazette. Stepping into the newspaper office, Mike looked around and saw a complex set up. Behind a counter were trays of type, bottles of ink, stacks of paper and a large printing press staged around the back half of the room. Hannah Calder, the editor, stood at her desk, working on a layout of a hand bill for the fourth of July. The last time he saw the office it had been nearly destroyed by the Senator's men.

"Hi Mrs. Calder," said Mike

She looked up with a smile, set down her ruler and pen saying, "Mike, please call me Hannah, after all you took down those men in Topeka."

Mike liked the tone of her voice. It was pleasant and better yet, friendly.

"Of course ma'am, Hannah."

"Is this a business call or a friendly call?"

As a gambler he showed a calm poker face, but inside, he grinned. Her question hinted that she might be receptive to a friendly call. He made a mental note to follow up on that idea soon.

"Unfortunately Miss Hannah, it's a business call. There's trouble hanging over our town by the name of Kelly. You keep up with news from back east, what do you know about Kelly and New York?"

Hannah gestured to Mike to have a seat at one of the customer's chairs, as she pulled a stool and propped up next to her desk.

"I have noticed that gang of toughs around him at the T-Hall saloon. A crime organization called Tammany Hall is operating in New York. They practically run the city. It is mostly Irish immigrants that control many of the wards in New York. Graft, payoffs, and kickbacks bring in millions of dollars. A man named Tweed ran it for years. He started as an enforcer, and moved up the ranks to boss. Kelly may have started the same way too, I don't know. Tweed was finally arrested in 1871 and went to jail. There was a lot of competition to get his job. I'm sure Kelly was involved in the struggle. Apparently, someone else got the job, and Kelly decided to take the system here."

"That makes sense, Miss Hannah. Ah've seen a lot a schemes and cons in N'arlins and steam boats and Kelly's oper-a-tion smells like a cooked up plot."

Hannah stood with hands on her hips, looked right at Mike and said, "Marshallville may become the seat of El Paso County, and that is a good start for political favor paybacks. One of the scams of Tammany Hall had contractors pay kickbacks to get city or state jobs or, in this case a county job. The other rumor is that the Colorado territory will become a state soon. A county or state or even a federal position would be worth a lot of money."

"Well, Miss Hannah, sounds like Kelly could be settin' himself for money and power. If he can take over Marshallville, he might just do it."

"He's already trying to run the saloon district with his gang. Who's going to stop him?"

"We'll see, ma'am, we'll see."

Mike made another mental note, it may be a while before he paid that 'friendly' visit.

Chapter 24

Rustlers down

Van and John, with Levi and Lefty, met up with Skinner and Wild Shot to set up an ambush for the rustlers that had been stealing the Gentry's cattle. Skinner had been following sign for a couple of days and found their campsite late one evening. Light rain had made tracking the stolen cattle a little easier and now they had gathered and a plan was taking shape.

"Listen boys," Van whispered, "we'll wait til dawn for the attack. Those crooks'll be rolled up warm and tight with only one guard lookin' around and he'll be half a sleep. They won't be able to tell us apart from other night critters sneaking around. Streaks of daylight will give us enough light ta make out the camp."

"What's da plan?" asked Wild Shot and the others moved in close to hear.

"Wild Shot, I want you to take out the night guard, and

then cover our backs. Skinner, you injun over to their string line, and get ready to cut loose the horses. John, Lefty, Levi and I will soft foot it around the camp and throw a surprise party for the rustlers. Wild Shot, wait till you see us set up. There'll be enough light comin' up at dawn for you to follow our set up. When you see us ready, take out the guard, and Skinner, when the guard goes down, cut the line, and shoo off the horses. Let's go."

One shot took out the guard. Skinner let loose the horses and Levi blew a blast into the campfire. The men jumped up to sparks flying in their faces and on their bedrolls. Yells of profanity broke out, and the rustlers reached for their guns. Another blast from the shotgun into the fire sent the message that any fast moves would bring lead flying in their direction. Pointing his gun straight out at one rustler then another, Van shouted, "Stand easy boys, there are six guns aimed at you so empty your hands, and sit still. Make a play and you'll be plugged silly."

Six men were at the camp. Five were sitting on their bed rolls; one was on the ground, flat with a dark red stain growing on his chest. Van and the boys circled the rustlers, guns out, ready for trouble. Gesturing with his fist, the biggest of the men shouted out, "You boys'll be sorry when we get back to town; we have a lot of friends there."

"I don't think you rustlers appreciate your predicament. You ain't gonna get back to town," said Levi.

Some light was dawning on the rustler's faces, more shouts of profanity and a half-hearted attempt at disbelief.

"Skinner, truss these boys up like a turkey settin' up for Sunday supper," barked Van.

More obscenities, but a little pistol whipping by Skinner settled them down quickly.

It didn't take Skinner long and five men lay on their sides, on the ground, tied tightly, unable to move. Scowling with a gash on his head, the mouthy one looked up and growled, "What'd you mean we ain't goin' back to town, you gonna kill us in cold blood?"

"Hey Skinner," asked John. "How many buffalo'd you and Wild Shot skin out a year or so back?"

"Maybe a thousand, that about right Wild Shot?" Wild Shot nodded.

"You ever skin a man?" asked John.

"I could I suppose, but never have. An old Indian friend a mine splained to me how to do it." Looking at the rustlers he said, "I could maybe give it a try."

The rustlers looked at each other, struggled with their ropes, turned pale and one of them threw up.

Feigning bravery, the mouthy one said, "we done nothing to you, took a few cows maybe, but that don't deserve no skinin'."

This time Lefty spoke up, "I suppose we could do some dealin'. Tell us who your boss is."

"We don't got no boss, we work our own jobs."

"Skinner, how close can you shave a head and still leave a scalp," asked Van.

"If I can skin out hundreds of buffs, I reckon I can shave a head down to the skin, ….maybe."

"See what you can do to this mouthy one."

Skinner went to his bag and pulled out an eight inch skinning knife. He wiped it a few times on the sleeve of his shirt and said he was ready. He walked over to the mouthy one who was hog-tied lying on the ground.

Wide eyes stared at the knife hovering over his head. "It was Kelly," he blurted out, "now get that knife away from me and I'll tell you more."

Skinner looked at Van with a smile and eased up.

"Go on."

"If I tell you more, you'll keep that butcher away from me."

"Sure."

"Mr. Kelly got a lot a men and a lot a plans. You and this town be his soon. If you let us go, I'll put in a good word for you'all."

"Here's the thing, you guys picked the wrong ranch, the wrong town, and the wrong boss. We aim to point out the error of your ways. We're gonna let you live, but you'll make yourselves scarce round these parts. Skinners gonna show you how to skin a buffalo, but he is gonna use your heads for demonstration. We hope that will give you incentive enough to follow our suggestion bout leaving these parts. Go ahead Skinner, shave them all, and no need to be too careful with the trimming, oh, and no need for water or shaving soap."

Another round of obscenities followed, with pulling at the ropes to get free. With fear dripping from their faces, they knew what was coming.

"Hey", the mouthy one said, "you said if I talked you'd keep him away from me."

Van scratched his head. "Now, I don't rightly remember sayin' that. Let me think on it a bit."

"The more you boys wiggle, the harder it is to scrap a clean shave. You mightin' hold your head as still as you can, or a little scalp mightin' just stick to ma knife." Skinner grinned.

Forty minutes and a lot of screaming later, five men were lying on the ground, heads shaved clean. They all had blood oozing from their heads showing a nick or two. Two were softly crying, and one had thrown up again. To his credit, the mouthy one didn't make a peep.

"Skinner, you did a great job. I may hire you at the barber shop when we get back," said Wild Shot.

Looking at each one and pointing a finger, Wild Shot said, "If'in any of you boys shows up in town, Skinner'll try out what that old Indian splained to him. We don't call him Skinner for nothin'. If ya heads north along the trade route, you might'n git to Denver in a couple oh days. I suggest you'all keep going north, maybe hitch a ride to the Oregon territory."

Van spoke up, "We are going to untie you, but leave all your gear where it lies. Throw your friend in a hole and cover him with rocks. Then you can ride 'Shanks mare' to Denver. We'll watch you for few hours. If you want to keep your skin, better keep going."

After the rustlers hobbled out of sight, Lefty said, "Well we whittled off six of them fellas. Mr. Kelly should be wondering what happened when those hombres don't make it back. I'm guessing he'll send a few of his gang out looking for them. Let's leave them a little message."

"Wha'ch you got in mind," asked Skinner.

"Let's take their bed rolls and fill them with rocks and lay them around the fire like they was a sleepin'. Pack their

319

saddlebags with rocks and set them next to the bed rolls. Now, what'd you think those 'no goods' are gonna think when they find a rock camp but no cows or fellas?"

One by one, the guys laughed. They all admitted they liked Skinner's idea.

Chapter 25

David Kelly

Cal knocked on the Mayor's door and entered after the "Come in." Walking over to the Mayor's desk, Cal offered a hand. "Hi Mr. Mayor."

"Have a seat Cal, what brings you in today?"

The office was new, laid out nicely with a large oak desk, a hard wood floor, pictures of Jane and little Jane were on the wall, and two high back chairs set in front of the desk. Taking off his hat, Cal took one of the seats in front of the desk. "You were from New York, did you know Kelly back then?"

"Yes, Sheriff, I knew of Dave Kelly in New York. Tammany Hall was very influential in New York, and Kelly was an enforcer for Boss Tweed. He's an Irish immigrant. He grew up on the streets of New York." Gesturing with both hands, Marshall went on, "He was big, tough and street fighting gave him boxing skills. He fought in the ring and rarely lost. That's how he became an enforcer for Tweed. Tweed liked him, brought him into the business. When Tweed went to jail in '71, Kelly tried to take the head job."

Leaning forward Cal asked, "What happened?"

"There was a lot of competition for boss. There was a man named Plunke, a powerful alderman, and in the New York assembly, who eventually took over. Kelly wanted to be boss, lost out, so it looks like he took his training on the road."

"That throws some light on Kelly's past, but what do you figure he's up to now?"

"I heard Kelly moved to Topeka, Kansas and set up an operation there. Don't know why he left Topeka or how he saw Marshallville as easy pickings, but here he is. He has been to a couple of city council meetings. He just sits, looking, and listening. He may feel he can use Marshallville as a stepping stone to Denver, then to Congress. We aren't a state yet, but we will be soon. We don't want another Tammany Hall here or in Denver. Did you notice the name of his saloon; T Hall saloon. We need to shut him down."

"Mr. Mayor, I am doing all I can to keep things legal. I

322

can't tie him to anything yet. We have some verbal comments, but nothing to take to court. As long as he keeps his business according to the zoning laws, he can continue to operate."

"What about this fire protection scam he is running?"

"It's a legal business. Private fire departments are legal. We can't prove he's forcing people to buy insurance.

"I'm worried Cal," said Marshall. "He grows stronger each day. Those employees of his are nothing more than enforcers like in New York. People in town are scared. We need proof of illegal activities. How did he come to own three saloons and a hotel?"

"He said he bought them from the owners. He showed me the deeds and bill of sale. He claimed the owners just left town with a big wad of money. They wanted to head for California."

"I hate to see you call on our former lawmen again, but maybe they'll have some ideas," said Marshall.

"Mr. Mayor, they may be our only chance."

*****

323

It was two weeks before the fourth and a week after the rustlers' party. Another meeting was taking place at the closed Short Keg. Molly brought in a platter of biscuits and bacon and Sundowner filled coffee cups around the table. The men smiled and thanked Molly.

"We need a plan if we are going to shut Kelly down," cautioned Ken, taking a sip of coffee.

"I have an idea said Van Gentry. John and I've made friends with a few of the Kiowa close by. If we head a few cows their way, I think we can get them to stage a small raid on the liquor warehouse back of the T-Hall saloon. No use us getting involved. Kelly can complain to the sheriff, and Cal can pretend to scout out the Indian tracks, but Mr. Kelly will be without drinks, and we won't get blamed. I think a week before the fourth of July is perfect. There'll be a lot of celebratin', and when Kelly's places go dry, the other saloons'll get all the action. I have a feelin' most of his boys will be hangin' where the drinks are flowin'."

"I was going to say we won't see hide nor hair of those rustlers, but it struck me they got no hair to be seen." John laughed at his own joke, mouthing a piece of bacon. "But that's six down and about thirty more to go."

Miss Kitty spoke up, "I've talked to the cooks at the T-Hall saloon, and the other two saloons Kelly owns. We have a plan. The sportin' ladies routinely use Aloe Vera as an ointment for their skin. The better the ladies look, the nicer their skin, the more money they can get. Freight haulers come up from the Arizona territory with crates of the cactus pads. It turns out that drinking a little juice of the Aloe cures constipation. In other words, a lot of juice in those cowboy beans, and those boys be running to the privy every hour. If the liquor warehouse burns down, and those boys get the runs, some of them may look elsewhere for an easier job."

"Great idea, Kitty, the timing needs to be just right," said Short Keg. "Let's wait til July Fourth for the bean fix. They will be out of booze, and spending the day in the privy. That should throw a horseshoe in Kelly's plans for the fourth, especially for the big boxing matches."

"Miss Hannah gave me zee low down bout Kelly's possible plans. We thenk he plans to take over zee town and create a crime organiza-tion like they did in New York," said Mike

"Cal told me that John Marshall said the same thing," replied Ken.

Chapter 26

Kelly's Plan

Kelly had lost the fight for New York Tammany Hall so he planned to move the same set up to another town. He started in Topeka, Kansas where an undercurrent of crime was already active. He picked out a small, one owner saloon for his first mark. Late one night he got the owner alone in his office and tortured him until he signed over the ownership of the saloon. Once he had the papers, he killed the owner, took the body out of town and buried it.

Thinking back on his play, he smiled to himself at how easy ownership came about. He was surprised that plan wasn't used more, so simple. He began with a few gun hands and went about collecting more saloons, killing and burying the owners. Topeka already had several crime bosses so taking over was not going to be as easy as he thought. He knew he was smarter and more vicious than anyone else in town, but winning would take time and a lot of money. He almost laughed out loud thinking about seeing a flier promoting the virtues of a town called Marshallville. It was an invitation, come get me, he thought. A small town, close to Denver, looked like a sitting pigeon for his plan.

Sitting in his office in the back of the T-Hall saloon, David Kelly leaned back in his chair thinking about the progress of his plan to set up a western version of Tammany Hall. His plans for the Fourth of July were coming together. He had sent for a few men from New York who were big, mean, Irish, Boxers. They had been street fighters growing up in New York, and he figured on making a lot of money on the boxing matches he set up. The horse races he figured he could fix with a bribe here and there. Kelly was figuring with the Fourth of July income, he would be able to buy enough votes for himself, and some of his cronies to take over the city council. Once that happened he could set up kick-backs, protection, zoning changes, and a blackmailing scheme involving the railroad and its' station. He stood up and walked around his desk and puffed out his chest a bit. It was just a matter of time before he owned the town and made a small fortune. All a stepping stone to setting up in Denver, and when Colorado became a state, he could be governor or US Senator. Mr. Kelly was chewing on his cigar with a smile on his face. He had no idea he was about to be derailed.

*****

A week before the Fourth at two a.m., a small Indian band broke into Kelly's liquor warehouse. They helped themselves to many bottles and set the place on fire. By the time anyone saw the flames, a roaring fire had engulfed the warehouse. The bottles were popping from the heat, pouring alcohol on the fire and kicking the flames higher. His private fire department was able to get a pumper to the warehouse spraying water and keeping the fire from spreading to his other properties, but could not save his warehouse. The Indians left enough clues, moccasin prints, an arrowhead amulet, strewn bottles, etc. to take the blame, and not make any town folk look guilty.

The next day, Mr. Kelly had to dig into his cash box to get to Denver for more alcohol. He sent five men to Denver to buy more whiskey and beer, and to guard the wagons returning to Marshallville.

Nevada Slim ran down to the Short Keg and told Kenny that five men had saddled up and were headed to Denver.

"Perfect," said Ken, "we can ambush them on their way back. Wild Shot and Skinner can give them a haircut, and Skinner can threaten to skin them alive just like the Indian told him. We take the booze for the Short Keg, and Kelly has spent more money, and still has no drinks, and loses five more men."

"Hey," said Slim, "Levi and Lefty have 'wanted posters' for two of them boys headin' to Denver. They'll go to jail, and Levi and Lefty will put some jingle in their pokes. I'll spread a little of that jingle, and drink mongst the freight haulers, and they'll ramble back to Denver after the ambush, taking their time. I know most of them haulers, and many owe me a favor for helping them with their rigs over the years. Whip Lash sorta heads up them boys and he'll see to it they'll sit tight in Denver. Kelly'll be stumped, that's for Simon pure. We'll still be hiding in the dark."

There were several places outside Denver for an ambush. Everything went according to plan. Three more got haircuts; dry cuts, no soap, no oil, just a sharp blade dragging across a scalp. Two others went to jail in Denver from the wanted posters. The haulers got some extra money, and a few bottles of whiskey. The Gentry brothers brought back some whiskey in their wagon for the Short Keg, and Lefty and Levi picked up about $3,000 in reward money. Of course the best part would be, five more gang members gone, and the balled up look on Kelly's face when no one showed with his whiskey.

*****

The city hall was packed with folks excited about the fourth.

They were buzzin', and jokin', and anxious to know the plans.

John Marshall stepped up to the podium, "Well, folks, it looks like the plans are in place for a great Fourth of July. Decorations are done, picnic food is being baked, and fire pits are set up. Harold tells me the Marshallville marching band is ready. Fireworks are set. The old court house is ready for a dance. Miss Apple has games, and prizes for the kids. The 200 yard horse race track for the kids is done, as is the mile track around the rock outcrop. Mr. Kelly has the boxing ring set up, and betting tables are ready. Mr. Haupt will bring the beer over on the fourth, and Mr. Arthur and the Gentry boys will have the meat ready for cookin'. It looks like most of the shops in town are having specials for the day. Is there anything we missed?"

"Mr. Mayor, I was able to get the tightrope walker from Denver for the day. She is staying at the Marshallville hotel and thanks to Mrs. Belle, she is staying for free. I have seen the show and it is thrilling. It will be an exciting start to an exciting day," grinned Mark. "I have a couple of men helping me set up a rope across Main St. for the event. The Arthur and Franks' kids will pass plates around before, and after the event so people can donate."

"Good job, Mark, we will start with the tightrope walk.

The band can play a march after she walks. When she is done, we will start the parade. It looks like we have fifteen groups marching in the parade. The parade takes us to the park for the picnic. The races will start at 12:30, and boxing starts at 4:00."

A lot of whoops, and hoo-rays sounded and the crowd headed outside.

Chapter 27

The Fourth of July

A warm, clear, cloudless day had the town folk gathered to see the tightrope walker in action. Many were eager for the show, saying they had never seen such a spectacle before. One woman said her husband and kids had tried to walk across a log over a stream before, but this was on a rope tied to the top of two buildings, about fifty feet across Main Street. Similar murmurs buzzed through the crowd, looking at a rope that high in the air brought a lot of head shaking.

Lily Lightfoot stepped out onto the roof of the bank building. She was dressed in what looked like tight, white bloomers, a white blouse with fringe hanging from the sleeves, ballet slippers, and a small, white hat with two white feathers sticking out of the back of the hat.

The rope stretched from the bank to the top of the Marshallville hotel, with no safety net below. Earlier that week, Hannah Calder had posted fliers, around town, and in the shops, with a picture of Lilly Lightfoot. Seemed like hundreds of people were crowded on main street to see the event. Alice and Richard Arthur and Cameron and Mary Frank passed through the crowd with a collection plate to pay for the act.

When Lily walked out, the crowd oohed and aahed. The white figure seemed to glow in the sunlight. They held their breath as she stepped on to the rope. Holding a long pole for balance, she started across the rope. A hundred people stood watching with mouths and eyes, wide open.

Insensitive to the danger, Dave Kelly was taking bets whether she would fall or not. He stood to make money if she fell.

Slowly, she walked, step by step, across the rope. A light breeze floated down Main Street. Mark Jones and Bill Williams walked along, under the rope, thinking they might be able to catch her if she fell. She floated like an angel. The crowd was mesmerized. About halfway across, she fluttered her arms, the pole wavered and the crowd gasped. She caught her balance and continued. The band had decided not to play while she walked. They did not want any distractions. They were ready to play when she finished her walk.

A giant roar went up when she stepped onto the roof of

the hotel. The band played a stirring war song, and people were hugging, clapping, and congratulating themselves. The collection plates were filled up, and the band started the parade. Spirits were high, music played, and the crowd moved toward the picnic grounds smiling, and happy. The anniversary of the fifth year of the founding, of the town, had started.

Mark Jones escorted Lily Lightfoot from the roof to her room to change, and then they worked their way to the picnic grounds. He beamed, and she seemed to enjoy his company. Most of the men at the park couldn't keep their eyes off Lily. The wives even admired her, but laughed at the menfolk for acting silly. A couple of the younger girls handed her flowers and told her they would like to tightrope walk someday.

Chapter 28

Races

The Fourth of July races turned out to be the largest races they ever had in Marshallville. Dozens of horses from miles around, showed up. There were several ranches in the area now, and each bunch knew their horses were the fastest. Several Indians brought strings of ponies they thought were fastest. As it turned out, the surprise horses were brought in by farmers; farmers from Kentucky. The farmers didn't talk much about their horses; their thoroughbreds were beautiful.

There were several kids with horses. After lunch, the kids started the race day from 200 yards out. They won ribbons, some penny candy, and had a blast. The parents were happy, and the racing day was off to a good start.

For the mile race, the entry fee was five dollars per horse, but it wasn't just the purse the racers were counting on, the betting that would bring the big money. Kelly knew how to handicap horse races, and the number of horses coming in, had him smiling. He could see his safe filling with money.

There were thirty horses so Kelly figured five races
with six horses each. No ranch would have to race against their
own horses. Kelly set up the program with horses, names, and
numbers. All the owners bet on their own horses to win, so a
betting pool was started. Kelly wrote the bets on a betting sheet
for all to see. The bettor was given a ticket with the horse
number, and amount of the bet. With the town folk betting, the
betting pool got larger and larger. First place bets got double
their bet. Second was original bet plus fifty percent, and third
was original bet plus thirty percent. The money bet on the
losers paid the winners, the extra went to Kelly.

As long as two of the favorites didn't win, there would
be a lot of money left in the pool, and Kelly would stuff his
pockets. If the favorites won, too many people would pick up
money, and there would be a negative pool, and Kelly would
lose money. Kelly was not new to graft. He figured on making
a lot of money on the races. Before the first race, he talked to a
couple of the Indians about bumping certain horses (the
favorites) at the turn. He gave them a few dollars and a bottle
of whisky. He ran each race every thirty minutes to get as
many bets as possible. That also gave him time to see who the
favorite was, and have that horse 'bumped'.

The first race went off as Kelly had planned. The
Indians were able to crowd out the favorites enough at the turn
that the longshots came in. Kelly made hundreds. The Indians
were quick to realize their horses did not finish in the money
either, and wanted Kelly to give back their bets to make up for
being out of the money. Kelly reluctantly offered them a few
more dollars, two bottles of whisky, and no more.

That arrogant attitude cost him a lot of money on the
next four races. Being from the east, Kelly did not understand
the Indians' dislike of the white man. This had the feel like
another treaty broken. The next four races the Indians helped
the favorite to win. They also bet on the favorite. That would
bring in a lot more than the $5 entry fee.

Quickly the crowd recognized true horse flesh. Money
flowed to the Kentucky breed and that proved costly to Kelly.
The other horses ran for second or third. With the Indians
bumping the non-favorites, Kelly lost thousands of dollars.

Miss Kitty had the cooks, "juice" up the beans, bacon,
and eggs the boxers were to eat for breakfast that morning.
They were big eaters. Kitty knew in a few hours, all hell would
break loose. She smiled when she thought of the word 'loose'.

*****

David Kelly planned to make a lot of money on his boxing matches. He needed the wins to make up for the horse race losses. He had eight matches set up. He had brought in several of the toughest fighters he knew from the streets of New York to augment the men he already had. He looked at his boxers sitting along one side of the ring, with a strong man's appreciation for violence, he smiled.

He had made the ring slightly smaller than regulation; he didn't want any of the opponents to have room to dodge punches. He was almost giddy inside. He knew his boxers like to pound opponents to the ground. He could see the blood flying off beaten faces.

Walking by his men he said, "Okay boys, put on a show. Start with body punches to soften them up. Then I want to see blood." His boxers nodded their heads and chuckled hoarsely.

He printed up a boxing card for his fighters and signed up opponents. He even gave odds of two to one against his fighters to encourage bets, and took on all wagers. Farm boys, cowboys and one big Indian filled the fight card. Every one of those boys had friends that were sure their guy would win. With odds of two to one, they piled on the money.

338

Kelly knew how to put on a show. He had ribbons tied to the corners of the ring. Some of his sporting ladies were dressed in colorful dresses, handing out penny candy. He set up a beer keg outside near the ring, and poured out free mugs of beer. One man played an accordion while his partner played a fiddle. With music, beer, candy and ribbons, the boxing festival was crowded with cheering, applause and an explosive tension in the air.

Kelly's top fighter was known as Big Mark. Mark was 6'3", weighed 245, and looked chiseled out of stone. Head shaved with a mustache drooped into his bearded chin, he had the profile of a bald eagle. His piercing eyes cut through the face or body of anyone who stood against him.

He liked to play with his opponent. He'd pound on a guy for a few rounds until almost unconscious, then back off a few rounds, and let him recover. He'd even drop his guard, and let the other guy get a glancing blow off his steel-like jaw, making him think he had a chance to win. Then Mark would pound him some more, then back off, then pound him some more. When Mark was done the guy's face would look like hamburger, he'd have a few broken ribs, and kidneys that barely worked any more. Big Mark thought that was fun.

Kelly started Big Mark in the first match in an effort to intimidate the fighters in the next matches. The bets were in, if a man backed out, the bet was lost. As big and mean as Mark looked, his opponent in the first match was an Indian who was bigger. At 6'5", and tipping the scales at 280 pounds, the chief resembled a mountain. The Indian did not have a chiseled look, but looked more like something wild out of the forest.

Big Mark smiled when he saw him and planned on having some fun. He knew Indians didn't box, they wrestled. The Indian turned out to be tough and could take a punch. Mark had to work hard those first few rounds, he landed blows that would crumple a normal man, but the big Indian still stayed upright. Ready to back off a bit to let the Indian think he had a chance, it happened. The rumbling in Big Marks stomach started to rage. His bowels were getting loose. The Indian scored a couple of hits to the midsection, and the loose feeling intensified; Mark blew a gust of gas that could be heard around the ring. A large gas explosion was not something one heard around a boxing ring, and a lot of spectators started to laugh. This distracted Mark, and the Indian landed a few more hits, and Mark took on a distressed look. Those loose bowels told Mark this fight had to end quickly. He wasn't about to ask the referee for a shit break.

As big as the Indian was, he could not weather the sudden barrage of blows erupting from Big Mark. It had to be a strange feeling for Mark; throwing punches, trying not to shit. As soon as the Indian was counted out, Mark ran to the privy around back of the T-Hall saloon. Anyone watching him run would notice a strange gait, like someone running with a stick up their butt.

Mark's fight would be the only fight Kelly's fighters won. Normally, the Irish boxers would be able to pound their opponents to the ground after eight or ten rounds. Shitting your pants is embarrassing, and those big Irishmen weren't about to be caught with shitty pants. More than a few times the matches had to wait between rounds while the Irishmen went to the privy. Diarrhea weakens you, dehydrates you, and opens you up to severe reactions when punched in the belly. Kelly felt his money slipping away. Instead of making thousands, Kelly was losing thousands.

His whiskey sold out early, and his saloons were empty. His boxers were spending most of the day in the privy. His men sent to Denver never showed up. Mr. Kelly was living a nightmare, and he didn't know what happened.

*****

341

After the races and boxing, the picnic started going full on at the city park. Kids were playing games, the marching band set in the gazebo, and lively tunes were sailing over the park.

John Marshall watched the fun and activities. He felt both happy and sad. He wished his wife could be here to see the growth of a happy town. Even after five years he missed her. It was little Jane's birthday. She was playing in the park with the other kids, laughing and happy. He felt proud of the town and what the six families were able to do in a blank open space. Even in the midst of a celebration, he had a sense of foreboding, he sensed David Kelly looking over his shoulder. Would the sheriff and his ex-lawmen friends be able to hold the reins of a wagon gone wild.

At 6:00 pm, the set up for the dance began. The tables and chairs were moved along the walls, leaving room to dance. People from out of town, who could not get there for the picnic, came in by the wagon loads. Nobody missed a dance if possible. Musicians brought out their instruments, and warmed up for the evening. Single boys and girls, men and women, gathered laughing, and flirting, and doing what young people do. A game called "Clap in, Clap out" kept the teen-agers busy for a while. Women formed gossip groups, while men sipped from their flasks, told jokes, and compared farming, and ranching stories. After midnight the lights were finally dimmed, and wagons pulled out to go home.

After the dance, the Short Keg hosted several men including the Mayor, and several old lawdog friends. They all agreed the 5th anniversary of the town came off successfully.

"Well, men," said Ken, "I think we can say, not too loudly, that Kelly suffered a huge defeat today." A lot of beer mugs were held up, clinked, and drained. "The question is, what comes next?"

Chapter 29

Down but not Out

Pacing up and down in his office, anger started to build. He walked across the broken glass on the floor from throwing his bottle of Bourbon against the wall. Temper, temper, he told himself, hold down the temper. He could not figure out what went wrong. It seemed everything went wrong, his plans blew up. He felt ready to explode. He went downstairs, around the back of the saloon, with his fists clenched. A man staggered down the alley trying to get home. Kelly attacked him, punching left and right, pounding the man senseless. Little by little he felt his anger subside. Kicking the man, he headed back into the saloon and upstairs to his office. He felt better, tension released.

David Kelly had spent too many years in New York fighting his way up through the slums as an Irish immigrant to quit now. Scraping by on petty crimes, and boxing matches had hardened his resolve. Tammany hall showed him how to use the system to make money. He took a deep breath and reviewed his plans.

He dressed as a dandy, not an enforcer. He wanted to portray an image of a successful businessman. He hired ex-cons, drifters, and gunmen to do his work. He learned from New York that money and gifts hold an organization together. His men all had a place to stay, three good meals a day, a few shots of whiskey, a turn or two with the girls upstairs, plus a weekly salary. His gang had never had it so good, and they wanted to keep the good times rolling. They knew it would take some muscle, and some gun play, and they were ready.

Kelly's gang sat about twenty-five men. He had used up much of his ready cash and came up a little short on his weekly salary. A few of the gang started grumbling. He assured his men it would only take a few weeks before his safe was full again. Gambling, girls, whiskey, and protection paid well. They would need to get more 'protection' policies signed.

He had three saloons, and he had brought in another wagon load of "fallen doves." He had sent ten men this time to Denver for several wagon loads of whiskey, and barrels of beer. He restocked his shelves after the Fourth, and continued to cut the whiskey with turpentine, ammonia, water and even chewing tobacco; rot gut would be served again. He put the word out that he needed more gun fighters. He felt confident again about taking over the city council, and running the town; it just would take a little more time.

*****

Lefty and Levi went to see the police chief of Denver to collect their bounties on the men caught for rustling. The chief at the time was a man named David Cook. He had been a sheriff in Colorado, and was now the police chief in Denver. Cook was a no nonsense law man. One motto, he frequently shared with other lawmen was, "Always have your gun ready, it is better to kill two men than have one kill you." He also said, "Never trust the honor of prisoners, nine out of ten have no honor."

"Sheriff, do you mind if we look through your wanted posters?"

"Help yourself, hope you find a familiar face."

"Check these guys out Levi, I've seen them in town."

They left the sheriff's office and sent telegrams to a few friends in Kansas with information about men found on the posters. They gave the friends directions to the Gentry brothers ranch, told them the fishing barrel was fully stocked.

A few weeks later, three bounty hunters found their
way to the Gentry's ranch. Levi and Lefty shook their hands
with a smile on their faces.

"Good to see you boys," said Levi, "I think I can make
it worth the trip. Come in, sit a spell, have some coffee and
hear my plan."

The three men were some of the toughest men in the
old west. Years of tracking, chasing, and trapping outlaws had
honed these men to a fine edge. Interestingly, one was Chinese,
short, only 5 feet, 4 inches. He seemed like a push over, an
easy man to beat. Most men did not regard a 'chinaman' as a
danger. Many men in jail right now had underestimated
'shorty'. As a walking arsenal, he had two .44's in a holster rig,
three hideaways including a spring loaded sleeve gun, and a
knife in each boot. He also had a metal lined hat that he used as
a back handed fist. The other two were built like bulls with
arms the size of a normal man's leg. They had trained in
boxing, wrestling, and eastern martial arts. Their best asset was
lightning fast reflexes. Many men had tried to draw on them,
and in a blink of an eye a throat punch had them gasping for air
as they dropped to the ground. If you were within arm's reach,
count yourself caught, and handcuffed. One had been a buffalo
hunter, and could shoot a fly off the head of a cow without the

cow even knowing it happened.

Levi introduced the three men to Van and John. He pulled out the wanted posters he had collected at the marshal's office in Denver, and spread them out on the table. He poured coffee all around, pulled out the makins' and rolled a smoke. The men squared up to the table looking at the posters.

"I've seen at least three of those boys in town. Trouble is they hang out with about twenty other hard cases, and having a shootout with that many men, ain't good odds. They do stay at a boarding house at the edge of town with several of the gang. We got to smoke'em out where we can get the drop," said Levi.

One of the bounty hunters said, "I have a method I think is funny but it works, and the outlaws get very pissed by it. It takes a least two people, three is better. When nature calls, and the wanted man heads for the privy, my partner beats the guy to the privy, and locks it. The guy rattles the door a couple of times, get antsy, and then has to loosen his gun belt to take a piss on the backside of the privy. That is when I show up. What's he gonna do? His hands are holding his pecker, and my hands are holding a gun, works every time. I handcuff him while his pecker is still out, I take his gun, then we march to the horses, and we saddle up. Believe me; they are very careful, and not likely to run. I don't let him button up until we get to the sheriff's office. It may take a long stake out, but it works."

The room erupted with laughter, the plan seemed perfect. The three bounty hunters would be in the bar watching and waiting for the trip outside by one of the wanted men. One would rush out to the privy while two would cover the area. At the right time, one did the arrest, and the other backed his play. It only took one day, and three more of the gang seemed to just disappear.

Chapter 30

The Fight Begins

When the big mouth rustler saw some of his Marshallville gang in Denver, getting a wagon full of liquor, he joined up. His hair was about a half inch long and he explained what happened. "Let's get back to town, I need to tell Kelly what's going on. Maybe you boys will help me get even with those bastards that scraped the top of my head."

Back in town with the wagon load of whiskey, big mouth explained to Kelly what was going on. "Damn, so that's what happened on the fourth. Those old men will be sorry they ever messed with me. We need to move tonight."

That night Kelly's men burned the barber shop and tannery. Wild Shot and Skinner were at their cabin on the edge of town. Kelly's men headed for the cabin while the fires raged. Surrounding the cabin, they opened fire.

Seeing the smoke and flames brought out the volunteer

fire department. With the fire bells ringing, four of the townsmen pulled the double pumper to the barber shop. They stretched a hose to the town water tank. A man on each side of the double pumper pushed and pulled while a third man positioned the hose and sprayed the shop with water. Several other men set up a bucket brigade for the tannery.

The sheriff, Shady Mike and Short Keg heard the fire bells ring. When they heard the gunfire they strapped on their guns and headed toward the shots. They came up behind four men shooting at Wild Shot's and Skinner's cabin. One minute later, one shooter was down and three others high tailed it back to town, one limping badly.

Cal haled the cabin and they went in to check on Wild Shot and Skinner. Both men were wounded, bleeding, but not life threatening. Bandanas covered the wounds and the bleeding stopped.

"It looks like the fight has begun," said Short Keg, "but how did they know you two were involved?"

"I recognized one of them men. He was the loud mouth rustler that Skinner give a head shavin' to. He musta sneaked back ta town and ratted us out," said Wild Shot as he grabbed his shoulder and winced in pain. "We better get right cause they be comin' for all us. I have a plan. I saw the Indians pull this on the cavalry once't, it should work."

Cal said, "We better get the rest of the guys in town and load up. This ain't what we wanted, but with your help, we can lick this thing. Looks like you'all gonna be deputies one more time."

"You're right Cal," said Short Keg. "We've had enough gun play in our careers, but our backs are against the wall, and now it's 'come to Jesus' time."

"Ah think Mr. shaved head is gonna want to get revenge on the Gentry brothers out at the ranch," chipped in Shady Mike. "Cal, if you send one deputy out to the ranch right away, they can set up a welcoming party for anyone coming with revenge on their mind. Van and John have three ex-Calvary men working for them so they can handle the job. That also means fewer men coming at us."

"Good suggestion, will do, Mike, let's head to the Short Keg, and meet up with the rest of our guys. Wild Shot, you can tell us your plan there."

All the guys were there and Wild Shot opened up. "Ah like to call it the 'jaws O death'." Wild Shot holds his hands together at the heels and slaps his fingers together. "Don't ya think that has a nice ring to it, 'jaws-O-death.' Da way it works is this. We place a lil bait, three of us, in the center of the street to draw them in close. We've our udder guys in shops along da street. Da bait looks like easy pickins', a few old men, and they start to back up like they be afraid. The gang moves down the street towards them like dey shootin' fish in a barrel. When we haves dem in a crossfire, then we cuts dem down."

Looking at Wild Shot, "That sounds like a good plan, so, who's the bait?" asked Short Keg.

"I figure you, Skinner, and Coop. Skinner will have his arm a sling, you be limping, and ole Buzzard Cooper looks like a paunchy old man, bout to fall down. Those boys be thinking easy pickins'. You stand in the street and as they come toward ya, slowly backs up like you is scared."

"That shouldn't be a problem," scoffed Coop.

"Meanwhile, we got the rest of us on da roof, in doorways on each side of da street and they comes walkin' into our trap. Mike, George and the sheriff will be on one side, Levi, Lefty, and one deputy on ta other side. I be on the roof with my fifty, lookin' for hide outs. Miss Kitty will close da door behind them. Slim will be at the jail house if we need to

353

fall back and he can cover us."

"Is there anyone else we can get," said Slim, "you can never have a posse that's too big."

"That be it big fella."

"We need to make this legal like," said Cal, "as much as I want to, we can't just gun'em down."

Wild Shot went on, "Make dis legal by yelling out for dem to drop their guns. When they don't, we can plead self-defense. They'll have bout twenty-five guys so they'll figure they have us outnumbered, which they will, but when we cut loose, dey won't know what hit 'em and there be less than twenty."

"I want to be out in the middle", said Bryce, "let Coop shoot from the side. I have found a home and I want to defend it."

Short Keg put a hand on Bryce's shoulder, squeezed and nodded approval.

"Well, like you said, I'll ask them to drop their guns. We'll let them make their play first, keep it legal and all."

Looking around at his friends, concern in his face, Ken asked, "When do you think this shindig is going to start?"

Mike spoke up, "Ah know guys like Kelly. He's goin' move fast. He's not a defensive fighter. When he real-izes we've played him for a suck-er, he'll be hop-ping mad, and move strong. He'll come chargin' like zee bull and that will be hees mistake. I figure he'll make his move at high noon."

Cal sent a deputy to the gentry's ranch along with Lefty. The rest of the ex-lawmen rounded up their guns and met at the Short Keg.

"Load up." With a grin Coop nodded. "Here we go again. The court of last resort is now in session. Let's hope this is the last time. I'm getting too old for this shit, and I don't need no more holes in my body."

As the men pulled their guns, Coop went on, "Better load up two guns boys. These cap and ball revolvers take about four minutes to load. At four or five minutes per gun, there ain't no time to reload during the fight. Kelly's men'll probably have one gun each, with our extra guns, we should have more fire power."

The double barrel shotguns had cartridges that could be

shot, emptied, then reloaded, and shot again in only a few seconds. Buzzard Cooper carried a repeating Spencer that was capable of seven shoots. He had extra cartridges, and the Spencer could be loaded quickly. Miss Kitty carried two, six shot .22s with extra cartridges that could also be reloaded quickly. The .22s would not kill in one shot, but if hit several times, a man would be laid out face down. Wild Shot pulled out his buffalo gun, and headed to the roof.

The men took their places in the store shops along the street. The shop owners knew the score. They were tired of paying protection and being bullied. They were proud of their town and would fight to protect it. They cleared most of their shelves and got down on the floor carrying their own six irons. Any shoppers in the store were waved away.

Boot Hill Bryce, Skinner and Short Keg stepped out onto the street as planned. They looked a bit "rag tag", but were heavily armed. All three were excellent shots and could easily hit a man at thirty yards. Kelly's men were already forming up in front of the T Hall. They out-numbered the Marshallville men by nearly three to one.

When they saw the three, elderly ex-lawmen, they had a good chuckle. A few laughed out loud and yelled obscenities with robust enthusiasm. They started walking right at them, guns in hand, Kelly urging them on.

Anyone still on Main street knew trouble was about to explode. Parents grabbed their kids and quickly ran down a side street. Main Street was empty and ready for a gun fight.

Bryce, Skinner and Short Keg started moving backward putting worried looks on their faces. The outlaws moved even faster sensing a quick and violent death for the three old men in the street. The plan worked well. When most of the gang were in range of the side shooters, Cal stepped out and yelled for them to drop their guns, and that they were under arrest. Almost in unison, they laughed and told the sheriff to come get their guns if he wanted to try. Levi stepped out a shop door and blew off both barrels, dropping two men quickly to the ground. Bryce, Skinner and Short Keg pulled their guns, turned sidewise and let loose three quick shots, dropping another gunslinger. They unleashed several more shots, and more men dropped. The rest of the ex-lawmen stepped out and opened up.

Lead was flying everywhere, and smoke clouded the street. Windows were breaking, men were shouting, and yells of pain filled the air. Kelly's men suddenly realized they were in the fight of their lives. The smell of death filled nostrils.

Shouted obscenities were drowned out by the explosion of rifles, pistols and shotguns. Watching other men die nearly stopped hearts from beating. Fear pumped the nerves of the fighting men to extreme distortion of reality. Hammer back, pull the trigger, hammer back, pull the trigger, killing was now in session.

The Marshallville men had the surprise and dropped a few of Kelly's men quickly. But these men were not first timers. They had been in gun fights before. They ducked, turned left and right, firing as they did. Coop stepped out with his Spencer, and levered off seven shots, dropping two more men and winging another. He caught some lead in the same leg where he had been shot before. He stumbled back into the hardware store, slumped to the floor, and grabbed his leg. The hardware owner's wife rushed over and tied a bandana around his leg to stop the bleeding. Coop was sweating and breathing hard but he reloaded the Spencer and looked outside.

A letup in the fight as people ducked, found cover, and sought out targets let the smoke clear. Several of Kelly's men were down, bodies were on the street, some not moving, some trying to crawl away. The Marshallville men looked to be winning. Cal shouted out again for the men to drop their guns. Several bullets flew his way, these men knew it was going to be a fight to the finish. Kelly was no stranger to fights; he always had an ace up his sleeve. From out behind his saloon, three men pulled a small wagon out onto the street. It carried a Gatling gun. Kelly knew it was all or nothing. If he took out the sheriff and these men, he would own the town.

The men opened up with the Gatling gun, shooting straight down the street. Boot Hill Bryce went down. Skinner was spun around like a top. Short Keg was barely able to dive to one side in time and rolled into an alley. The bullets cut through the buildings. There was no way to fight a Gatling gun. Kelly's men cheered. Some of them had ducked into the alleys and were out of the line of fire but now felt a surge. The sheriff and his men dove behind any post or wall they could find while the Gatling gun, pumped shot after shot down Main Street.

Wild Shot, on a rooftop with his Sharps on his buffalo tripod, zeroed in on the men. About thirty seconds later, the men lay on the ground, not moving. Levi stepped out with his shot gun, unloaded both barrels on two of the men that had cheered, and had moved out from the alley. Miss Kitty closed out two more that had retreated with four .22s into each one. Shady Mike caught one trying to sneak back toward the alley and sent a ball into his chest.

Gentleman George had caught a slug in the same arm where he'd been hit before and had stuffed a bandana under his shirt to stop the bleeding, but sent six balls into three more men with his big Walker Colt. The rest of the Marshallville men stepped out of the shops, all at once, still loaded for bear. Most of Kelly's men were down or wounded. The few still standing were out of ammo and noticed several guns pointed their way. Hands went up, and guns went down.

As they rounded up Kelly's men they noticed that Kelly was not in the bunch.

Kelly would not go down without a fight. His temper screamed for revenge. He could see his plan, all his efforts, going up in smoke. No bunch of old men were going to stop him, he was David Kelly. He was tougher than this town and all the people in it. *I'll show them.* He stepped out of an alley holding two sticks of dynamite, one in each hand. The fuses had been light and ready to blow. "Here's a little something for you boys," he yelled.

From the top of the roof, Wild Shot had seen him in the alley and was already taking a bead on him. As Kelly reared back to throw the dynamite, Wild Shot took his shot. A red blotch sprung out on the chest, and Kelly flew over backwards still holding the dynamite. Five seconds later, the dynamite blew. Kelly was spread all over the street and alley.

A couple minutes later, the Gentry brothers came riding fast into town. Looking over the chaos and destruction in the street and shops, they quickly dismounted, pulled their guns, and looked sharply for their friends. Seeing their friends still upright holding guns, they breathed a sigh of relief. Behind them Lefty, one deputy and three ex-Calvary men rode into town leading five horses. Two had bodies draped over the saddles, and three others had Kelly's men, taped, and bandaged, riding astride their horses. The big mouthed, head shaved, outlaw was still alive, but, looked dismayed and angry.

At the other end of the street the town doctor, Short Keg and Nevada Slim were looking at Bryce.

"I'm afraid he's dead," said the doc, "nothing I can do."

Ken and Slim took off their hats and bowed their heads.

"He finally found a home," said Ken. "He died protecting it; looks like he'll be staying with us for quite a while."

When the counting was over, Bryce was dead, Skinner,

361

Buzzard Cooper, and Gentleman George were wounded.

"Damn it Coop, I keep getting hit in the same spot," George moaned, holding his shoulder.

"I feel your pain, actually, I feel my pain in the same spot too. Another hole in my leg and I'll have to give up dancing."

"You two can stop whining, I got two in the same shoulder," griped Skinner.

From the street fight, the Dave Kelly gang had three alive and clean, ten wounded, and seven dead. The Gentry boys brought in three more wounded and two dead. Parts of Kelly were found blown over a fifty-foot area.

Evert Mitch, the town's undertaker, and his helpers brought up a wagon and started loading up the dead. The three clean men went to jail. Cal set up a wounded man area in the T- Hall saloon. His deputies kept them covered until Doc could get to them. Nevada Slim brought over some chains from the blacksmith shop and locked all the men together.

They weren't going to run away unless all thirteen guys could get up together and take off in the same direction. After they were bandaged, they would be taken by wagon to Denver, where there were enough cells to lock them all up. Denver had a sitting judge so the trials would start soon. Murder and attempted murder charges would put those men away for a long time.

It took a few weeks to put Marshallville back together. Wood posts, doorways, water troughs and boardwalks, all needed repairs. Bullets from a Gatling gun can rip holes in just about anything. John Marshall and the city councilmen saw their town ripped apart, but also knew it would heal and be stronger than ever. The town folk practically cheered as they repaired the damage. Their town had survived a vicious attack, but they had won the battle.

Cal breathed a sigh of relief knowing the town was saved and law and order would be restored.

Skinner, Cooper and George were healing from their wounds. Cooper and George each had a noticeable limp. Several other men had glass cuts from the broken windows, but those too would heal. There was a lot of hand shaking and back slapping and a feeling of optimism in town.

Speaking to the hundreds of people attending Bryce's funeral, Ken said, "He had come into town just wandering from place to place and found friends, and a home." Continuing as Bryce was lowered into the earth, "His piano playing lighted up the evenings at the Short Keg. He came into town a lost soul, but went out a hero. He will be missed."

Wild Shot was treated as a hero for his marksmanship that literally saved many lives. After his wounds healed, Skinner packed up and headed for the gold fields. He was given a "going away" party at the Short Keg, a gold pan and $50 from the city council. The city council awarded a prize of "no taxes for five years" to Gentleman George, Short Keg, Buzzard Cooper, Nevada Slim, Wild Shot, Shady Mike, and the Gentry Brothers. They also paid to rebuild the barber shop.

At the city council meeting following the shoot-out, Gentleman George spoke up, "Cal, Mayor, we are done with shoot-outs, tracking, and saving the town. We're done being deputized. The city council can hire more peace officers. We intend to spend the rest of our days enjoying life, socializing at the Short Keg, and having Bar-B-Qs at the Gentry's ranch."

A few weeks later, Short Keg looked at his friends sitting around a table having a beer, joking, with Buzzard

Cooper reading stories out of the newspaper. He had come to Marshallville looking for some peace and quiet, away from criminals and gun play. He felt discouraged, was past forty, with a bum leg, and skeptical about starting in a new town, with a new business. But, even though trouble found him, and life wasn't always peaceful, he had found friends that would stand together and stake their lives when faced with trouble.

He had found romance that seemed impossible. He had found a town to build a life. He felt good about life. In the end, it wasn't peace and quiet that were important, it was friends and place to call home.

Fate can play cruel tricks. Marshallville and its men might be in for it again when it is least expected.

About the Author

John West grew up in Santa Monica and now lives six months in Scottsdale, Arizona and six months on Bainbridge Island, Washington. He has a wife, Valerie, a daughter, a son, and five grandsons. John is a graduate of CSULB with a major in Biology. He retired in 2001 after thirty-three years of teaching science.

He enjoys writing, golf, cowboy fast draw competitions (2018 National champion), chainsaw carving and sculpting. John self-published a children's book titled *Being Three* and a non-fiction book titled *The Nature of Men and Women, The X and Y Factor or I Didn't Say it was your Fault, I Said I was Going to Blame You.* He produced a DVD on Cowboy Fast Draw and recorded a CD of original cowboy poetry.

A western history buff, "Marshallville" is his third book.

Made in the USA
Middletown, DE
04 January 2023

17264243R00222